Praise for *The City Beneath Her*

"Beth Hahn's *The City Beneath Her* is an extraordinary novel; lyrical, gripping, insightful, and compelling. A literary thriller that's a pure pleasure to read and one that's not easily forgotten, there simply aren't enough superlatives to describe this book. Highly recommended!"

—Karen Dionne, author of the #1 international bestseller *The Marsh King's Daughter* and *The Wicked Sister*

"In *The City Beneath Her*, Beth Hahn brings to life a 1947 Los Angeles simmering with danger and allure. As a serial killer stalks the shadows, two women navigate a treacherous maze of deception and hidden truths. Hahn's skilful storytelling plunges readers into a world where glamour masks peril, weaving a literary thriller that keeps pulses racing. Hahn has created a mesmerizing blend of historical ambience and heart-stopping suspense. *The City Beneath Her* is a must-read literary sizzler."

—Ann Garvin, author of *I Thought You Said This Would Work*

"Beth Hahn's masterly new novel, *The City Beneath Her*, is the story of a lost girl in a lost era, the heyday of old Hollywood, but also a cautionary tale for our own time—that wherever there are young women with big dreams and small means, there will be human monsters to prey on them. Inspired by the still-unsolved murder of Elizabeth Short, 'The Black Dahlia,' Hahn's harrowing and compassionate narrative will be savored by fans of true crime, but it is so much more than that. This gorgeously written tragedy of blighted dreams could move a heart of stone."

—Jacquelyn Mitchard:

THE CITY BENEATH HER

Beth Hahn

Regal House Publishing

Published by
Regal House Publishing, LLC
Raleigh, NC 27605
All rights reserved

ISBN -13 (paperback): 9781646035540
ISBN -13 (epub): 9781646035557
Library of Congress Control Number: 2024935102

Cover images and design by © C. B. Royal

Regal House Publishing, LLC
https://regalhousepublishing.com

Printed in the United States of America

AFTER

Los Angeles, 1947

A fingerprint is made up of whorls and arches, the detective explained. See the friction edge? This is a radial loop, the peacock's eye—

He stepped away from the microscope so that the others could have a look. He stepped away because matching prints could become dizzying, like staring into a hypnotist's wheel.

Two sets of prints had been lifted from a woman's black patent-leather handbag—one belonging to the victim, the other, unknown. The handbag had been left atop a trashcan that morning along with a pair of shoes—the toes tucked into the mouth of the handbag as if they were part of a display in a department store window. The sun bounced off the garbage can's aluminum lid, making the garbageman blink. He paused over the handbag and shoes, but he had one job to do, and he went ahead anyway, and later, in the city's trash dump, patrolmen sorted through heaps of stinking refuse to find the items.

Are they *her* things? the garbageman asked when the detective called him into the station. They sat across from each other, the shoes and bag on a table between them.

We don't know yet, he said—*but, yes*, he thought. *I'm almost sure they are her things.*

The garbageman described how he'd found the evidence. He used his hands, which were as big as the shoes on the table. He felt self-conscious. He'd argued with his wife about the tie he wore. He said it was too bright, but she said it was the latest. It will make everyone happy, she'd said, straightening it. It's beach colors—that's all.

There was nothing else in the handbag? Do you remember? Was it heavier? Pick it up, he said.

The garbageman nodded. He stood, picked up the handbag, then put it back down. I don't know, he said. I don't think it felt any different. The shoes were in them. Sorry we tossed them. That must have been a bad job for someone.

It wasn't too bad, the patrolman who'd found them said. He was standing at the back of the room with his arms folded, listening. The patrolman described the way the patent leather of the bag shone like a beetle in the sun, catching his eye. The shoes weren't far away. One, then the other.

The garbageman was staring at the shoes. It's sad—

The detective nodded. Thanks for coming by, he said, standing. When the garbageman was gone, the detective bent over the shoes. The suede was still clean. No mars or nicks. Size five and one-half. The bottoms of the shoes had been capped with metal: a cap at the heel, and another where the ball of the foot touched the pavement.

She wasn't careless, he murmured. Can we get some pictures before we box these?

The photographer was called. He brought out his Graflex Speed Press Camera from a polished leather bag. He noted with satisfaction the click of the film plate sliding into place, the pop and blizzard-white light of the flash.

This picture—*his* picture—would be in the newspaper the next day.

The detective took the elevator down to the basement. The elevator jumped on each floor like it was playing a prank, but he was used to the machinery's joke and folded his arms and looked at the ceiling.

In the morgue, he stood over the woman. He opened the fingers of her left hand. Inside, a black circle drawn on the palm. It was drawn from ashes, already smeared. Her nails had dirt beneath them. She'd been one place, then another. He

didn't know what the first place was yet. He shook his head.
Can I get a better look at this? he asked the medical examiner.
He held her hand for a moment longer, examining the scrapes
on her knuckles.

Her nails were short and painted pink.

The examiner passed him a magnifying glass. Black soot.
Sweat. She could have pressed her hand into something—some
coiled instrument, a bit of machinery, maybe. This mark, it
could be nothing, or—

The edges were too even. No, someone did it to her.

At the newspaper, the woman who labeled photographs for
the *Daily* studied the black-and-white image of the shoes and
handbag. This is the last photograph of her, she thought. She
shook her head. Shoes and a handbag. They were bought for
show, but they were private too. Where you went, how you got
there. Who saw when you arrived.

Already there were ghost stories. At night, on the road
around the canyon that led to the sea, a barefoot woman in a
black dress might appear. Sometimes she raised her hand like
a white flag, her face strained, her eyes set briefly ablaze by the
headlights.

Stop.

And then—the brace of the body, the release of its spring
tension—just as the driver pulled over—she disappeared.

BEFORE

Los Angeles, 1946

1

MAY

May had the feeling that you could be a ghost and not even know it—you could be haunted by what hadn't happened yet—by your own ghost, trailing around a chain and screaming backward through time.

Oh, stop—

A cup of coffee would set her straight.

She and Lily crossed the street, heading for the drugstore—the one near the Hamilton with the green-and-white striped awning and the black-and-white tiled floor—where you could get eggs and potatoes for three cents.

May and Lily wore their day dresses, cotton, in two shades of blue, Lily's lighter, faded from washing, and May's bright with small white dots. Lily walked a little ahead of her, and May could see the vivid twist of her high blond ponytail, the determined set of her shoulders. When Lily brushed her hair out, cast it over one shoulder, powdered her skin, painted her mouth, she became the other Lily. The movie star Lily—the same woman who lived in the silver-shadowed rooms of the photographs that Lily took on auditions. Serious and serene, pale as paper.

May's Lily wanted a glass of water. "I drank too much last night," she said, turning toward May.

May had had too much to drink last night too. She'd danced with a boy who'd just come back from overseas—James—she reminded herself—because she'd promised she'd have dinner with him. He was from Kentucky. He had a gap between his front teeth and freckles across his nose. He was in love with her. He said so. "You can't possibly—" she'd insisted. But he swore it.

She met Hazel too—a girl who worked as one of the models at Robinson's. When a new line of dresses came out, the department store hired models. Hazel pinched May's waist. "You're just right," she said. Hazel told May she'd have to go when a certain salesman was working. He was the sort you could talk to, Hazel explained. "You know what I mean—" she said, looking at May's eyes. "He'll get you lunch too. He's got hands, but they all do. Come on and work with me."

There were always people to meet. There were places to go. And the funny thing was that no one knew anyone else, but as soon as you met someone, they were your friend. Where are you from? they asked each other. How long have you been here? Will you stay, then?

If May got the job at Robinson's, she could make things up to Lily—pay for everything for a week. At least. Lily had been talking to a man in a black suit and a woman wearing a long white dress. They'd clustered together at one end of the bar, the woman laughing at something the man said—one hand on her hip, her back to May, the fabric shivering over her pale skin. But Lily wasn't laughing. She was standing against the wall and was looking up at the man. For a moment, it reminded May of a scene in a monster movie. Lily was the heroine, and she was shrinking beneath his shadow. But the man wasn't monstrous at all. His clothes were elegant, and his face, when she saw it, was not frightening. It was similar to David Niven's—a heavier brow, the jaw more angular, and he didn't have that secret, joking joy.

Hazel followed May's gaze. "Is that—" she started.

"It's not," May said. *David Niven*, she would've added, but someone jostled her shoulder, and she didn't finish.

"Oh, I thought—" but then Hazel started talking about the job again. She put two fingers beneath her own chin and tilted her face up. "You have to walk like this. Like a snob."

The man in the fine clothes left Lily and the woman in white and sat down at one of the small tables. He leaned back, one elbow on the table. He crossed his legs and lifted his chin as

Hazel had. It was a position of casual ownership—that way rich people had of scanning a room. He regarded May until she looked away. She'd had the feeling that if she kept looking, he would point at her, call her out, and if he pointed at her, who knew what might happen. Perhaps everyone would turn to stare. The music would fall silent. May would stand alone in a white light.

"Come at four tomorrow," Hazel said, but May was hardly listening. When she looked around for the man again, he was gone, and so was the woman in the elegant dress, and then Lily was by May's side, only she was smiling now, saying how late it was even though it was only midnight.

That night, back in the room they rented at the Hamilton, May asked Lily about the couple, but Lily said she couldn't remember talking to anyone. May didn't buy it. No one else was nearly as glamorous. They looked as if they were on their way to Ciro's— just stopping in for cheap drinks to get the night started.

May and Lily shared the oval mirror above the sink in the small, brightly lit bathroom. Lily rolled her hair, her elbows bent like a pin-up girl, and May worked slow circles of cold cream across her cheeks. May held Lily's gaze in the reflection, waiting for her to tell the truth, but Lily paid no attention. Finally, May said, "I have to do my teeth." She needed the bathroom to herself. She didn't like anyone to see her when she opened her jaw wide and scraped out the bits of wax that made her teeth appear opaque and healthy. When the wax was gone, her teeth were yellowed, translucent in places, brown in others. Every morning, she softened part of a pale stub of candle, molding the pliant wax into her bad teeth while it was still hot. Her fingers were often singed, and she'd come to detest the sulfuric stink of a struck match.

In front of the drugstore, Lily turned to May. "You get a paper and I'll get us a spot at the counter." She passed May a few cents.

At the end of the block, a newsboy was sitting on the sidewalk in the sun, his ankles crossed in front of him, his shirt untucked. When he looked up at May, she thought how pretty he was: his soft round cheeks, his small cherry mouth. "You'll be dead before long," he said to her.

"What? What sort of thing is that to say?" She couldn't see the boy's face. The sun was bright, and her shadow fell over him. She stepped back. "What kind of horrible boy are you?"

The boy looked at her, his face blank of expression. "All I said is 'Would you like to buy a paper?'"

She stared at him, her mouth slightly open. Hadn't she heard him say it? She looked up and down the street. "I'm sorry," she said. "I thought you—"

"It's very hot today, ma'am," the boy said. "Maybe you feel the heat. I do feel it."

"Yes, yes." She handed the boy three pennies and took a paper from his stack. She scanned the headline as she walked back to the drugstore. The Raptor had killed a fourth woman. The police didn't know who the victim was yet, but the Raptor had been seen.

Seen!

The Raptor could arrive out of nothing, out of the night itself—like the bat who, by some trick of the film and light, settles into the skin of a man. May and Lily lingered on the details of his crimes. If they knew his habits, his tricks, it wouldn't be either of them. Lily showed May how to hook her fingers inside a man's nose, how to gouge the eyes. Kick like this, she said, putting her hands on May's shoulders, lifting her knee. Like this—

Surely it wouldn't be long now until he was caught. *Seen!*

"Look." May put the newspaper down on the counter in front of Lily. She pointed to the drawing of the man's face. "Does he look like anyone to you?"

May watched Lily study the drawing. She frowned. "He looks like *anyone*, all right," she said.

"And everyone," May added.

The waitress came over, a coffee pot in her hand. The three women leaned over the paper and read.

"It's a damn shame," Lily said. "A girl comes all the way out here, does the hard work of getting herself a place to live and a job, and then ends up murdered."

May stared at the counter, at the water left behind from the cloth, a quickly disappearing streak across the aluminum.

Murdered.

Lily opened the paper. "I'm going to read the funnies. I can't think about something like that happening." She nudged May. "Read the funnies with me."

The waitress straightened, turned. "There are plenty of sex maniacs in this town. I could tell you a story or two."

May raised her hand. "I could too. Honest to god sex maniacs." The boy she'd bought the paper from had come inside for a glass of water. He turned and looked at May as she spoke, and May took a deep breath, holding it for moment. She brought her hands to her neck, touching it all over, and then to her hair, pressing her fingers into her skull.

"Say—" Lily turned to her. "Are you all right? Do you need to go lie down?"

May shook her head. "No, I just—" She smiled and opened her eyes. "It's crazy but I felt like I had to touch my head. To keep it—" And then she began to laugh. "To keep it on."

Lily stared at her. "Hey, it's all right. That's a terrible story. Here—" She pointed to the comics. Dagwood was taking Blondie on a date. "Let's see what stupid thing he does to ruin it."

May looked at the cartoon strip but didn't read the bubbles. She rested her elbows on the counter and kept her hands braced around her neck. She thought about the story she and her sister Ann used to tell when they were little, whispering in the dark when they were supposed to be asleep—the story of the woman with the velvet choker—how she insisted on wearing the black band around her neck, only saying she could never take it off, wearing it on her wedding day even, and then every day and night after that, and how one night, when her husband could no longer stand the idea of the choker, he decided to untie it, to take it off while his wife slept, and she opened her wild, searching eyes briefly before her head rolled away, off the pillow and then the bed, to hit the floor with a dull thud.

AGNES

At her desk at the back of the newsroom, Agnes wrote notes to herself on scraps of paper: *Put yourself in the path of good fortune. Get lucky. Have the sense to know when something is good and when it just looks good. Walk away from fool's gold. Play the stocks. Get a driver's license.*

No one can see around a corner, though.

The morning newspaper showed a drawing of a man with a wide brow, a thin mouth. Agnes held the paper at arm's length and looked down her nose at him. The drawing was neatly done, better than average. He looked the type who owned things: railroads, oil, hotels. A conspirator leaning toward her across the table. A man with a tip.

She didn't want what he was selling. No one did. Certainly not the unidentified woman he'd left half-buried in the dunes.

Agnes turned the paper face down and went back to work. She worked for the *Daily*, writing captions for photographs. Engagements. Weddings. *Mr. and Mrs. So-and-Van-So are happy to announce— The bride wore— The wedding was held at—*

Every day, the photographs landed on her desk in large paper envelopes. Sometimes they came with notes, or the backs were scrawled on—a place, a date. If she didn't get notes, she couldn't do much in the way of labeling people, but she could do some research and label events, intersections, buildings. *Acrobats on Venice Beach. A night out in Hollywood.*

Danny tapped one knuckle on her desk. "Lunch?" he asked. She smiled up at him, nodding. Danny was the paper's best photographer. He had a flair for the dramatic, for narrative—the show girl who murdered her married lover, her eyes two black circles as she was caught getting out of a car. The petty thief, his cheek bloodied from a police officer's fist. A holdup. A victim. Detectives standing over a body. He antenna-tuned his car radio to police dispatch and raced to crime scenes, sometimes arriving before the patrol cars.

She wanted to ask him about something. Who did he think was doing the best writing about the Raptor? *I can do better,* she wanted to say. She wanted to give her writing to Elgin—the editor—and naturally he'd say, *Who knew that Agnes Crandall could write? Get her off labels. Put her on crime.*

Never mind that she hadn't actually written anything yet. Or that no one ever put a woman on crime. The most she might hope for was a sideways move to the society pages, but she didn't have the pedigree for that. The women who wrote about fashion and flowers had inherited the practiced smiles of easy fortune, and they exchanged these smiles over the argent plates of philanthropic luncheons. Agnes had labeled the women in photographs, sought them out in blue books, filed their stories away in her memory like characters from novels. Their husbands too—the ones who ran the city. The oil men and the water men. The land men. The financiers. She knew the names of criminals, of conmen. She saw them all intersect through the city, the links between the upper world and the lower. No one was ever one thing or another. They depended on each other. The rich just knew how to keep their dirty work at a distance, to pass it off to someone who could manage it the way their maids did their soiled clothing. Every once in a while, a man of the world was caught: some financial scheme was uncovered, the criminal exposed. But then it was up to their lawyers to rewrite the story, to gain sympathy, to clean the image. And it usually worked. Men of the world were not held accountable.

It wasn't that the drawing of the Raptor looked like one of them, but it was his brazenness, his lack of concern in being caught. That was it.

The job at the *Daily* was a lucky accident. She'd gone in to interview for a telephone operator, but that job had gone to a reporter's sister. They'd asked to see Agnes's handwriting, which was neat. How fast could she type? And that very day, she found herself sitting in the back of the newsroom, her scuffed handbag on the desk next to a typewriter. No one really told her what to do. It was Agnes's job to decipher the hastily scrawled notes, to make proper labels, and then to take the photographs down to the long tunnels of the basement archives and file them away.

To celebrate the job, Ben had taken her out to dinner and given her a silver pen. When she opened the box, he said, "You're a newspaper woman now." She liked the feel of the pen, and the black ink ran smooth and even over the heavy paper she kept for letters. The pen was from Argentina and came in a shining red case. She liked the small lie of being called a newspaper woman.

He gave her cut lilies, the white petals trembling against the waxy paper. "One day," he said, leaning over the table, "I'll shock you and give you a ring."

She smiled at him. When he said such things, she imagined her grandmother's china cabinet back in Portland. She thought of the way the key slid into the lock and turned, the silvery rattle of stacked plates.

Don't wait for someone to give you something, she had written. *Take it.*

Did she want what Ben was waiting to give? She wondered why he said such things. Was she supposed to beg him, then? To ask *when, when,* as she cut into the plump pink of her creamed chicken, and when he didn't answer, was she then to raise her hand to the waiter, order something stronger—a stinger, perhaps, the burn of the brandy hidden by the sweet mint, and sit there smoking and drinking, smoldering away while he finished his food? She was not obsessed with the ring which he may or may not present to her. For the moment, anyway, their future was a lie that they both understood. The ring was a lie—perhaps bigger than the newspaper woman lie—but a lie nonetheless.

She would decide for herself whether the lie would hold or turn into something else.

She would decide.

Back in the office, she imagined herself walking to the front of the room and pushing a reporter out of his chair and sitting down. Or the reporter—say the one who called her *doll* and breathed down on her at Christmas parties and was tapped to cover the Raptor—Max, oh, that man—Max would come in one day and find her in his seat, and she would refuse to move. "Shove off," she'd say. "You're a hack writer, anyway."

It was November, the light golden, the days short.

She and Danny walked to the automat. She liked it when he came and found her. It was always a surprise—as if it had never happened before. Him arriving at her desk; she knowing it was him before she looked up. At the automat, they sat beneath the white lights and discussed the day's news—the trials, the open cases. They talked about the Nazis in the newsreels—the monsters who looked like rich foreign uncles with their little round glasses and neat haircuts.

They ate turkey sandwiches on toast, too dry, and drank weak tea. Someone had left a newspaper on the table beside them. Agnes tapped the drawing of the man's face with one finger. She leaned toward Danny. "I have a proposition."

"What's that?"

"Let's catch the Raptor. You and me."

"All right." He winked at her. "Easy. How should we do that?"

"I write. You take pictures. We go early. We go late. Say you'll do it. Say you'll give it a try. I don't know if we'll catch him, but we can act like we will."

"All right," he said. He smiled at her. "What's in it for me? Early, late. That's a lot of sleep to lose."

She suspected he didn't sleep much already. He had circles beneath his eyes. "Your photographs on the front page. The money, of course. That's always something. And the chase."

The chase. That's what would hook him, she knew. She knew from the way he talked about the police when he turned up at a crime scene—how they asked, Where did you come from? You're some detective, they said. You should be one of us.

He nodded. "What sort of man would let himself be seen walking along the side of the road like that after he'd killed a girl?"

"I'll tell you who. A brazen one, that's the kind. And someone who feels safe—he'd know that even if someone *saw* him they didn't really *see* him. You know what provides that sort of disguise?"

"What?"

She waited. "Money," she said. She pointed at him with her fork. "That's what does that."

Danny stared at her. "I see, yeah. Someone with prestige—but not so much that you'd recognize him right off. Not an actor or a politician. So you think the Raptor's got some money?"

"It's a theory."

"They're not thinking like that," Danny said. "The cops. They're thinking of a bum, a typical suspect. You're a real case cracker, Agnes."

"Shake on it," she said. She took his hand in hers. "Let's catch him. Another thing—"

"What's that?"

"Can you teach me how to drive?"

When Agnes got back to her desk, instead of labeling photographs, she wrote down everything she knew about the murders. The Raptor liked dancers and actresses. He liked to find a girl who believed in alchemy—a trick reserved for Hollywood—a regular flesh and blood woman transformed into a goddess. If the girls wanted, he could pretend—couldn't he—to be a producer or a director? What did they know, anyway, about a director's job? Even the ones who had some means—they didn't know, either.

Whoever the Raptor was, the women didn't suspect him.

Maybe he could offer them jobs, money—if he had it, and Agnes suspected he did.

One of the newspapers had started to call him the Raptor, and then they all took it up. They called him the Raptor because the women were—she didn't like to think it. They were in bad shape, that was all. It seemed personal to Agnes. A knife. A rope. Never a gun. The police couldn't decide if the crimes were linked. Some were, others—they *varied* so much. But the papers always tied the murders to the Raptor. Write it in blood, the men who covered the Raptor joked.

They didn't have to worry.

Canyons. Dunes.

They called him the Raptor because he was able to disappear so quickly from the scene of his crimes—as if he'd lifted himself into the sky and flown away. The man who'd seen him, the one who described him for the police, had been disembarking a city bus. He'd been so close as to nearly brush the suspect's shoulder. The witness's house wasn't far from the dune where the murdered woman was found, and sometimes, if the night were pleasant, he went down to the sea before heading home and smoked a pipe and looked at the moon. That was just what he'd planned to do, but then he'd been stopped by a woman's open palm, and then, looking more closely, he saw the body, the strange angle of the head. He rushed back to the road to catch the man, who'd been, when he thought of it, walking too quickly. But the man was gone—he hadn't boarded the bus, and the sidewalk was well-lit.

He'd simply vanished.

There must have been a car somewhere, but he hadn't heard one. Agnes pictured this man. She saw him standing on the street, looking one way, then the other. He'd found a telephone booth and called the police.

Agnes stayed late, labeling the photographs she'd neglected. *Summer fair. Miss Orange County.*

It was past seven when she left the building.

On a crowded bus, a man stood behind her. She was aware

of his presence, could feel his breath on her neck. She put her hand on her purse, bending her elbow so that the sharp point stuck in his ribs. She pressed until he stepped away from her.

Strangers had always told Agnes stories—even when she was a child, waiting in a grocery line with the grown-ups—they told her things. "Look at the cost of this—" a conversation may well begin. "Why when I was your age—" and she'd smile up, waiting. Strangers had the most wonderful secrets. What she'd especially loved was a story about a bad child. When someone told a bad-child story, she felt as if she were anticipating a jump—or was in mid-air already. Orphans interested her immensely, and being a bad child herself, she imagined she might be abandoned or sent away—

"Reform school," her mother had said when she'd discovered a stolen pencil set in Agnes's school bag. "That's where you'll end up if you don't learn how to behave." Her mother confiscated the pencil set. She held Agnes's chin in her hand. "The way you act—*you* were born under a bridge to a raggedy woman."

A raggedy woman! *Of course* her real mother was a raggedy woman.

She'd only wanted the pencil set so she could write down what strangers told her. Questions were pathways—secret ways into locked rooms—alleyways, the back steps, a raised windowsill. She learned to ask without seeming to press, but press she did, her expression placid, her smile frozen. The back way to anything was the lonely way—which meant there might be something or someone there you didn't want to meet. A man with a brown bottle, his hat pulled down—or a rabid dog, his head hung low, his mouth dripping.

Did your wife survive the fall? Did they catch the man who took all your money?

One teacher, writing that Agnes was the first to raise her hand in the classroom, noted that this might betray a propensity for over-confidence. *It's unbecoming*, she wrote.

Un-be-com-ing, Agnes sounded. To become. To unbecome.

She would unbecome.

When school ended, she wanted to go to college, but there was no money for that, so when the war started, she packed a suitcase and took the train to Los Angeles. She could get a job at one of the bases—doing what, she didn't know. It wasn't done, not really. Living alone in a city. It wasn't done until that moment, when all the men were called away and their jobs and rooms sat empty, papers across the floor, hastily erased blackboards, ships half-built. Everyone gone to fight the Nazis.

The only people left were the women—or so it seemed.

She found work with the army, interviewing men who'd just returned from overseas at one of the veterans' hospitals. Some of the men had a terrible time. They came home and couldn't sleep. They drank. They dreamed of flying into black, arsenal-filled clouds, of waking to fire. Soon enough, they began getting arrested. It seemed Los Angeles was teaming with men who were crawling out of their skin, who smashed beer bottles over heads and left each other bleeding in gutters.

She sat across from them and asked a battery of questions: *Yes or no—do you ever have violent thoughts? Do you see things that aren't really there? How many hours a night do you sleep? One to three hours, less than that, up to eight? Do you hear conversations when no one else is in the room?*

Sometimes the men didn't answer. They stared at her. She looked at a poster on the wall of a woman sitting at a typewriter, smiling. Agnes did not smile at the men. She held her sharpened pencil over the form and waited.

She delivered their answers to the doctors, who listened solemnly as she converted the answers to percentages. Some of the men were sent home; others were wheeled through the heavy doors and down the long white corridor where Agnes had never gone. She looked through the hatched-glass window at the hallway. She could not see the end.

On breaks, she and Rosemary, one of the hospital's nurses, would stand in the courtyard, leaning against the wall for the shade and cool stone, and murmur to each other about the heat.

They weren't supposed to discuss the men with each other, but Rosemary told her things anyway. The doctors were eager for any treatment that worked—even the new surgery that was meant to soothe a patient but left some of them as dependent as little children. "It's shameful," Rosemary said. "If I were a doctor, I'd never do that."

The Raptor barely registered then—he'd killed already, but the papers hadn't started calling him the Raptor yet. Agnes and Rosemary talked about the murders. "He could be one of ours," Rosemary said. "He could be just behind this wall." Agnes's back felt cold when Rosemary said that.

Agnes let Rosemary talk about the cold-water treatments, the ice baths. When she wasn't talking about work, her sentences began "My husband, Arnold—"

Did Agnes have a steady? Rosemary wondered aloud. "Oh no," Agnes said. "I just got here—" And that was how she met Ben. Rosemary invited her over to dinner one night. Rosemary sat Ben across from Agnes at the table so they could have a look at each other.

Ben and Arnold were chemists for a paint company, and neither of them had gone to war. Arnold had a bad back from a fall, and Ben was a year too old for service. He lived with his mother in Glendale, whom he described to Agnes as *infirm*.

After dinner, the group played euchre, the windows open, the sea in the distance. Ben wore glasses and was gray at the temples, but Agnes liked how polite he was—too old, she thought—but he looked her in the eye when he asked her questions, and then listened to her answers. She became animated in front of him, as if he were shining a light on her. She laughed and ordered them all to allow table talk. "We must do it," she said. "It's such a lot of fun."

"But that's cheating!" Rosemary cried.

"It's not cheating if we're all doing it," Agnes insisted.

The game grew uproarious, the score forgotten because everyone was laughing. What did Ben mean tugging his ear that way? What on earth does patting your head imply?

Ben offered to drive Agnes home, and on the way, they stopped at an all-night hamburger place and drank bitter coffee.

"What do you do at the hospital, Agnes?" Ben asked.

"I talk to men," she answered. "I ask them about what's gone wrong with their minds."

2

MAY

After breakfast, they wrote letters in their room, but May couldn't decide who to write to, so she drew shoes instead—the black-bowed toes like little cat's ears, the wooden heel stacked with clearly drawn lines.

When it grew too hot to stay indoors, Lily went into the hall and called a girl named Dora who owned a car. May and Lily wore their swimsuits under their shorts and blouses and went downstairs. They leaned against the Hamilton's white stucco façade, arms folded, hair pinned back, big Bakelite sunglasses, their bathing suits hot, waiting for Dora to appear in her car. In the heat, the woolen bathing suit itched, and in the water, the suit sagged, but May's was navy with a white belt—like a sailor's—and she thought it was a kick.

She liked clothes: the whisper of a stocking's toe, a new set of gloves with a mother of pearl button at the wrist—small and white as a baby's tooth. She liked the mirror shine of black patent leather, a carefully cut and well-laid collar.

May told Lily about Hazel and the job at Robinson's.

"That would be swell," Lily said. "Can you imagine what it would be like if you never needed to make money? Dora's like that. Her parents have a lot of dough. They own a department store back East." Lily was chewing gum. She blew a bubble and let it pop over her lips. She said her own parents lived in a tarpaper shack. She laughed when she said it, pulling the gum away and putting it back in her mouth, but she reminded May of a girl who'd gone to meet a boy and found him instead with another girl.

"My father's nuts," May said. "He left my mother after he lost all of our money."

"Where'd he go?"

May covered her mouth and laughed. "He jumped off a bridge."

"Oh, that's bad luck." Lily stopped chewing and looked at May.

"He was fine. He didn't do much of anything right. Not even that. He broke a leg is all."

"Why'd he do it?"

"He was in love with another woman. She left him. And then he lost all our money in the Crash."

When May's mother found out about the woman and the money, she locked the doors and for a whole week sat at the kitchen table staring at the stove and shaking her head, until finally she got up and put her hands on her hips. "I guess he may as well have gone on and died," she'd said, and went back to work.

Lily blew another bubble. "Pop drinks a lot of beer. Mother likes scotch. You can't ask the two of them to do anything. They'll show up drunk and ruin things. They're like something from a cheap novel."

"Mine is too. My father, I mean. My mother never drinks." After May said that, neither of them said anything. Had she hurt Lily's feelings when she said that her mother didn't drink? She looked at her friend sideways. Maybe Lily thought May was full of herself. Some girls thought that about her. They called her Mother-May-I, mimicking her careful manners, but Lily wasn't like that. Lily was wonderful. If it weren't for Lily, May might be back in Boston, standing on a corner in a drab wool coat, her feet wet from the sleet, waiting for a tram, but here was Lily beside her, golden as California.

May's mother and her sister, Ann, told her to come home all the time. If it weren't for Ann's friends William and Edith, who'd moved out West after the war, her mother never would've let her come—not that she could have stopped her—but she would have made it harder.

But there were Edith and William to oversee her—real people, Boston people. May had gone to Edith's wedding—caught her bouquet when she'd thrown it high in the drafty church hall. May had carried the bouquet into an alcove where she could sit by a window and examine the doubled blooms: the rouged rose, the pinwheeled dahlia—wrapped her fingers in the trail of smooth fronds, the living green against the white. She closed her eyes and saw Errol Flynn standing on the deck of a boat, one foot lifted onto the bow, his shoulders thrown back, a sword at his side, triumphant.

He winked at her.

At the end of the night, her mother passed her a slice of cake enclosed in brown paper and told her that if she slept with it under her pillow, she would dream of her husband—but May dreamed she was being chased by skeletons, their rattling white bones crashing together like china plates in a pitch house, and she was hiding—below the floorboards, in a cupboard beneath the sink. She woke and reached for the cake. The stiff glazed icing scattered on her sheet when she opened the package, but she devoured the cake, sucked the sweetness from her fingers, licked the paper when she was finished.

When they moved to Los Angeles, William and Edith bought a stucco bungalow in Leimert Park that was surrounded by newly planted rose bushes and lemon trees. They had May over to dinner once a week. Ann called them *nice people* and said it in a way that reminded May she needed to be influenced by *nice* people. But May could not tell sometimes if they were nice. Edith envied a woman called Betty who lived down the street. Edith said Betty was perfect, and though May had never met Betty, she heard the way Edith said it—which was the interesting part—as if Edith were throwing something over her shoulder and walking away.

Perfect.

"Do your parents ever tell you to come home?" May asked Lily.

"Come home?" Lily said. "Are you kidding me? Gosh, no. If I'm not careful, they'll come down here and move in with us."

A man walked by and whistled at them. "I'd like to be the fellow you're waiting for," he said to both of them at once.

"Wouldn't you?" Lily blew another bubble. "Here she comes—" Lily said. She pointed to the traffic light, but May didn't know which car to look at. "Say." Lily turned to May and touched her lightly on the arm. "If Dora says anything strange, just try to ignore it. She's a little—" and Lily made a gesture, turning her index finger in circles. "Loopy."

"Really?"

"She's an actress," Lily said in explanation. "We're all a little—" and she made the gesture again.

Dora owned a blue convertible with plaid wool seats that made the backs of May's legs hot. As Dora drove, Lily sat in the front and sang a song they'd heard the night before. Dora laughed. She wore her hair cut straight across her forehead, and reminded May of fairy drawings, or the children in *The Water Babies*—that small nose, the pointed chin, the red cheeks. She could picture her using a flower as a parasol. She might be tucked into the wing of a sparrow.

A boy jumped onto the motor board and hung on for a stoplight or two. "What's your name?" he cried, leaning in. May shook her hair in the wind and smiled at him. She lifted her sunglasses and winked at him in the way James had winked at her. His cheeks were red from the sun. His neck was brown. "June," she lied, and he leaned in to kiss her cheek, then jumped back on to the sidewalk. "I had to know!" he called out as the car sped off. "I hope I see you again, June."

At the beach, Dora put a blue-and-white striped blanket on the sand. May and Lily struggled with the heavy umbrella. Dora and Lily were talking about a girl they knew who hadn't turned up for work. Joan was a dancer at the Venetian Gardens and Lily was filling in for her. Lily had lied and told the manager that Joan had already asked her to fill in; that way, Joan wouldn't get fired when she got back from wherever she'd gone. "I heard she has a bun in the oven," Dora said. "Maybe she's gone off to take care of it."

"Really?" Lily lay down on her side with her head propped in her hand. She was reading a book by F. Scott Fitzgerald, but she put the book face down to hear what Dora had to say. "That's not what I heard."

"What did you hear?"

May wanted to know how Joan was in trouble, but she was hot, and she felt left out of the gossip. She didn't know Joan. And she didn't want to hear about Joan's baby. She didn't care in the least. She wrapped a scarf around her hair so it wouldn't get wet. When she finished, she set out across the sand. She stood knee-deep in the tide, watching the children play in the surf. She kicked the waves, letting the eddy carry her farther, and decided not to resist the rush and swell. Soon she was waist deep in the water. She saw a ship on the horizon, and she watched it, shielding her eyes from the sun, wondering where it was going. Richard had talked about taking her to Europe. He wanted to show her things, to travel to England, to France, to stand beneath the Eiffel Tower and look straight up to the top. He told her these things over dinner one night, leaning toward her, grasping her hand so hard that it almost hurt, and she wondered, looking at him, how she was so lucky.

She thought about Richard walking across a hot Florida air strip, the back of his neck damp from sweat, and climbing into his plane on that last trip. She imagined him waving to her. He wasn't wearing his uniform, but something dapper— something that Charles Lindbergh would have worn—a white linen jacket, open and flapping in the wind as he climbed into his plane. She didn't cry when she imagined Richard waving goodbye.

Richard's mother sent her ten dollars once, and Ned—a boy from home—sent money. Ned wrote, *I know I'm a fool to keep hoping.* "Don't encourage Ned," her sister, Ann, had said. "If you're not serious." But maybe she *was* serious. She might ask him to come out West. *It's better here,* she told him. *You're missing so much life,* she wrote, and then crossed it out, even though it was true. Ned worked in a garage. He spent his days beneath cars or in the cramped back office, the air thick with the smell of oil and gasoline.

What did it matter if her hair got wet? She floated on her back, gently moving her arms and legs in the water. She could see a plane overhead, and she watched it pass, pretending that Richard was flying it, and that she was with him in the plane, and that they were on their way to France. She imagined herself holding a baby in her lap. The baby was naked except for goggles and a diaper.

They all waved, flying higher and higher, moving up through the mist of clouds until they disappeared.

That was love. That was goodbye.

May swam back to shore and lay down on the blanket. She listened as Dora and Lily gossiped. They were still talking about Joan. May closed her eyes and listened. *I bet she just went back home. A bun in the oven. A baby and all.* May was sleepy, and their voices mixed with the surf, the call of gulls. *This is not a place to raise a baby—especially if you don't know who the father is.* May was standing on a stage in Robinson's and she could not see the floor. *She didn't know who the father was?* Her dress was white, the stage was white, the walls, and sunlight poured into the room. *How could she?* She was floating. *You know her better than I.* That was Lily. *You know her better than I.*

"There's a party tonight," Dora said when they were back in the car. "Do you two want to come?"

"I have to work—" Lily said. She was brown from the sun. Her hair was white blond and stiff from the ocean. She was pushing the sand off her arms, sitting sideways in the passenger seat with the door open. "But maybe after the show ends." Lily was dancing that night at the Palace, in a show called "The Circus." She had to wear a mouse's mask—a giant gray head made of fabric and paper. She'd been learning the steps, filling in for Joan. The mask made Lily's shoulders ache, and she'd shown May the bruises, the rash on her neck from the heat of the thing. She said the mask was grotesque. *Grotesque,* May thought, turning the word over, as she'd watched Lily dust powder over the rash. Lily explained the premise of the story—that there was an evil ringmaster who possessed the animals and made them dance—but May protested. There were so many more animals and only one ringmaster. If the animals wanted to go back to the forest or wherever, they could just do away with the ringmaster. Lily stopped powdering the spots on her throat and looked at herself in the mirror. She blinked twice and then looked at May. "But that never happens," she'd said. "Not even in real life."

"What sort of party is it?" May asked.

"It's at Claude's house."

"I don't know him."

"Lily does. I've heard so many rumors about Claude. Do you think any of them are true?"

"What do they say about Claude?" May asked.

"Why, all sorts of things. That he practices black magic, for one—" Dora's eyes were wide. "I don't believe it! He's been absolutely *charming* with me. He's not at all sinister."

May looked at Lily, but Lily didn't say anything. She pushed the sand off her legs and shut the car door. "Next time," she said. "Claude's parties are boring."

"Claude's parties are *not* boring!" Dora laughed and started the car. "Boring," she repeated, shaking her head in disbelief. "There wouldn't be all those rumors about him if he were boring. He's a financier, you know." She looked at May. "He makes a lot of money for people. He knows *everyone*. But what do I know? I saw Claude the other night at the Palace. He was with—" Dora looked at Lily. "Oh, I'm sorry, kid."

"What?" Lily was listening, but she didn't look at Dora at all.

"Weren't you seeing him for a while?"

"You're all mixed up, Dora. I was never seeing Claude."

"Did you work for him, then? I really thought—"

"What sort of work could I do for Claude?"

"Well, it's not unusual that I'm mixed up. Anyway, they

looked like a couple of movie stars. He had on this impeccable black suit and she was wearing a dress I could die for—with that new kind of cross strap, just this gorgeous satiny white. I told them I didn't know they were getting married." Dora laughed.

"Didn't we see them the night we went dancing?" May said to Lily.

"Oh no, I don't think so," Lily answered, and Dora looked from May to Lily as if she'd missed something important, pausing before she pulled out and into traffic.

⁓

On the U to Leimert Park, May wondered what Edith would cook. Edith would have been to the butcher, wearing one of her brown-checked dresses, her hair freshly waved at the beauty parlor, her nails clipped. Errand day. Two for the price of one. Edith had big white teeth, and when the butcher showed her a cut of beef, she would smile, exposing her good fortune.

"Edith's lucky," Ann always said.

May read the evening paper over a woman's shoulder. *Dancer Dead in Raptor Spree*. They weren't releasing details—only that the woman was a dancer in one of the clubs.

May imagined Lily seeing the headline—another of the dancers coming in for the night's work, asking, "Have you seen this?" holding up the paper. The rustle of fabric, *Do you have a pin?* the ripped stocking, changing, *Can you help me with this?* All the idle chatter interrupted as the dancer with the newspaper spoke. "What if it's Joan?"—and then the way the women's faces looked in the mirrors and light—ashen and fearful against the shimmer and wink of their costumes.

May almost missed her stop. But missing her stop was the way she'd learned the city—pulling the trolley's bell cord before she should, walking in the wrong direction and then turning around, a map in her hand. If she missed a stop, she pretended that she knew what she was doing, and more often than not, a man would stop, take his hat off, and ask her if she needed help.

If he seemed too certain that she did need his help, she would say, "No thank you," in a way that made it seem he'd insulted her, and she wouldn't even smile, but lift her chin a little in a haughty way that she knew her mother and sister would not approve of.

After all, May could find her way.

She'd come clear across the country—across the desert, along the red banked roads, traveling from one ocean to the other. She passed through towns where children waved at the train from dirt embankments, where women looked up from hanging laundry, shielding their eyes in the sunshine. She saw cemeteries and ball fields and factories. When the train passed through those towns, she could almost feel the china shaking in the grandmothers' cupboards, hear the pause in conversation, see the finger held up, the smile.

There were lakes as big as oceans and there was Chicago on a blue day, rising up out of nothing.

At school, May had liked to look out of windows at swaying trees, her chin resting in her hand until the teacher came over and slapped the edge of her desk with a ruler.

Boring old brute.

There was something about the freedom of the leaves.

In Iowa, she had ridden in the back seat of a car with the children of a family she'd met, taking the candy they passed her with their sticky hands. She sucked, trying to take care with her teeth, which ached. She didn't really like candy, not as she once had. It reminded her too much of Mr. Perry.

But it was worse to be hungry.

It couldn't be Joan.

Edith served chicken casserole, the top browned with butter, and green beans. May tried to eat slowly—not the way she ate sometimes in her room at the Hamilton—straight out of a can, hardly chewing between mouthfuls.

"Are you working now, May?" Edith asked.

"I'm a dress model—" May blurted out, thinking of Hazel, but it was too late. Edith nodded politely, but she was looking down at her dinner instead of at May. May kept talking. She said Robinson's was hosting a spring show at the Biltmore, and she would be in it. She said the room would be full of flowers, as it always was, and the smell— She began to describe it, but it was impossible to describe a smell, wasn't it? And anyway, she might describe it as a funeral smell—all those flowers. But it wasn't like that at all.

"Say," William said. "The Biltmore? I wonder if they've got any entrances."

"Well, of course they have entrances, silly. How do you suppose people get in and out?"

"He's talking about the tunnels."

"What tunnels?" May asked.

William put his fork down and cleared his throat. "There are tunnels that run all over Hollywood—into Los Feliz, even."

William was an engineer for the Department of Transportation. During the war, he'd located bunkers in Germany and France. The bunkers were hidden in the sides of mountains, with steep steps leading downward. When he came home, he said, he thought a lot about those bunkers—about how there could be cities beneath cities. "This city is too new for any of that," he told May, "and we don't have bunkers, not really, and certainly not catacombs. But there are old mines and unused train lines. Those could easily be turned into bunkers."

"But we don't need bunkers here," Edith said.

"You never know what the future will bring. You've seen what the H-bomb can do. We might like to live underground someday," he said.

"I don't think I'd like to live underground," May said, but William kept talking. He'd read a novel about the future and in it, everyone lived underground. They took trains that somehow ran on air to each other's cities. All the cities were in the same places as they'd always been, but they were underground—just upside down—like a reflection in a lake on a clear day. William put his fork and knife down and looked straight at May. "You've never heard about the tunnels?"

"I suppose not," she answered. "No. I've never heard of the tunnels. Is that something I should know about?" If she lived underground, she'd miss the gardens, the smell of the grass. She liked to float face up in swimming pools, the sun on her skin. But how strange it would be to walk beneath the city! How cold it must be, with no sunshine, and the cool smells of underground things: dirt and water and rock.

"Do you like secrets?"

"It depends on what they are."

"That's a funny answer." He looked at her for a while before going on. "Bootleggers used the tunnels in the twenties to get liquor into the bars. That's why I thought maybe the Biltmore, but—" He looked at Edith, and something swift passed between them.

"I'd like to ask May something, dear," Edith said, turning to May. "Would you like to come to church with us?"

May smiled up at them. "Church on a Saturday night?" The dining room windows were open and she could smell the lime trees outside. She was supposed to meet Lily and Dora for a drink.

"We have church most nights."

Everything—even a meal with William and Edith—cost something. It wasn't a high price to pay for a chicken casserole, green beans, sweet rolls, and a glass of lemonade. "Sure, I'll come."

"That's just wonderful. Isn't it, William?"

"It certainly is."

Soon Edith stood and began to clear the table. "Tell me about the tunnels," May said. "Does anyone use them now?"

William shook his head. He frowned. "Hobos. Derelicts. I don't think you'd like it down there."

"You've been, though."

He nodded. "I have. A few times. There's a place to get in downtown, and another in Hollywood. They don't all connect.

I'm trying to map it out." William looked down at the white tablecloth, pressing his fingertips there as if it were a piano and he was trying to decide which song to play. "I'll show you." He stood and went to his study, and then came back with a flat portfolio. It was black—the sort a death certificate might be kept in. "Have a look," he said, untying the ribbons that held it closed. "It's not organized yet."

He stood behind her and put the portfolio down in front of her so she could have a look. She opened it. Inside, there were maps of Los Angeles. There was a large commercial map of the trolley and train system, full of blue waving lines and careful print, a key with red dots. Atop the map, William had affixed a sheet of translucent paper. He'd marked it, the lines first drawn in pencil, then traced in black ink.

"These are all tunnels?" she asked, running a finger lightly over the surface.

"Yes—" He came around and sat down next to her again. "I've tried to include the offshoot tunnels here, from the closed trolley lines. I haven't explored those. They seem unstable."

"Especially if there were an earthquake," Edith called from the kitchen. "He doesn't go into those. Do you, darling?"

William winked at May. "Of course not."

There were other maps, clippings from old newspapers, notes. "What is this for?" May asked. She was looking at a clumsy drawing. Six circles, each containing a different animal, but the animals were hybrids of one another. A bird had the legs of a horse. A horse's head was perched on a feathered back. A cat's face, an ostrich's torso. It was like a game that required matching and rearranging.

"How did that get in there?" William took the drawing without comment and put it face down and in the back of the folio. "It's a silly thing. It's nothing." But his voice didn't sound like it was nothing. He rubbed his cheek absently. "It's a silly thing," he repeated.

May went back to looking at the map. An entire second city lay beneath Los Angeles, with new, unnamed roads—paths, some cut through rock for mining. "What will you do when you're finished exploring?"

"When I finish?" He raised his eyebrows. She didn't know. Would he put in a shop—a garage, perhaps—or buy property?

"Oh dear, no. Nothing so practical. I have some friends I work with. We're a club, maybe. If you like. It's a hobby—" She studied the map with him. It was an awful lot of work for a hobby. "Some of these are just guesses—" he went on. "They're based on what I've seen in the more finished tunnels. Would you like to go sometime?"

"Oh, William," Edith said, arriving with a coffee pot. "I doubt May wants to get all dirty in these old tunnels. I know I don't."

William glanced up at her but kept talking to May. "There's a legend that there's gold buried in some of the tunnels. Knowing that makes it quite fun when you're down there."

"Yes," May said. "Yes, I could go. Let's find the gold." She laughed, a quick startled sound.

"If it weren't dark, I'd take you right now. There's an entrance near church."

May didn't understand how there could be an entrance near the church until she saw the church. Edith and William's church wasn't like the churches back home. It was in a big white tent in an empty building lot in Hollywood. There were lights set up, and they blazed against the whiteness of the tent, and inside, the parishioners' shadows danced overhead. Edith took May's hands in her own and squeezed them. "You will be changed," she whispered, and May imagined herself changed, breaking out a of shell, growing wings—like one of the animals in William's folio. She shivered. The drawings were ugly. And she didn't want to be changed. She was just fine.

All through the sermon, May thought of Lily and Dora waiting for her, the slow slide of trombone announcing the night, the tremendous beat of the drum. She could be dancing. Instead, the night stayed outside, enormous, asleep, like a coat waiting to be put back on. But Joan, she thought. *Joan.* Was it Joan?

It really couldn't be.

She wanted to look at Lily.

First this person spoke and then the choir sang, and then a handsome young man came up and waved his arms and said no problem could be solved without Jesus, and soon May realized this boy in the light blue suit was the main attraction, and women raised their white-gloved hands and rose and swayed, caught in some invisible, rhythmic wind, and the men pounded their thighs with their hands and wiped their brows in the heat. Some cried. Children raced each other in and out of the sides of the tent, and no one told them to sit down and be quiet.

William sat between May and Edith, and soon May felt his fingers on her own, his hand on her thigh, and she could not move. She looked at his face, but he was staring straight ahead, his jaw set, his eyes shining, and May decided it was a mistake—this touch. She stood, and his hand fell away. Edith looked up at her, her smile radiant, and soon she stood too, raising her hands and closing her eyes. May imitated the others, holding the pamphlets with their drawings of crosses and praying hands that had been passed to her above in the air as she swayed back and forth.

Afterward, there was cake and coffee. May took an extra slice, wrapping it in a napkin and put it in her handbag when no one was looking. She smiled at Edith when she came toward her through the crowd. Edith's eyes were large and hopeful, her cheeks flushed. "You felt it, didn't you?" she said. William stood beside Edith, and he'd softened again, turning again into lucky Edith's husband.

"Oh yes." May lied. "Oh, I sure did," she said, thinking she'd have to try to remember what time the cake and coffee was served.

AGNES

The dancer's name was Joan Reed. "We can't release that, though," Elgin told Agnes. "The police are still digging around—but go down to the archives and find out in which club Joan worked. See if you can get a picture of her. Then give it to Max," he said. "He's on the Raptor."

Agnes looked at Max's wide back.

"Sure thing, boss," she said. She didn't tell Elgin that she already knew which club Joan Reed had worked in—that she'd already been down to the archives, where the photographs were housed in filing cabinets, in long, low-ceilinged rooms. She'd called around that morning, and after talking to one of the patrol officers, he'd given the name up, saying, "Don't print it, darling. I'll never give you a tip again."

Joan had been a dancer in one of the big clubs—not the best club, but the second-best, maybe. The one that was affordable, where the drinks were watered down and the steaks were drenched in sauce to disguise the toughness of the meat. It was a cabaret place called the Venetian Palace, but Agnes had only ever heard it referred to as the Palace.

The police wanted to hold Joan's name back for a day, see what would turn up, so the *Daily* had called Joan *dancer* in the evening edition. The autopsy photograph landed on Agnes's desk in the afternoon. She'd covered the body with a sheet of typing paper and looked at Joan's face instead.

Dancer. Joan hadn't been the main dancer, but someone who'd stood in the back row with the other girls, circling and moving in formation, turning together. She was part of a backdrop, a shining wall that separated the audience from the seediness of backstage, the grease makeup, the louche nightclub owner—a man named Ray.

In the archives, Agnes had found a folder with Ray's name on it. She read a clipping that was mixed in with the photographs. He'd been arrested in the thirties, when he was just a boy, for getting bootlegged liquor into nightclubs. He was the sort who knew the price of everything—he knew backrooms, side doors, safe houses. There were photographs of him with men she didn't recognize, men in tailored suits. There were others she did recognize: an ex-mayor, the city commissioner, the head of an architectural guild.

It always seemed as if he'd walked into a photograph at the last minute. He was smiling while the other men looked serious. Ray extended a hand, reached for a shoulder—a practiced, seemingly unguarded, warmth. He'd been born poor, so his life had begun in close quarters—he was used to pressing for space. Agnes didn't disagree with that approach—only that it was, like everything else, easier for men to master.

Ray's empire existed in the world of night. Nightclubs, music halls, a string of bars between Los Angeles and San Diego. And it was his money, of course, that kept the city's attention. Everyone who needed it pretended Ray had gone straight, but everyone knew he hadn't. The city was full of men like Ray—rumored to be Cosa Nostra, swollen from expensive dinners and well-stocked bars. The middle button on their good suits always a stitch too tight. There was the rumor, the shade of something—but only that—just enough for that dark bit of gossip—the intrigue.

But no one talked.

No one told.

In the most recent photograph, Ray was standing on a stage at the Palace, his arm around a dancer—another girl, not Joan, but a girl like Joan, maybe. He held a drink, and both he and the dancer were laughing as if the photographer had said something funny. Agnes pulled a photograph of the nightclub's dancers. In one of the photographs, the dancers wore identical outfits: cross-over halters, pleated shorts, and shoes with a wedged heel. They stood on a stage arced like a quarter-moon. The walls behind them were black and the floor below mirrored. Each girl had one hand on her hip and twisted slightly to accentuate her waist. A cutout of a cutout of a cutout, hair tucked beneath a pale turban, lips and eyes darkened with makeup, but there. She tapped the photograph.

That one looked like Joan.

She found more photographs from the Palace. This one showed an elaborate production of a show called "The Circus." The dancers wore animal masks—there was a tiger, a lion. The masks were garish with paint, oversized, and gave the dancers an inhuman, burdened quality. The women's costumes were made of sequins and fur and colored tulle. A male dancer stood at the center, his hat tipped. He was the ringmaster with a whip. A girl wearing a horse's mask stood beside him, one hand on her hip. The tiger did a high kick.

Agnes kept the photographs, tucking them into an envelope in her satchel, and when Elgin came over, she had just been looking at her watch, thinking she should take the streetcar to the Palace and see if she could get any information about Joan before the police turned up.

Agnes stood on the sidewalk in front of the Palace. The building rambled in its lot, hardly regal, pulling along its various additions and attachments. There were faux balconies—decorative and too shallow to stand on—and columns too large for the entrance. It was painted light blue and salmon, and there were clumsily painted murals of dancing women, their arms stiff. They reminded Agnes of drawings a schoolboy would do on a piece of scrap paper, passing it to another while a teacher's back was turned.

Agnes discarded the idea of going in the front, and followed a side alley and went around back. The schoolboy's women followed her down the alley and then disappeared without fanfare as she turned a corner.

Go on in, she told herself. You could be anyone. You could be a cleaning woman, a bookkeeper, an assistant.

After all, you could be a *reporter.*

The back door was propped open with a brick. Inside, she followed the sound of laughter. She followed it down a short hallway, and walked into a room that two women were walking out of. The women looked at her and smiled and moved past her. In the dressing room, she found a woman sitting at a long mirror, the lights bright, the counter in front of her littered with lipstick, glitter, with pins and feathers and sequined sashes. Bright costumes hung on garment racks.

"You're early," the woman said to Agnes. She watched Agnes in the mirror. "Are you new too? Ginger is showing me the moves for tonight's show. Ginger, there's another girl here—" she called. "It's easy, but you can stay in the back until you get the dance."

A woman came out from behind a curtain. "It's just the mask that makes it harder. They're heavy." She was holding a papier maché lion's head under her arm—it's nose wide and pink, the mane blossoming in orange fur. "Ray's having lighter masks made, but we have to do with these for a while."

"I'm new, yes," Agnes said. "But I'm not a dancer. I'm a reporter."

"A reporter, huh?" The woman holding the mask glanced in the mirror, touching her hair. "I'm Ginger," she said. "This is Lily. We're actresses. Don't be fooled by all this. It's just temporary, right, Lil?"

Lily winked at Ginger.

"I'm with the *Daily*. Agnes Crandall." She put out her hand, but Ginger and Lily just looked at her.

"What's this about?" Ginger said.

"Do you know Joan Reed?" And then they knew why she was there. They stared, and it seemed the whole room shifted. Agnes noticed that the wooden floor was darkly scuffed and covered with the debris from costumes. She saw the strange masks—the elephant with its shortened trunk, the eyes cut out for the dancers, and the tiger—his coarse stripes, a rabbit's mischievous grin. The electric lights around the mirrors, the dark corners.

They didn't have to ask, "Was it Joan?" It was plain. Ginger cried out. "No," she said. She repeated it. Not Joan. No. Not Joan. No. But Lily was pale faced and silent. Agnes apologized. "No—" Ginger said again, looking at Agnes. "No."

"I'm sorry," she repeated. "I'm so very sorry."

Lily took Ginger's hands in her own.

"Soon," Agnes said to them, "when the police figure out some things about Joan, they'll want to ask questions. They'll make her sound—well—" She looked around the room, thinking of how to say it. She didn't need to explain it to them. They were watching her.

"They'll make it sound like she was cheap," Lily said. "Like it was her fault."

"I don't want that to happen. I want to know who Joan was," Agnes explained, holding Lily's gaze. "I want to know what was important to her—"

"I knew it, somehow I knew it—" Ginger said. "I knew something was wrong. Who can you ask when your friend doesn't turn up?"

"People say all kind of things—" Lily began.

"About girls like us," Ginger added. "For making a living."

Agnes imagined herself as they saw her: eager in her plain dress, a notepad out, her hair pinned back, her face bare. A girl from school, maybe, the one with the raised— But it was true, wasn't it? She *had* always been the first to raise her hand. If she hadn't raised it quickly, she would never be called on—ever. "I'd like to solve this," Agnes said. "I want to know who the Raptor is. Did Joan have a boyfriend?"

"A guy named Marty," Ginger said.

"Do you know how she met him?"

"At church of all places. If you can believe that. I want to know who did that to her. Will you find out?"

"How did it happen?" Lily asked. "How was she killed? Are they sure it was the Raptor? Was it as bad as the others?"

"Yes. It was as bad," Agnes said. She said it quietly, like she was holding her breath, and explained what she knew. She tried to sound like a doctor as she described it. She didn't even tell them the worst things. "Did you ever meet Marty?" she asked in the silence that followed.

"No, but someone must have." Ginger put her hands to her own throat. "*Strangled*," she said. "Imagine that."

"Do you know which church she went to—where she met him?" *Church. Marty or Martin*, she wrote.

"No. I think it was one of those churches in a tent though.

That kind. She liked to sing. Joanie had a pretty voice. It was practice. Harmony. The hymns. She could have made it." Ginger turned away.

Agnes wrote her telephone number on a piece of paper. "Call me if you want to talk about Joan. I'd like to hear about her. Who she was—"

Ginger nodded. "Leave it there," she said. "I'll let the others know too."

At home, Agnes let herself in, then stood in the darkening hallway and gazed at the lilies that Ben had given her. They were starting to turn, the high note of perfume mingling with a fetid edge, but the petals were still stiff with moisture, their white fingers blue in the evening light.

Where did a lily come from? What history of trade and craft had set them in a vase of water on the same table where she lazily dropped her mail? And why did she not stop and exclaim, *What an incredible thing!* each time she saw a flower?

She took off her shoes and cracked her toes. She unhooked her bra and rolled her stockings off. She stretched one nylon leg, tugged at it with both hands until it was a long, strong chord. What was it to wrap that around a neck? She released the stocking and balled it up, tossing it into a corner.

She began to write.

3

MAY

Lily's face was set, her lips thin and pressed together, her jaw moving like she was rolling a stone around in her mouth. She was sitting in a chair by the window in their room at the Hamilton. When May came in, she didn't need to ask, but said, "Was it—?"

"Joan, yes."

May sat down on Lily's bed. She looked out the window too. A sign flashed on and off. A door slammed in the hallway. Someone laughed on the street below. "How do you know?" May finally asked, and Lily told her about the woman who'd come to the Palace—Agnes, she thought her name was.

After a while, May got up and went to her own bed, but she didn't change into her night clothes or pull the sheet that separated their beds across the room. She watched Lily. Lily put her feet up on the windowsill and smoked one cigarette after the next. She wrote in her calendar book. May fell asleep to the scratch of her pen across the paper, aware of Lily's restlessness as she drifted into dreams. May only dreamed of travel, of rushing through the night on a crowded train, the world flying by. *Where am I?* she asked, but no one answered.

In the morning, Lily was still sitting at the window. Her calendar book was lying on the floor, and Lily had the same expression on her face. "I'm starved," she said to May, but she didn't look at her. She looked out the window.

At the drugstore, over eggs, May kept waiting for Lily to talk about Joan, but she didn't—nor did she eat her eggs. She looked at a newspaper. It said nothing about Joan. She was still *Dancer.*

"Maybe it's not her—" May tried. "Maybe that Agnes woman was lying."

"She wasn't lying."

Lily said she wanted to look at something beautiful instead of the dull old curtains in their room, so May suggested the gardens, and even though Lily insisted she wasn't tired, once they were in the gardens, Lily looked at a broad white stone bench. "I feel dizzy. I'd like to lie down. Do you think anyone will mind?"

"Why should they? You've had a shock, and you don't want to faint. It's hot." Lily's eyes were as red and small as if she lived underground. "Stay here," May said. "I just want to go down that path." She pointed to a place across a wide green lawn where a copse of trees parted. "I'd like to see if there's a cooler place to rest in the shade." She left Lily on a bench amid roses and crossed the lawn.

Where the white path split and the afternoon shadows settled heavily into the deep green of the ornamental trees, May came upon a man sitting by a fountain. "Why, hello," he said, and she smiled with her lips closed and nodded at him. "It's a beautiful day, isn't it?"

"Isn't it always a beautiful day here?"

"Are you from a place that doesn't have beautiful days?"

"Plenty."

He looked at her before saying anything—head to toe, as if he'd find a hint. "East coast, I'd guess. Not New York. Philadelphia, Baltimore?"

"You're getting too far south—" She laughed.

"Oh, a New England girl."

"Boston." She looked back over her shoulder. She could no longer see Lily. She would go back in just a moment, but she liked this man. He had a funny way about him. He had thick brown hair and a small mustache and wore a good suit. He looked like a film star in his clean white shirt and gray trousers, a jacket next to him on the bench.

"Of course! I should have known."

"Why do you say that? You say it like it's a bad thing."

"No, it's not a bad thing. You look, well, Irish in a way. There are lots of Irish in Boston."

"I suppose there are lots of Irish everywhere. And Mother's Scottish, anyway."

He uncrossed his legs and then crossed them the other way. He took out a pipe and tapped it gently against the bench, but then he put it down as if he changed his mind. "Visiting?"

"In a way." She looked at her feet. Her shoes were small and black and neat with a tiny silk bow on each toe. They were dusty from the dry weather, and she fought the urge to reach down and brush them off.

"Sit down. Talk to me." He gestured at the bench behind her. "You seem like the best thing that's about to happen to me all day."

She sat down, crossing her ankles and tucking her handbag into her lap.

"Call me Adams," he said.

"Aren't you going to smoke that?"

"If I do, I won't be able to smell the roses. And some ladies don't like the smell of smoke." His face was brown from the sun. He smiled and winked.

"I don't mind. It's just a little smoke." Still he didn't light his pipe, but sat gazing at her. She sat up straighter. "It's nice to make your acquaintance, Adams. I'm May."

"Where are you staying?"

She paused, considering whether she would tell him. Some girls said not to tell a man, not at first, but others said it was fine. She thought of a girl she bunked with for week or so, and how she'd come back crying, saying, *He knows where I live*— "The Edmonton," she said. It was one hotel over from the Hamilton and just a bit nicer too. She could meet him in the lobby of the Edmonton. She imagined herself on the red sofa in a black dress, waiting.

"That downtown?"

"Yes."

Neither of them said anything for a moment. May looked at her shoes again, and down the shady walk to the place where the path ended. The sun came through the trees, making shadowed patterns on her skin. She thought she and Lily could find a place there to sit and talk. Or Lily could sleep. She'd even let her put her head in her lap if she needed to.

It was cool enough in Los Angeles for some of the trees to lose their thick leaves, and they lay on the green grass, as big and open as the palm of one's hand. She opened her own hands and looked at the lines there. "Is Adams your real name?"

He laughed. His teeth were nearly as white as his shirt. "Of course."

"What do you do? Are you in the service?"

"Oh, I was—like everyone else. I'm in—" He looked around, as if he'd forgotten, and then said: "I'm a detective."

"Well, that's very interesting. I suppose that's how you knew I wasn't from here."

"Sure. It's practice."

"Tell me something else you've noticed."

He gazed at her. "You're rather upset by something."

She looked quickly up at him. "It's nothing," she said, not wanting to talk about Joan—or anything terrible at all. "Tell me something else you see."

"You don't mind being alone."

It was true. She didn't. She looked back through the trees for Lily. "Because I came in here by myself?"

"That too."

"What else?"

"You're single. You got on a train and came clean across the country. If I were questioning you, I'd try to find out why."

"But I haven't *done* anything." She knew she sounded petulant. Just a moment ago, when all the men were overseas, it had been fine to come out West. There would be some job to fill at one of the air force bases—but then the war ended, and people kept asking her why she was there at all. "You must be an actress," they said. "Or a model. You'll find a husband soon enough, anyway. You're so pretty." It was confusing, after all, the way the world kept repurposing her. They wanted one thing, then another, and soon she didn't know what she was supposed to be doing.

"Everyone's done *something*."

She tilted her head to one side. "*I* haven't."

"Then you *will* do something, some day."

"I won't."

"Are you an actress?"

"I'm a hat model," she lied. Soon enough it would be true, anyway. She'd go over to Robinson's and find that man that Hazel had told her about, and then she'd say, "Yes, in fact, I am a model," when people wondered what she was doing. She'd let the man at Robinson's fit her for a dress to see if it looked well on her, and then she'd be a dress model, a hat model, a glove—whatever sort of model they needed at the moment.

"Really? Is that so?"

"Why sure it's so."

"You're certainly pretty enough, and I imagine it's tough to find work as a hat model in Boston."

"Oh, it's not so hard."

"Is that why you came out here?"

"Somewhat."

He lit his pipe and brushed off his trousers. "What a mystery you are, May." He rose and put on his jacket. "I think your friend is here." May looked over and saw Lily walking slowly across the grass in the sunshine, one white-gloved hand shielding her eyes from the sun as she came. "Thursday at six?" Adams asked. "The Edmonton?"

"That sounds fine."

"Who was that?" Lily asked when she found May. She sat down next to her on the bench and took off her gloves.

"Adams," May answered.

"*Adams?* What sort of a name is that?"

"A funny one."

"Did he fall in love with you?"

"He may have." May laughed. "I told him I'm a hat model."

"Aren't you?"

"He's a detective."

"Oh dear. You lied to a detective?" Lily laughed. "He'll find you out."

"Yes. I'm sure he knows all my secrets already."

"You haven't *got* any secrets."

But she did have secrets. There were fragments—memories she couldn't quite unearth. It gave her some anxiety, some sense that the world wasn't what it pretended to be, even in all that sunshine.

They stood and walked the way Adams had gone, pausing at the stone fountain. It wasn't any cooler there but it felt as though it must be, in the shade with the sound of water. "We made a date."

"Did you?"

"For Thursday."

When Thursday came, May didn't get a message from Adams, even though she walked the block to the Edmonton three times, back and forth, asking the hotel clerk if there was a message for her until the clerk finally looked at her as if she were holding a tin cup out. He shook his head, and before she could ask, he said, "No one has phoned, miss."

She went back to the Hamilton and sat for a while in the lobby, opening her handbag and closing it again, pressing the small silver clasp in a way that it made a nice catching noise. She thought of Richard and all the boys in their uniforms. She'd met him at one of the dances. She was leaning against a wall because her feet hurt and she was tired, but she didn't want to leave. The night was just beginning. She looked around the room and found his broad back. He was talking to some fellows, and he was tall and had to lean a little forward to make himself heard over the band, who lifted their trumpets high in the air and then broke to take a drink and wipe their brows. Richard must have felt her looking at him because he glanced once or twice around the room as if someone had shouted his name. Soon he found her there, leaning against the wall, smiling, her hands folded behind her. He jogged a little as he came toward her, his long legs slightly bowed, imperfect. When he reached her, he stood over her, smiling, and then, instead of saying anything, he leaned against the wall beside her and found her hand there, and slipped it into his.

Later she found out about his eyes and how they could never be hard—even when he talked about the Germans—even though his jaw jutted and his voice changed as if his windpipe were partly constricted, the expression in his eyes, that softness—it never changed.

She left the hotel and walked along the street, looking at the people who passed, trying to see the expression in their eyes. She paused in front of a diner and saw herself in the window, but she was just a black silhouette, an outline of a woman. She opened her change purse and counted coins, looking up now and then at the menu taped to the glass as she made decisions. She went inside and ordered a chicken sandwich and a glass of milk, and when she was halfway through, she saw Adams outside, wearing a brown suit and looking at his wristwatch, but she did not knock on the window or wave.

AGNES

It was getting dark when Agnes and Danny drove up to Mount Hollywood. They went all the way to the peak on a dirt road that was really too narrow for a car, but they managed, and Danny laughed that this is how he would teach Agnes how to drive. On roads like this. "No, thank you," she said.

At the top, she sat on the hood of the car and held a flashlight for him as he set up his tripod, his camera. He rolled his shirt sleeves and crouched in the dirt to level out the tripod, certain in his movements. When he stood, he brushed his hands together and brought a cable shutter release out of his pocket.

This was his project. He photographed the city at night, finding perch after perch. He opened the shutter at different intervals, testing the way light traveled across the film. He usually worked alone, but tonight he'd invited Agnes, and because she sometimes wondered what he did when he left the station, she'd said yes.

He came back to her and sat down next to her on the hood, which was still warm. Wasn't it pleasant to be up there with him, next to him, with a thermos of coffee or a silver flask of gin between them? "Your choice," he said, holding the thermos in one hand and the flask in the other. She took the coffee, thinking she'd save the gin for later.

Soon she sighed and brought her hands together, saying it would be dark enough soon. He agreed, and then she told him about Joan—about Ginger and Lily. *Marty*, she said. "I'd like to find him."

"How—" he said, wanting to know how she'd found Ginger and Lily, and she told him about the archives, about the Palace. He whistled. "You could be a detective."

She laughed. Oh, it was nothing—no, really. But it was something. It was a great deal. And he thought so too. "Do you know anything about a church in a tent?" she asked.

"In Hollywood. Used to be a streetcar station there. It's all the rage if that's your style." He laughed. He'd heard about it from a friend who went out of curiosity—which might be worth doing. People went for the show—the boys carrying snakes, the healings, the baptisms in the big white bathtub set up near the alter—and sometimes, if you were lucky, the exorcisms, the women fainting, the men crying.

"That sounds dreadful," Agnes said, laughing. "Do you get out alive?"

"Sister," Danny rested his hand on Agnes's, "you get out better than alive. You get out *saved*." He smiled at her.

"I'm nearly afraid to go." She studied his hand on hers, wide and soft and warm, and fought an impulse to wrap her fingers around his. She was glad when he took it away and picked up the shutter release again. She thought of Ben reading the newspaper in the morning, his face serious, his glasses low on his nose.

Danny was younger than Agnes, and sometimes she noticed and sometimes she didn't. It wasn't but a few years, not even a handful, but people made a big deal out of something like that. No one said boo about Ben's age. When she told them he was fifteen years older than she, they smiled as if that were a good thing. "He knows a thing or two about the world, then," Rosemary had said when she first brought him up. "He knows how things are set."

Danny had done communications in the army—transmitters and receivers, radio waves, and he'd tinkered with the radio in the car until it picked up police calls. He turned the radio up so they could hear. The police dispatcher's voice cracked and jumped with the announcement of each staticky ten-code. They listened, impassive, to calls for robberies, assaults. Below them, pickpockets roamed the boulevard, men fought in bars, partygoers made too much noise. There was a fire in a warehouse, and someone broke into a hardware store.

"Close your eyes," he said, and she did. He took her hand again in his and lifted it so that she pointed over the city. "Maybe that's where he is. Or there." He let her hand go. She opened her eyes.

"Might as well be. He could be anywhere," she said.

Danny took his first photograph. They counted the seconds together in intervals, "One-chimpanzee, two-chimpanzee, three— " She waited for the shutter release to sound, the cock and click of the aperture. The city brightened with light below them. The lazy curve toward the observatory, headlights, the ebb and flow.

When he finished a pack of film, they got into the car. She put her head back on the seat and closed her eyes, listening to the ten-ohs. "Let's try it," she said. "Next stick up. Next fight. Let's see how fast we can get there."

"Practice," Danny said.

There it was: a purse snatching. "Go," Agnes yelled, and Danny pulled out. The car screeched at a turn, and then another. "Faster—" Agnes cried out, while Danny kept his Graflex at his side, driving with one hand on the camera, trying to beat the police. Agnes and Danny arrived with the police cars, their headlights blanching the faces of the small crowd. The woman who'd had her handbag stolen had been knocked to the ground, and one of her knees was bloodied.

What happened? Who saw?

"Lucky it wasn't the Raptor," a man said.

"Maybe it was. Maybe you saved my life by turning up." The victim stood in the center of the semi-circle, her hands clasped in front of her as if she were carrying the ghost of her bag. "He got away—" she said to Agnes.

He always does, thought Agnes.

When Agnes and Danny got back to her house in Pasadena, it was late but they were giddy. She invited him in for something—coffee, even, or a glass of water. He was hungry, so she cooked him eggs. "Are you a good cook?" he asked.

"Not particularly," she said, and they laughed, but he said the eggs were the best he'd ever had.

"This is another bit we can do." She carried the telephone to the table while he ate, the long black cord swishing on the floor as she moved. She dialed the police stations, district by district. She got up and walked around the room, carrying the phone with her. She perched it on her hip, and cradled the receiver between her chin and shoulder. "I'm at the *Daily*," she told them. "Got anything for me?" after a pause—"Agnes Crandall." He watched her. "That's right. The *Daily*." She took the pen from behind her ear and came back over to the table, writing. "You think it might have been the Raptor?" She shook her head at Danny. *Not tonight.*

It was four a.m. He lay down on the couch. "Stay for a minute," he said as she was rising to go, and she did. She sat on the end of the sofa and held his feet in her lap. She rested her head

on the back of the sofa and looked at the ceiling, wondering if
he had a steady girl, and then wondered why she was thinking
that. She closed her eyes. When he started to snore, she got up
and went to bed.

On Saturday, Danny taught her how to drive in the parking
lot behind Ralph's, and soon she was on the streets. She could
feel the weight of the Packard when she stalled out on hills,
laughing as the car horns sounded behind her.

When the call came over Danny's radio, she relinquished the
wheel to him. She was still too slow. "Go," she yelled, and they
ran around the car so that he could take the driver's side. She
did not like to speed—not yet—and they had to get there fast.

At the apartment house in Silver Lake, Agnes only saw the
victim's feet, which were bare, the ankles swollen. A patrolman
held her back from getting into the apartment. "Come on, Joe,"
she said to him. "I'm a reporter."

"That's why I'm not letting you in." It was a lie, Agnes knew.
He let Danny through without a second thought. A man with
a camera! Agnes could see the flash of the Graflex through the
doorway.

Men in suits. Men in uniforms. Men blocking doorways. You
had to find other ways around. Take the back stairs. Call the
police station. Make a man laugh. Let him think what he liked.

She turned toward the crowd gathering in the hallway. "Who
lives here?" she asked a woman in a checkered robe.

"Beverly. Beverly Dean."

"Did you know her?"

"A little. She was friendly. Always said hello. Who could do
such a thing?" The woman peered past the officer in the doorway, gazing at Beverly's swollen ankles. She held on to Agnes's
arm. Her hair was still wrapped for sleep, the salon's curls pre-
served beneath. She turned her face to Agnes. "Who—"

"Did she have a boyfriend?" Agnes asked. "Did you hear
anything?"

"This shouldn't have happened." The woman's face was

pale, her eyes dark in the bright overhead light of the hallway. "Why did this happen?" Her fingers dug into Agnes's arm.

Agnes shook her head. She imagined them from above. She was a camera floating over the crime scene. Below was Beverly Dean's body splayed on the bathroom floor, the black-and-white tiles, the detective squatting over her. If she could just see them all that way, she thought, from above, encapsulated, frozen—she would see the clues.

4

MAY

"You stood us up the other night," Dora said. "Where'd you go?"

"Church."

"You're *not* serious. You stood us up for church?" They were waiting for Lily to finish her audition and sat at a soda fountain near the lot, sizing up anyone who came in. They crossed their legs and spun on their stools. "Actor," Dora whispered. "I think I've seen him in that— Oh, *what was* that film—" But she couldn't remember, and she tapped her finger to her forehead. "You didn't miss anything. We were mostly just distraught," Dora said. "About poor Joan. We got exceedingly drunk."

"Did you know her well?"

"Hardly. I met her once. Still—" Dora gazed past May at the door. "Still," she repeated. "It's so horrible. I can't really believe it."

"I know."

"*Lily* knew her, though. She was shaking awfully."

Lily had told May she hardly knew Joan at all. So either Dora was mistaken, or— But Lily didn't talk much about the people she'd met in Los Angeles before they'd become friends. Lily talked about her family and acting, but she'd never heard her mention Joan until that day at the beach with Dora. "How did you and Lily meet?" May asked.

"She came up to me out of the blue and struck up a conversation. She took me to a party at Claude's. I was so thankful. I didn't know anyone here, practically." Dora had met Joan at Claude's too. Just that one time. "There are always a lot of pretty girls at Claude's house. Actresses—that sort."

"And are the men very handsome?"

"They are—*old.*" Dora laughed. "Oh, I guess you'll see someday. But you always meet a lot of interesting people. Everyone wants to be someone. That's the thing—if they aren't someone already. And Claude can make that happen. He knows everyone."

"I'd like to go."

"Would you? I'll bring you if Lily won't. She acts like she doesn't want to hang around there anymore." Dora looked at May for a moment. Was she waiting for May to tell her why Lily didn't want to go? May didn't know. Lily kept quiet about Claude. "Just don't stand me up for church!" Dora finally said.

"Oh, brother." May chewed on her pinky nail. "What a church too."

"Tell me. Tell me something funny."

"It's in a tent. Everyone throws up their hands and says, Praise Jesus! They get the fits." She rolled her eyes, laughing. "Praise Jesus!" she said.

"Oh—are you a friend of Jesus?" Dora smiled. She looked at May sideways.

Aside from Edith, May didn't know anyone in Los Angeles who went to church. It was as if all the old things had been tossed away. A church was in a tent. A girl could live on her own forever. There were women who didn't have children, who lived in apartments with animals. They didn't even cook their own food.

"Are you his *lamb?*" Dora rested her chin on her hand.

"I'm not. Not really." But May felt funny saying it. Perhaps a lightning bolt would shoot from the clear blue sky. "I suppose I'm a *friend* of a friend of Jesus."

"Who's the friend?"

"A friend of the family."

Dora gasped and clapped her hands together. "Say it with me."

"What?"

She took May's hands in hers. "A friend of a friend of Jesus is a friend of the family." She swung May's hands back and forth as she sang the words like a hymn.

Laughing, May covered her mouth. "You mustn't," she said. "It sounds just like something they'd sing."

"It sure does. Did they have snakes?"

"Snakes?"

"You'll see. If you keep going."

"But how do you know so much?"

"A gang of us went once. We wanted to see. We were all a little drunk. It was scandalous. And the preacher is ghastly. He's this tall fair creature whose face is always red."

"I wonder if you went to this church?" May told her where it was, but Dora said they were popping up all over the place since the war.

May chewed on her straw. "I guess people need a new way to look at something old. Like resewing a coat for a new season."

Dora stopped spinning on her stool and faced May. "I like that. I've never resewn a coat."

"No?"

"I just get a new one. Do you have a fellow?"

"I have a lot of fellows, but no, not anyone. Not really."

"But Lily said you did. She said your fiancé died in the war."

May nodded. "Just after. He was coming home."

"That's terrible luck. Is that why you're way out here?"

"In a way." May didn't feel like telling a story. One day she'd have to stop talking about Richard. She tried to imagine that day. She saw herself sitting in the sunshine on a park bench with white birds around her. It didn't make any sense, but that's what she saw. She might carry something of Richard's with her still. She'd keep the photo of them together, tucked into her bag. "That's not Daddy," her children would say. "Who is that?" and maybe she would tell them and maybe she wouldn't. She wondered if Richard's body existed anymore after the plane crashed. It was no good to think like that. That's what her mother said. Don't think about it. Turn your thoughts to pretty things instead.

Dora was staring at her. "Hey—" She smiled. "Hey, kiddo. Sorry I brought it up. I should keep my mouth shut." Dora began to tell her a story about a man she'd gone to dinner with the night before. She said she'd elope with him if he asked, but her parents would never approve. He wasn't their sort.

"What's their sort?"

"They like a man who has his nose in the air." When May didn't say anything, Dora went on: "A rich boy with phony ways. An Ivy League man. I like artists. I want to live in Paris. I want to drink wine and live with a man who writes poems for me. *About* me. I want to have revolutions."

"That would be swell."

"Swell?" Dora shook her head. "You're a funny one. You're adorable." May tried to see if Dora was teasing her, but she didn't think she was. She leaned her elbows on the counter and called to the waitress. "Have you got a match?" The waitress came over and put a box down in front of her. Dora took one out, lit it, then blew it out. She opened her left palm to May. Inside was a faint circle, a spiral, a twist. She traced over it again with the snubbed match. "Lily showed this to me," she said. When she was finished, she took May's hand in her own—and opposite-side handshake—and held it tightly for a moment. "Make a wish," Dora said. "Close your eyes and make a wish." May did as she was told. She shut her eyes and saw Richard sitting in the kitchen with the red-checked curtains. He was looking at her and smiling. His legs were crossed. She knew she was holding a baby. Even though she couldn't see it, she felt the baby's soft breath on her neck. "All right," Dora said, and May opened her eyes again. "Look at your hand."

Inside May's palm was the faint outline of the mark Dora had made on her own. "It's for good luck," she said. "Lily knows all sorts of things, doesn't she?"

This is where you kick. This is how to hit.

Dora spun on her stool. "I want to go dancing later. Let's go to the pier. If Lily doesn't want to go, we could just the two of us."

"All right." May liked going to the pier. Sometimes she pretended it wasn't quite nice enough to like. It could get a little wayward and cheap feeling, everyone on a hustle, but Dora liked it, so in that moment, May liked it, too, and when she said, "All right," she said it like it was a treat.

"I skip around a lot. Sorry. Anyone will tell you."

"What do you mean?"

"I have so many thoughts in my head. They all want to jump out at once."

"That happens to me sometimes, but mine don't jump out, they stay inside."

"Really? I was in the hospital for it. That's why everyone calls me crazy."

"I haven't heard that."

"Yes, you have. It's all right. I don't mind. Everyone knows. It makes me interesting. It was when I was in college. I had to leave college. It was a very formative experience."

May was about to ask what happened, but Dora talked into the pause.

"Do you know what I learned from the whole thing? Never tell anyone you're not just like they are. Well, you can tell *some* people, but not everyone. I can tell *you* what I think about. I can tell all the artists."

"But I'm not an artist."

"You're not?" Dora raised her eyebrows. "I assumed. You live like one. You've gotten outside of the lines. Most of us are."

Dora was making things up. She didn't know May hardly at all anyway. "What lines?"

"You came out here. You got on a train and came all the way out here. That's remarkable." She was excited, moving her hands through the air as she spoke. "Lily's outside the lines too. No one told her to be an actress. No one told you to get on a train. You live outside the lines. You've got something you want to give the world. You know? That's how you can tell someone's a real artist. They take chances that other people don't take.

It's like they've got to. But what's hard is to get back in the lines once you've been out awhile. My parents want me to come home and get back in the lines. That's the thing. You see what it's like and you want your freedom."

"I never was in anyone's lines." May tried it out. It was like standing on top of a table, saying something like that. She said it again, this time with her chin lifted, but Dora's face was dark. She pointed to a man reading the news. "Look at that," she said. "*No leads in the Raptor case.*" The headline was black and bold. "I get scared out of my wits sometimes."

Dora looked around. "A woman called Agnes Crandall wrote about me when I was in the hospital. I heard she works for the *Daily* now. She's a very clever person. She could see clear past all the lines. Even farther than the doctors could. She wanted to publish a story about me, and I thought that was very interesting, but when my mother found out about it, she was in a terrible rage."

Wasn't that the name of the woman who came to talk to Lily and Ginger? Didn't she say her name was Agnes too? "I think Agnes is the one who told Lily about Joan," May said. "I can't imagine having someone want to write a story about me."

"I bet it is. She's very clever, as I said. I liked her a great deal, but Mother thought she was too ambitious—but that's what Mother says about people when she thinks they don't know their place. Agnes doesn't know her place, but that's wonderful. I'm always so very glad when people don't know their place."

Dora looked back at the man who was reading the newspaper. May thought she'd say something about Joan, but she didn't. She rubbed her cheek, and when she spoke, she didn't look at May. "The doctors wanted to give me an operation," she said. She tapped her forehead. "Here, but Mother and Father didn't want it, and I didn't really either because I hate medicine. I really do. I really hate medicine. A girl gets outside of the lines and no one knows what to do with her. There's only a general panic to get her back in or hush her up. I've always been outside the lines. *That's* why I was in the hospital. They were trying to press me in again." Dora turned to May. "Let's get out of here. Lily's never coming, and I'm terribly envious of her right now. They've probably got her doing more scenes. Her facial features are *terribly* symmetrical, don't you think? She'll forgive us. I'll drive to the pier so we can dance. I want a beer, don't you? It's hot. It will be so nice by the ocean on a hot evening. This way, Lily will miss out on something too." She smiled at May and dipped her chin, opening her purse and taking out money. When she looked up again, she said, "You must think I'm awful." But May didn't. She thought Dora was wonderful. And May was jealous of Lily, too, though she'd never have been the one to say it.

Dora drove with one hand on the steering wheel, the other resting on the open window, her palm open, as if she were letting that spiraled mark breathe. Every time Dora and May stopped in traffic, some boy would try to talk to them, calling out from another car, or coming up and leaning in the window. Dora and May laughed. It was too much, wasn't it? The way you could never get away. Even if you were just on your way somewhere and not thinking about men at all.

By the time they reached the ocean, it was almost dark. The sky above the sea was blue-violet and orange at the horizon. Above them, the Ferris wheel's cars rocked, silhouetted against the setting sun until the lights blinked on, and May caught sight of herself in the glancing mirrors of the carousel, and amid the garish horses' grins, she saw herself smiling, walking beside Dora, who had her hands in the pockets of her dress and her small face turned toward the ocean. May yelled to be heard above the crowd, leaning toward Dora. They pointed, setting off in the direction of the band, which they could hear playing in the ballroom that sat near the end of the pier, its wide door-ways open for the clean air, seducing the passerby with color and motion.

The dancers were from different places, from the Midwest or the South or the East, so their moves were varied and nuanced by place and attitude, and you could choose what you wanted to learn and then a boy would teach you, or a girl would stand off by the side to show you, letting you follow until you got it.

When May and Dora passed each other dancing, they called out, *A friend of a friend of Jesus is a friend of the family*—or some version of it—and laughed. They danced on the beach, even, shoeless, the sand cold between their toes. They danced with music and without. They danced into the small hours, past closing time, never wanting any of it to end.

May didn't like endings. She didn't like closing time—the lights switching off, watching cars leave a parking lot. It was the absence of pleasure, like her mother's careful nightly dinners: scraps from the butcher, gristle and fat. She thought of the girls from the Common, imagined they ate stuffed fowl glazed brown at long shining tables, the skin crispy as they pulled at it with their even white teeth. Sated, whole, they were allowed the pleasures of life—not the pain of it, not the poverty. The way they danced in mirrored rooms, not at tawdry halls, a man's palm light and respectful at mid-back—the arm straightened gracefully, the pale dresses caught in the wind of motion, safe in the orchestral wave, the night settled and still beyond the well-lit room.

With each dance, May imagined she was passing on the good luck spiral that nested in her palm. She imagined it becoming deeper, a gully, a rivulet, a scar. The black water rushing, becoming a part of her. It became her heartbeat, her very pulse. But when Dora came laughing back to her at the end of the night, they walked into the light to find the car, and May opened her hands and looked down at them. The mark was gone. It had only been a smear of ash after all.

AGNES

Between piles of unlabeled photographs, Agnes wrote down what Ginger said when she finally called. She was glad for Ben's silver pen and the typewriter paper shivering against her hand. Ginger said that Joan was from Ohio, had wanted to be an actress, and that she hadn't been in the city for very long—two years. In two years, Joan had lived in seven different places. She moved from hotel to rooming house, back to a hotel, and had briefly lived with a boyfriend somewhere in the Hills. That ended, and she moved again. She'd always worked at the Palace, though. At first as hat check, then a cigarette girl, then finally, as a dancer. On free afternoons, she auditioned for film parts. She'd just gotten a part in a movie. Ginger sighed. "Joanie was going to take some time off from the Palace. She called it her 'actress time.' I thought she was, you know, playing hookie."

"But she wasn't."

"No." Ginger sniffed—but Agnes pressed. Did Joan tell her anything? Was she afraid of anyone? Did she say anything, anything at all, that seemed odd to Ginger?

"Once we met for lunch—just after she found out about the part—and we were laughing about some fellows, and I said I wanted to a marry a man with money—or at least one who had a job—and Joanie said, 'No, don't marry a man with a lot of money. Don't do that.' And I said, 'Why wouldn't I do that?' and she said, 'You wouldn't *believe* what people with money get up to in this town'—and it wasn't *what* she said, really, but the *way* she said it. Like she wanted to tell me a secret."

"Did you ask her what she meant?"

"Sure I did. Sure."

Agnes wrote it down: *You wouldn't believe what people with money*— She could hear Ginger crying on the other end of the line. "I'm glad she got that part," Agnes said. "That must have made her happy. I'm glad she had that."

"Me too. She told me once— 'Well,' she said, 'this isn't a lucky break. I did something for this. I gave something—'"

"What did she mean?"

"Oh, I don't know! I wish I did. She was so serious when she said it, and she was different. I noticed it. She didn't laugh as much—she had *secrets*. And I couldn't find out anything about any Marty. I asked everyone I could think of. Maybe I was the only person she mentioned it to?"

"Maybe. Did you know Beverly Dean?"

Ginger paused. "No—though she looked familiar when I saw her in the paper. I couldn't say how. Maybe we crossed paths somewhere." But Beverly Dean seemed like someone Ginger would remember seeing, didn't she? She had some of her own. She had an apartment. She wasn't like Joan.

Before they hung up, Ginger invited Agnes to come by the Palace. She'd spot her a free show.

Agnes looked at what she'd written about Joan: *No enemies. Can't live like a vagabond forever. You wouldn't believe—*

She wrote for most of the night, the clatter of the typewriter's keys echoing through her body even when she finally fell asleep.

Agnes and Danny met for lunch at the automat, and she passed him her work. While he read, she was careful to look away from his face. She looked at a wall of cakes instead, or into her tea.

"We've got to get this to Elgin," he said when he finished reading. "You should be on crime full time."

"He won't put a woman on crime." It was nonsense, what she was doing. She felt it then—the futility—when she heard herself tell the truth. A weight hitting the floor.

Danny raised his eyebrows at her. When they stood to go, he held her coat. They walked back to the office without saying anything, Danny whistling a tune. She wished he'd be quiet. Her own thoughts were noise enough.

When they got back to the office, instead of leaving, he followed her to her desk and sat down on the edge. "Give me a pen, Agnes, and your story." She passed him both. "Watch and learn," he said, and blackened her name out. He took her work and tossed it on Elgin's desk. She watched Danny as he talked to Elgin—the way he shrugged his shoulders as if saying, *I don't know who wrote it.* He came out and sat on Agnes's desk. They watched Elgin, who stood reading.

"He's forgotten to sit down," Danny said.

Agnes couldn't look. "Is that so?" she asked, and then, a moment later: "What's his face look like?"

"Puzzled. He's looking for a name, I bet. Wondering where it came from."

"What now?" she asked a moment later. She was staring at a photograph of a U-bomb test—a house in the desert with all the glass blown out.

"He's coming out."

"Has he still got my story?"

"Yep."

Elgin came out into the office and looked at all of them. He held the typewritten pages in the air. "Who wrote this, fellas?" But no one said anything.

Agnes stood slowly, her damp palms pressed against the rough wool of her skirt.

Elgin looked at her for a long time. He read from her article again, this time aloud. When he'd finished, he said, "That's damn good, Agnes."

Max turned in his chair to look at Agnes, and soon the others did too. She lifted her chin. "Thanks," she said. "There's more where that came from."

Max shook his head and laughed. "Well, I'll be," he said, turning back to his typewriter.

Elgin did not move her desk. There would be no fat paycheck. "Let's see what you can do," Elgin said, explaining that she wasn't getting a new job. She was getting more work. She would split her time between labeling and writing.

But she knew. She was a *reporter*. Downstairs, she picked up her press card.

A press card. She kept it in her wallet. She locked herself in the women's room and looked at it. Agnes Crandall. Reporter. She put her hand over her mouth.

To celebrate, she and Danny went to a better place than the automat for dinner—a restaurant in Hollywood where the waiters wore dark vests and knew to pronounce certain words with a flourish, in the French way. At the end of the meal, she paid, taking the check from Danny. She showed Danny the pen that Ben had given her.

"It's very nice," he said. He leaned his elbows on the table and gazed at her.

"What?" she said, sitting back. "Give a man credit. He knows what I want."

"He does, doesn't he? Is it, though, what *you* want?" He put his chin on his hand. "A pen?" *He's drunk,* she thought, but he wasn't. "Tell me something. Did you choose him, or did he choose you?"

She didn't answer him. She looked, instead, at his eyes, which were hazel. He was squinting in the late afternoon sunlight that came through the window. She didn't have to answer him.

In Pasadena, Agnes lived in a small, dark wooden house that backed up to an alley full of other small, dark wooden houses. The stillness of the night was only broken by the call of a cat in heat, or the whistle of a man coming home late. And it was late. She heard the cat. She heard the whistle. She was writing about Beverly. The press card sat beside her, propped against the base of the gooseneck lamp.

All the women besides Beverly lived in the hotels and rooming houses in Hollywood or nearby. Agnes felt far off, a spectator. She knew that if she wanted to understand the lives of the women, she would have to go where they did.

She'd learned that when she first began writing—when she wanted to write about what she'd seen at the veterans' hospital. It was best to be inside, to have easy access. She'd wanted to interview Rosemary, but when she told Rosemary what she wanted to do, Rosemary folded her arms and looked at Agnes as if she'd insulted her. "They'll find out it was me who told you," she'd said. "I'll lose my place. I can't let that happen."

"You won't," Agnes argued. "I'll make it anonymous."

"I didn't know you were a writer. I never would have told you."

Agnes hadn't been sure that she even *was* a writer, but she wanted to try. She began asking the doctors questions about treatments. She made notations about the patient's answers in her own notebook, placing stars next to the names of the men who were taken beyond the hatched glass. She wanted to talk to the veterans housed in the sterile white rooms, to pass into the long hallway beyond the locked metal door, but the staff wouldn't let her. Her first attempts must have been clumsy, because soon she was reassigned to the general office's typing pool, and Agnes couldn't even get into the hospital building.

Rosemary and Arnold stopped inviting her and Ben over for dinner, and she apologized to Ben, but Ben only laughed and said it was between women. "That's the way it is with women sometimes," he said.

But Agnes was determined to see what sort of story she could write, and that's when she read about the Mary Thomas Home for the Mentally Unsound.

Everyone who had anything to do with the Mary Thomas Home called it the Mary T.—like a ship or a hotel, but it was neither of those things. If you had to be locked up, the Mary T. was the place. It boasted a view of the ocean, painting classes, music recitals. It was a private hospital, of course, but the surgery—the lobotomy, Agnes learned it was called—had made its way to the Mary T., too, over the carefully manicured grounds and through the heavy wooden doors. Agnes petitioned the board, asking for access, telling them that she wrote for a ladies' magazine. One of the doctors was enthusiastic and told her about the new procedure—how sanity was achieved by tapping into the front of the brain. "Just here," he said, putting a finger on Agnes's forehead.

She didn't like the feel of his finger on her skin. It was as if he'd frozen that spot or burned it. She could feel the press of his finger for the rest of the day. She rubbed at it when she interviewed a girl from a wealthy family—Dora—who the doctor said was a perfect candidate for the procedure. "There's really no need," Dora said of the surgery, watching Agnes rub her forehead. "I'm a little nutshell, myself. Sealed up and solid.

I like it just fine." In the end, Dora's parents protested the operation, and Agnes never finished her story.

Unlucky for Agnes—she would have seen the way Dora changed, been able to chronicle the before and after; but lucky for Dora that the doctors hadn't cracked her head open. The idea of the surgery scared Agnes. It was taking something away, even if the something made one miserable. Sometimes Agnes swore she could still feel the doctor's touch, the slight pressure of his skin on hers, left like a fingerprint at a crime scene.

One person's good fortune was often made up of another's misfortune. The half-finished story about the Mary T. stayed in a box at the back of Agnes's closet for a long time, but one evening, she carried it down to a filling station that burned refuse for the neighborhood. She threw it into the oil drum filled with embers and watched the black smoke jump and plume into the air.

Until misfortune was your own, you took what luck the world offered.

Luck, if there were such a thing, worked like money. If you didn't pay attention, it was gone. If you worked to turn that money into more money, well, then you had more money. Lucky you. But she remembered the poverty of the thirties— sometimes there was no way to turn money into more money because someone else had all the money, and luck bled out.

Agnes packed a bag. She'd check into one of the hotels on the boulevard—the Edmonton. She'd seen it advertised in the newspaper. Two dollars a week with a telephone in the room and a fresh linen rental. She could write long hand until she returned to Pasadena, and that would be less conspicuous than the bang of the typewriter. She could work at the *Daily*, too, of course. She thought of the envelopes accumulating on her desk, the pictures that would need to be marked and filed away, the long tunnels of the archives.

Beverly Dean was not like the other women. She was not destitute, and she did not seem, anyway, to have yearned for that transformation into starlet. She was a bit older, closer to thirty than twenty. Agnes wondered, like the police, if this was the work of the Raptor. She sensed something in it, though— and Ginger had said that Beverly looked familiar. She thought of the photographic archives again, the images pressed together, and wondered if she could find a photograph that linked Beverly to Joan.

5

MAY

Lily paused to lean dramatically on the stairway railing, posing like Rita Hayworth, her head tossed back. She made it all look glamorous: that less than polished railing, the stairs that were never washed, her old shoes. And May, nodding at her, could see—she could see that Lily would be famous. "It would be my *own* role," Lily said, telling her about the audition, running out ahead of May, pushing through the Hamilton's front doors, turning and laughing.

"Don't forget about me!" May called. Maybe she was an artist, too, somehow, like Dora said. But what kind?

They were both pretending. The police had talked to Lily about Joan, and Joan's family had come to claim their daughter's body. When Lily had gotten back from the police station, she shut herself in the bath and cried. May sat on the bed, listening. She got Lily two aspirin, and at the drugstore, the waitress gave her a glass full of ice cubes. May wrapped the ice in a bath towel and told Lily to hold it to her eyes. She ran her hand over Lily's back and stroked her hair—but it had been Lily's idea for May to phone up James and see if he and a friend could go to a late dinner and then dancing.

Out on the street, they looked around for James and his friend but didn't see them. A black sedan idled in front of the Hamilton, and then a man got out. He got out from the passenger's side, slowly, looking at Lily.

Lily took a step back. "What are *you* doing here?"

"Waiting for you, beautiful. Where are you going?"

"None of your business."

"Aren't you going to introduce me to your friend?" he asked

Lily, clicking his tongue. There was another man in the car, on the driver's side. He sat with his hands on the steering wheel. He looked straight out ahead, as if he thought the car were still in motion.

Lily's lips were pursed, the pink O of a painted mouth, her cheeks pale. "No. I'm not going to introduce you. I told you to buzz off." She pointed at the sidewalk, and then lifted her arm straight out, like a scarecrow. "I told you—"

"I don't buzz, sweetheart," the man interrupted. "You know that." He smiled at May. He took off his hat, pressing it against the breast pocket of his black overcoat. "Since Lily here is too rude to introduce us—" He bowed a little and extended his free hand. "I'm Ray. I own a few nightclubs. You like to dance? You like shows?" His hand felt big and soft and slightly damp. "Maybe you've heard of me."

She pulled her fingers from his grip. "I'm May." She looked up and down the street, but she didn't see her date. She didn't see anyone.

Lily took May's arm, linking it to her own. "Let's go." They began walking away.

"Hey," Ray said. "I'm just being friendly. Claude is wondering about you. He misses you."

"It's all right," Lily told May. "He won't bother us."

"We could wait inside." May thought of the two sofas that faced each other in the lobby, the lamps with green glass shades, the ashtrays that always had a cigarette butt or two in them. She thought of sitting on the edge of one of the sofas with her legs crossed, waiting, waiting for a man, waiting for dinner, waiting for the night to begin.

"Don't you remember how you and Claude met?" Ray called softly down the street, almost too quiet to hear, and Lily slowed, turning. He whistled. The whistle was like a sigh. "So romantic. It's such a beautiful story to tell the world."

"You see—" Lily's voice shook. "I don't mean to be rude, but we're waiting for some fellas. We already have dates. They'll be here any minute. You should go."

"Oh, those two. They're not coming." He leaned against the car and crossed his arms. "They were here, right?" He took a cigarette out of a thick silver case. "But I told them you girls made other plans."

Lily's arm was still linked to May's, her fingers were white against the black of May's dress.

Ray flicked the lighter several times without touching it to the cigarette. "We've got to go. We can't be late." But he said it like he had all the time in the world. "Claude hates it when we're late." He shook his head, finally bringing the lighter to the cigarette.

Who did he think he was—telling their dates to go away, scaring Lily? "We don't have plans with you," May called out. She pulled a little on Lily's arm. "Come on. We'll go back upstairs." But Lily didn't move.

"Aw jeez, kid. Don't be angry. I'm just a guy who likes pretty girls. I'm harmless. You can't stay out here when the—what do they call him? The Raptor?—when the Raptor is loose."

"Lily?"

"I have to go with him."

"No, you don't."

"You don't understand."

"Tell me."

"I fouled up."

"How?" May wanted to know, but Lily only shook her head.

"You stay here. Go back upstairs. Forget this ever happened."

"No. I'm not letting you go alone." They walked toward the car together, whispering.

Ray opened the door, stood back. "Do you like to dance?" he asked May. She looked at him. He had a small, thin-lipped mouth, teeth like a child's with gaps between each, and a soft chin. His eyes were gray and blank. He smiled at her. "Do you like parties?"

She got in the car after Lily, sliding across the red fabric to sit close to her friend. When the door shut, she had the sudden urge to bang on the windows with her fists, to yell for help, but there was no reason. Ray was humming. She tried to place the song. It was the same Nat King Cole song she'd danced to with James. He stopped humming and turned to look at them. "Oh, Claude is going to be so happy to see you two."

May looked out the window as the streetlights slid by, and then she saw James and his friend. They were walking toward the Hamilton to meet them, and they were both carrying flowers wrapped in cones of brown paper. James tilted his head back and laughed at something his friend said. She remembered the way he danced, his joints loose, the minty smell of his aftershave mingled with hair wax. "Hey," she said, turning to Lily. "Hey!" She knocked on the glass, but it was too late. They didn't see her.

"Just in the nick of time," Ray said, laughing. He tapped the driver on the shoulder. "Right, Karl?" May studied the back of the driver's head as he nodded. "Just in the nick of time," he repeated. "A fella's gotta do what a fella's gotta do to get a date with a pretty girl." He laughed. "Life's a real joke."

He said it as the night moved inside and outside the car, as they turned off Hollywood Boulevard, leaving the lights behind. "Well, where are we going then?" May asked, but no one answered her.

They turned off the main road and drove up a hill, toward the observatory. They were at a midway point, somewhere in the hills, where the smell of sage made the city seem far off, even though it was not.

What sort of flowers had James chosen? She liked roses and dahlias the best—the flowers within flowers, that perpetual unfolding—though she did not like to see them cut. The sharp snip of a scissor blade against the green skin of a stem made her wince.

When the car stopped, Ray turned to face them, throwing his arm over the seat. He touched Lily on the nose. "Lily's been here before. This is Claude's place."

May stared. The house was not really a house—not the sort that was lived in. Not a Tudor with a serpentine path or a craftsman, but a house of glass—modern, aglow—framed by the black shapes of palm trees.

Lily nodded at her in the darkness of the parked car. "It's all right." She touched May's hand. "It's just fine." But May didn't believe her. Lily got out of the car and May followed. Lily took Karl's arm and walked toward the house and Ray smiled, offering May his arm. She let him lead her in, up the walk, slowing so as not to trip on the low, wide steps as the palm trees closed above her.

Lily frowned. "I thought you said it was a party." Lily stood with her arms folded. Her lipstick was faded. "Where is everybody?"

Ray laughed. "Wherever you are, Lily—that's the party. You know you've always been the party."

Lily looked at him for a long moment. She hates him, May thought, watching her friend. The tension in the jaw, biting down on the words that she might hurl at him. Why didn't she? Why did she go along? But it didn't take long for May to forget. This was Claude's, and Lily walked in ahead of everyone else as if she owned the place.

"Isn't she a doll?" Ray took off his hat as he spoke. "She's a sweetheart. She's the party. This way," Ray said, going out ahead of May. They passed down a hallway and through a doorway and into a dark courtyard. May could hear water splashing, a piano playing in another room. She had no sense of the space. She looked up at the sky and saw the stars.

A marble statue of woman rose out of a black fountain. She was running, caught mid-motion—between tree and woman, or woman and tree. She reached upward, a look of surprise on her backward-glancing face: her arms were elegant branches! Leaves sprouted at her fingertips. Water shone on the pale stone of her body, and her feet disappeared beneath the mirrored fountain's surface.

"Is that you?" May heard a man call. "Did you bring the showgirls?" The man came toward them out of the dark carrying a torch. He wore a white shirt and dark trousers. May noticed his feet were bare. "Is that you?" he said again, holding the light up. "Oh, it *is* you. Don't take any offense—" He stood in front of them, one hand in his pocket. "I know you aren't showgirls. Sometimes I call all pretty girls *showgirls*. And you *are* pretty girls." His features were lost in shadow, but May knew that he was the same man from the bar—the one she'd seen Lily talking to. This was Claude, then. He held the light high, looking at his guests. "Hello, Lily."

"Hello, Claude."

"I didn't think I'd see you again so soon."

"I doubt that's true."

"Well—" He paused. "It is, my love. You said you weren't coming. I sent Ray over to see if he could change your mind. I'm so glad he did." He smiled at May. "All the guests are here. Shall we?" He took May's arm. "I don't think we've met before. I'm Claude. And who are you?"

"May." Her voice was too soft. He leaned toward her.

"*May*," he said loudly, taking her arm. "Soon you'll know everyone here. You'll make such friends." He sang: "The merry month of May—so frolic, so gay, and so green." He stood still, staring, and held the light toward her face. He hummed, singing—*the merry month of May*, and then turned away. "This way, then," he said. He stabbed the torch into the ground, and they passed from the courtyard into the house, into a well-lit room where a few men were leaning against a fireplace, smoking cigarettes and laughing. Dora was playing a grand piano and singing. They all turned to look at Claude, at May. "So green, so green—" Claude finished. "This is merry May," he called to them. "Isn't she lovely?"

Everyone looked at her. Dora was pale in the bright light. The light bounced around the room. A white couch, the walls white, the fire in the fireplace, the shining floor, and May stood on a rug that was cut into the shape of a pale bear—or once a bear. She could not tell. There was so much light that it was like standing in an overexposed photograph, where everyone's face looked flat, their eyes dark and unreadable. May expected the

woman in the white dress—the woman from that first night—
to emerge, to rise up, shimmering like heat at the edge of the
desert, but she did not.

Lily glanced at May. "Here we are, then. Sorry about this,"
she said, rolling the rock again in her cheek, her jaw tight—but
May smiled at all of them. They were expensive in that white
room, the colors and patterns of their clothing vivid.

And she was one of them.

She had never seen a house like this—and the guests—
dressed up as if they were going to the symphony. Dora wore
yellow silk, and Claude remained shoeless, looking for all the
world like a diplomat who'd unexpectedly landed on some far-
away tropical island. He handed her a tall glass.

"This is for you," he said. "Lily invented this drink."

She took it and watched the bubbles catch in the light. "Isn't
it champagne?"

"Never miss a detail, May. Taste the berry."

"What is it?" The berry was dark red, almost black.

"You'll see."

She put it on her tongue. It was bitter. Lily watched her, and
Dora, from the piano, shook her head *no*.

"Swallow." Claude nodded at her and smiled. He touched
her lips with one finger.

She swallowed it. "What was that?"

"Nightshade."

She coughed. "But you've poisoned me."

"Only a little. Don't worry." He laughed.

"Will it hurt me?"

"No. The world will just shift a little. Drink up."

"But it's deadly, isn't it? Don't they call it *deadly* nightshade?"

"The roots are deadly. The rest—" He waved his hand
through the air as if clearing cobwebs. "Colors. Colors, *l'obscu-
rité*. Imagine the depth."

"Excuse me?"

"Oh, ignore me. It's something I'm writing." He touched his
pockets. "It takes five berries to kill a child. I need a pen," he

said, but went to the piano instead and sat down next to Dora. "This is Dora. Dora, this is May. Isn't she lovely?" They both looked at May.

"We've met," Dora said. "Once or twice."

Why—it was all so strange! Dora seemed solemn over the keys, her fingers picking out a mirthless tune, and Lily—she had walked across the room to the window and had her back to May. May looked around at the others—at Ray and the driver, Karl, and at the other men—men leaning against the fireplace, their eyes wandering over to her, a nod, a murmured greeting. Who were they? One came toward her, a tall angular man in a blue shirt with gray hair, and he put his hands around her waist but Claude said, "She's not for you, Thomas," and he stepped back and apologized. He did not look at her again, and the men took their stares away and gave them to Lily and Dora instead.

"Lily," Claude called. "Come here. Let's all play a song for May." Lily turned away from the window and took a seat on the other side of Claude. She and Claude and Dora conferred over the keys, and then he began to play. Dora and Lily sang—Lily's voice slightly higher than Dora's. They sang "I'll Remember April," and Claude laughed as he sang out *May* over *April,* and then Dora and Lily joined in, and the song was finished that way, and each time they sang her name, they all looked at May, who felt light and strange. She could feel her blood inside of her body, the way it moved and roved about, bringing a red pulsing light to her chest.

The colors, the shadows.

She thought of a tree—the maple whose leaves turned near black in the summer, and how strange it seemed in the sunshine, the shimmering black giant of a tree in a grove with its shallow roots and thick trunk. A grove of black maples, crimson maples, and how, passing beneath them, she became a shadow, unseen.

A sweet, fetid smell filled the room. It mixed with the scent from the vases filled with jasmine, the women's powdery perfume, the underscent of alcohol and the rank layer of cigarette smoke. "Have you tried this?" Ray passed her a tightly rolled cigarette. He took it from a silver box on top of the piano and offered it to her. He struck a match and held it to the tip.

"I don't like to smoke," she said, putting it to her lips.

"You'll like this."

She coughed.

"Hold in your lungs for a moment," Ray said, breathing deeply.

But she couldn't. Her lungs wouldn't allow it. Her chest hurt. *Mary Warner*, the boys in Florida called it. Giggle weed. She smiled at Ray, her lips closed. He moved toward her, touching her arm. For a moment, she thought he might try to kiss her, but Lily took her hand and led her away. "Come with me."

Dora left the piano and followed them into the courtyard. She looked once behind her. Claude had left the torch in the yard, and the trees loomed in shadow. "Hey, girls," Dora called out. "Wait for me." Dora's eyes were big and glistened as if she were about to cry. Dora was a bird—at once timid and excited.

"Shhh—" Lily turned to Dora. "Keep quiet. We're leaving."

"Where are you going? Maybe I want to come." She followed behind them. "Tell me."

Lily turned. "Home, silly. Nowhere interesting."

"Stay," Dora said. "Or let me come. Why don't you stay? The night will be over and then we'll leave together and no one— I'm scared."

"You've smoked too much Mary Warner," Lily said. "There's nothing to scare you." They stood in front of the statue at the fountain, where the woman offered her useless arms to the sky.

Beyond, May could see the house, the well-lit room where Claude was playing the piano. The sound reached them in the garden, where May held her shoes in one hand and Lily gripped her arm. When would the men notice the only women had left? What would they do when Dora was the only one? Would the enormous man called Thomas come and put his hands on Dora's waist, and would Claude warn him off, or would he let him? "You could come with us," May said to Dora, but Lily was pulling at May's elbow.

"Why are you so mad at me, Lily?" Dora reached for Lily's hand. "Don't you know—" she began, but Lily interrupted her, saying, "I'm not mad. I'm just tired."

"Oh." Dora brought a hand to the back of her head. She lifted her hair, piling it up. "Fiddlesticks."

"What?"

"I broke my shoe." She brought her hands to her face and rubbed her eyes. "Stay for a minute and talk to me while I fix it." Balancing on one foot, she held May's hand to steady herself. "You better take care," she said to May—pulling her close and trying to whisper, but her voice was more raspy than quiet. She's drunk, May thought. Dora is drunk. May looked at Dora's shoe. It hadn't broken—she'd merely stepped out of it.

"Take care?"

"We can't stay," Lily said. "Someone will realize we're gone soon enough."

"But I want to tell you something." Dora rose, and she came so close that May could feel Dora's breath on her cheek. It smelled like scotch, soured, but sweet like a geranium, too. "Something horrible has happened." She looked over her shoulder, at the house, and then around the dark courtyard. "You can't trust anyone—"

"What sort of thing?"

In the flickering light, Dora's face was all angles. She looked over her shoulder at the house. "It's Claude."

"What about him?" Lily sounded almost bored when she asked.

Dora's hands were hot on May's. "He killed someone."

"Who?" Lily asked.

"Beverly."

But Lily only shook her head. "Beverly?"

"*Beverly*. Don't you read the papers?"

"I don't know Beverly."

"Oh, Lily. What is wrong with you? You're such a liar." Dora

looked from Lily to May's face. "She lies so much. In his basement—" Dora looked over her shoulder at the door that led
back into the house. "We should find the book. Come back
inside with me. You'll see. It's the only reason I'm here. I need
the book. I'm going to bring the book to the police."

Lily laughed—a high bounce across the courtyard, an echo
that returned as empty as an overturned cup.

"What book?" May asked. She could see Ray standing at the
window, looking out.

"Who's out there?" he called. "Where did all the showgirls
go?"

Lily pulled at May. They ran across the courtyard together,
leaving Dora standing still in the grass in one shoe. They moved
down a stone walkway, and then they were out of the house and
down the steps. Lily laughed, pulling May along behind her.

May looked to see if Dora had followed, but she couldn't
even see how they'd left the house. Palms and climbing vines
obscured the façade. They ran farther, toward Hollywood, and
May's breath came hard. She wanted to stop, but she liked the
motion, and she could see Lily up ahead of her laughing, her
blond hair coming loose, her shoes in her hands. Finally, Lily
slowed. "Those parties last for hours, and eventually everyone
starts talking like Dora."

"About Claude killing people?"

"Oh no, just—" Lily caught her breath. "Any old thing." A
car swung past them, and Lily pulled May behind a hedge.

"Are you scared?" May whispered. "Why are we hiding?"

"I just don't want to go back."

"Would they come out looking for us?"

"You can never tell with that crowd."

They found themselves at a drive-in on the boulevard. They
walked past the cars with the trays propped in the windows,
radios playing. "We can get the bus from here," Lily said. She
went to the counter and ordered two hamburgers. "It stops out
front."

"What did Dora mean?" May asked, pushing her hair back

from her face. "Did Beverly know Claude?" And Joan—*Lily* knew Joan. Dora knew Joan. Did Claude? "Does she think Claude's the Raptor?"

"Oh, she's crazy. I told you. *And* she's drunk. Or high. Or both. She was in the bug house, you know. Do you have any money?"

"But what did she *mean*?" May fished in her handbag and pulled out seven cents. She didn't want to pass the coins to Lily. Ned hadn't answered her last few letters, and he hadn't sent money like he usually did. Soon she'd be out. She wondered what she would do then. She looked at the waitresses who darted back and forth across the parking lot to the cars. They moved quickly in their bright red dresses with yellow aprons. There was still Robinson's—tomorrow. She'd go tomorrow, and maybe she'd look so well in a dress that they'd even let her keep one. Something like that yellow silk Dora had worn! She would see about the man Hazel had mentioned soon.

"Last week, Dora thought that Claude killed Ruth."

"Who's Ruth?"

"Ruth was Claude's secretary, but poor kid. She died of a drug overdose a few months ago. Claude didn't kill her."

"How *awful*. But why would Dora say those things?"

"Because she's bonkers, May. She doesn't believe it. Why would she still show up if she really believed it? She's one of those stupid rich girls who smokes a lot of Mary Warner and runs around trying to meet actors. She's working that poor little rich girl angle. You know, the black sheep."

Lily sounded so mean. May studied her friend's face, waiting for it to soften. They sat down on a bench, and Lily held her hands over her tea as if it were a small fire and her fingers were cold. "But forget Dora. I didn't want you to get mixed up with them. They're a lousy bunch, but they aren't murderers. I don't even want to know them anymore."

"Did you know Beverly?"

"Maybe. I can't remember. I've met so many people." Lily squinted, as if she were trying to see something in the distance.

May looked, too, but the light was so bright, she couldn't see anything beyond. "And anyway—" Lily began, shaking her head. "Ruth didn't die in Claude's basement. They found her in her own apartment. She was a drug addict. She was old too. I mean in her forties or something."

What was it like to be old? May thought of her mother in her big checked wool coat, her breath visible in the cold, her gloves worn. "But what was Dora talking about—that book?"

"Who knows. I don't know." Lily laughed. She was still staring out into the darkness, and again May followed, looking where Lily looked, but she saw nothing.

May felt as though nothing existed but the bright false light that she was caught in. It was only the smell of meat, its grease thick on her tongue, and the bitterness of tannins—which she thought would make her stomach ache later—that taste of dirt and root. What a pleasure it would be to disappear into the shadows of night-black trees. She closed her eyes and imagined reaching into a tree, to find a heart at its center, passing her fingers through the deep-gouged lovers' initials in the bark, the bark like teeth, grabbing and biting at her skin, sacrificing her whole hand to the pleasure.

When she looked back at Lily, her friend was staring at her. "It's a coincidence about Joan and Beverly—" Lily said. She turned to look where May had a moment ago. "Did you see something out there?" she asked.

"What would I see?"

AGNES

Beverly Dean's income was a mystery. She had enough to live in a nice apartment by herself. She had a car, a maid, and closet full of party dresses. She had enough money to say that she *was* an actress—even though she rarely worked. The women who worked in the clubs, like Ginger, had to say, I *want* to be an actress. They signified that the club was temporary—it was a place to tap your foot until the train arrived.

But where did Beverly's money come from? She was poor too. A country mouse like the others. Someone transferred money into her account each month. Someone—

They were in her apartment. Danny knew a cop who knew another cop, and that cop stood in the foyer while Agnes and Danny looked around. "Don't let me see you touch anything," he said, and then went into the kitchen with one of Beverly's magazines and smoked a cigarette. In Beverly's desk, Agnes found a bank book. Each month showed a cash deposit of five-hundred dollars. Agnes whistled. In another drawer, a single black pearl on a gold band.

Agnes asked Danny to photograph everything at Beverly's so she could remember it exactly—a partly opened window, thawing meat that had begun to turn, the time on a stopped watch—anything that might tell her something.

Back in her rented room, she wrote, practicing the lede—less than ten words that would make anyone stop and read her story.

Rich Girl Kept Poor Company.

Girl Friday Killed on Monday.

She wrote about Beverly. Mysterious wealth. Party clothes.

She wrote about Joan, who'd came by train, from the center of Minnesota, in the winter, clutching a ballet-pink cardboard suitcase. Inside, two dresses and her dance outfits. Her trunk would sit on the unfinished dirt floor of her parents' basement until she found a place—buckled and black and dented on one side. From the train window, the desert looked like another planet. Maybe Joan had wished she hadn't come, but it was too late now, anyway. The light said so. It was like passing through a veil of dust, the silt shining like flecks of gold.

But I want—

Imagine a woman who has never seen the ocean, Agnes wrote.

Pictures, yes. Drawings. Seascapes in the museum, but not the real thing. In films, the white waves, the black line of the horizon. Imagine swollen feet, sleeping upright, counting change. Movement. The rush of green leaves and sunlight, the black of entering a tunnel. And then it appears: the sea.

Joan's trunk had eventually been shipped to a hotel that she'd shared with two roommates—not the Edmonton, but in a hotel and in a room that probably looked just like Agnes's. Single beds. A telephone table without a telephone. One closet with scuffed wooden hangers. The paint scraped. A dresser for clothes. In the drugstore across the street, Agnes had heard a girl say that the Hamilton had bugs. The Edmonton was just *that much* nicer. The girl held up two fingers and pinched the air. You might see a bug in the shared kitchen, but no one could help that. Not in the rooms. And you could eat in the drugstore if you didn't want to cook in the kitchen.

Agnes's room was rarely quiet: the chatter beyond the walls was constant. It ran up and down the hallways with the click of the women's heels or the soft shuffle of their slippers. She rode with them in the elevator on her way to dinner, and then passed them in the stairway, their knees pulled up to their chins, their shoes off, their hair in curlers. They looked up at her and smiled, thinking she was one of them, and then when she'd passed, they looked again as she disappeared, wondering about the newcomer.

They looked at her like she might mean luck.

In the daytime, Agnes sat in the newsroom. The pile of un-labeled photographs on her desk was growing, and Elgin nod-ded at them as he passed, reminding her. She ate lunch at the automat with Danny. She met Ben for dinner. Over white rolls and crab soup, she told him stories, and then, "Oh, heavens—" she said, taking out the silver pen and her notepad and writing something down.

"Are you all right?" Ben asked. She put her hands over his.

"You needn't worry. I'm fine." Was it because he was a sci-entist? Did all this movement make him uneasy? Unsettled. All was unsettled—living without a fixed address, an ever-changing group of friends. Gossip. Borrowed clothing. Someone else's nail polish. Someone else's dinner date.

Ben took her hand and held it. "It's just that I've never seen you like this," he said, his eyes gray, fixed. "Your hair—" He reached out and touched it. She'd had it colored red, set. Autumn sunrise, the beautician had called it. Ben didn't like it. She could tell. But she did. "You look like all the others now," he said.

She took her hands away. What did he mean—*all the others?*

He walked her back to the Edmonton with his hand on the small of her back. Mine, she imagined him saying. Mine. But she gave him a kiss at the door, anyway. Even though she felt angry. It was easier.

Upstairs, she looked at herself in the mirror. She'd only done it to blend in, but it was right—this hair, this color. She was *supposed* to be a redhead.

She went back down to the lobby and sat in one of the armchairs. She picked up a magazine and made herself visible, waiting for someone to talk to her. She smiled at a woman sitting on the couch.

The woman leaned forward. "Are you an actress or a model?" she asked, and Agnes affected the same bright-eyed astonishment—because it was true, and it was incredible.

"I'm neither," she whispered. "I'm a *writer*," Agnes said.

"Oh, brother, have I got a story for you—screenplays?" She introduced herself. "Hazel," she said, holding out her hand, and before Agnes could say the word *newspaper*, Hazel launched into a story. Agnes let her talk. One story led to another, and soon the next. "Just tell me to be quiet," Hazel said. "Everyone else does." But Agnes did not.

They went to the bar down the street for a cocktail. Hazel talked. Finally, sitting at the bar, Agnes laughed. "But I don't write screenplays," she said. "I write for the *Daily*."

"Holy moly," Hazel said. Her eyes darted over Agnes's face. "You write for a *newspaper?*" She took a sip of her drink and then reached into her bag. She lit a cigarette, blowing the smoke at the ceiling. She fixed her gaze back on Agnes. "Do you know the identity of the Raptor?"

"No one does—"

"We thought maybe the newsies had an idea."

"Did you know Joan—or Beverly?"

Hazel's nod was slow, deliberate. "Not well," she said. "Like we know everyone here—from a party or through another friend. I knew who they were." She stubbed her cigarette out. "I don't want to talk about that," she said. Agnes watched her. The way she picked at her nail polish, finished her drink, brought her hand to her forehead. "I'm tired," she said. "Let's go back." On the street, Hazel laughed. "I get so scared," she said, "when I think of it. I practically have a heart attack."

"I want to solve it," Agnes confessed. "I want to stop it."

"Someone should." Hazel told Agnes another story, on the street out in front of the Edmonton, shifting her weight as she talked. She'd heard it wasn't one man, but several. That's what the women said. They said it was a gang. She said it in a way that gave Agnes a shivery feeling on the back of her neck. Gang. How many men made up a gang? Agnes wondered.

"That's all I know," Hazel said. "That's what everyone says. You're looking for more than one man. Maybe it's not true. Maybe it's a rumor. Maybe it's just one man, or—"

"Or what?"

"It's crazy." Hazel looked up and down the street.

"What is?"

"I heard it was *magic*. But you hear all kinds of things from the girls who've been around for a while," she said. "It's probably nonsense. I heard the murders were a magic ritual." She wrapped her arms around her body, shivering. "Let's go inside," she said.

Hazel lived with three other women. Two to a bed, and there was a lumpy cot. The short end of the stick got blankets on the floor, though Hazel said it might be better than the cot. Hazel took to Agnes, who let her complain about her roommates or sleep in the armchair with the ottoman. They all wanted to be actresses. They were from Missouri or New Jersey or Ohio. Hazel worked as a dress model at Robinson's. She told Agnes about it. If a man came in to shop for his wife, Hazel tried on the dress for him. Did he like it? Would he like her to try on another? How does your wife wear her hair—up or down? Like this? Men bought dresses when Hazel tried them on, and women liked to see the new fashions without the bother of changing. Now that the war was over, the older women had taken to wearing corsets again. They were strapped-in, harnessed, immobile. They preferred to have tea and watch while another woman bent herself into dress after dress.

Hazel and her friends invited Agnes to go out with them. Agnes danced with sailors. She found corners and halls and passages and brought her notebook out. She wrote standing up, and late at night, back in her room, she finally asked Hazel if she could interview her talking about the Raptor. Danny came along. He took photographs of them, and flirted easily with Hazel and her friends. "Isn't he your fellow?" Hazel asked one night. She was drunk. She leaned on Agnes's arm, her face close.

"Fellow? No. I have another fellow," Agnes said, smiling, but when she saw them leave together, she wondered where they were going. She was nudged by jealousy, by possession. She called Ben from a telephone booth and told him to come to the Edmonton.

Hazel never told her what happened with Danny. She only called him *the gentleman* when his name came up and raised her eyebrows. "The gentleman," she said.

Hazel talked about most things, but never about Danny. She'd known Joan—not well, no. Just in passing. They'd both roomed at another hotel for a bit. "She was seeing a fellow, but we don't know who it was."

"Marty?" Agnes pressed.

"No, no. That doesn't sound right. One syllable. I'll come knock on your door tonight. Joan said he was rich. I think he lived on—" But she shook her head. She couldn't remember. She was standing by the window, her finger on her lip. She turned toward Agnes as if she'd suddenly remembered the name, but said, "Have you heard about the witches yet?"

"*Witches?*" Agnes repeated.

"I heard a rumor is all. A group of women—" She was interrupted by a soft knock at the door. Hazel got up. "I've got to go," she said.

When Agnes heard the door in Hazel's room close, she put her ear to the wall and listened. She could hear Hazel and one of her roommates arguing about something. "Do you want to end up like Joan?" someone said. "Well, then—" A door slammed. Footsteps in the hall. On the other side of the wall, a woman was crying. She guessed it was Hazel.

"I was right," Agnes said to Danny over the phone. "Rich."

"I'll be. Case cracker, like I said."

"Say—" She laughed. "Why does Hazel call you the gentleman all the time?"

"Does she?"

"Sure she does."

"That's for me to know."

Near the end of the week, when Agnes went to find Hazel again, the room she'd been staying in was empty, the door ajar for housekeeping. Agnes stood with her hands on her hips, looking at the closet, at the empty hangers, feeling that she'd missed her chance.

She consoled herself with work. This was how it went, she knew. You could lose a source. In the *Daily*'s office, Agnes wrote about Hazel and the Raptor, about the women who came to Los Angeles and lived in rooming houses. She focused more on Joan, whose life reminded her of Hazel's. When she was finished, she put the work in Elgin's inbox, her first assignment finished.

6

May

"Dora's missing," Lily said. "I've just spoken to Claude. He wanted to know if I'd seen Dora. Her roommate Lorelei is in a panic." She'd just come in. She held her hand to her chest as if she were catching her breath.

"Dora's not missing." May was making her bed, tucking the corners of a fresh white sheet. She straightened and looked at Lily. "We just saw her. And Lorelei's worried because we're *all* worried right now—"

"After the party—when Dora left—no one knows where she went. They thought she left with us. What if—"

May went to the open window. The sun was coming straight in. "Nothing's happened," May said.

"I should have taken her with us. I was mean. What if—"

"Don't say it." May stood still. She rested her hands on the windowsill. Outside, the sky was bright blue. Lily *had* been a bit mean to Dora, but Dora was drunk, and there was Joan too—Lily wasn't herself. That was all. Everyone was a little off. Dora had probably gone away to think.

The sign outside flashed during the daytime, too, though you couldn't see it as well. Ice-Cold-Drinks. Here. Here. Red at night. A barely perceptible pink in the day. "Let's go for a walk," May said. She dropped the curtain and the room fell into shadow. "I'm hot." She lifted her chin and closed her eyes.

"Yes, it's close in here. I need to go to Robinson's for a dress. For work. Would you come? I don't want to go alone."

May had just been thinking of going to Robinson's—either that afternoon or the next. Before Lily came in, she'd stood with her hands at her waist and twisted a little to the side, watching herself in the mirror.

In the lobby, they passed a man reading a magazine. He was sitting on the couch, and his hat was balanced on one knee. The cover of the magazine showed a drawing of a woman running through empty city streets. She ran beneath the spotlight of a full moon, her dress ripped at the neckline. Behind her, a shadow creature—half man, half bird. *He comes at night,* the cover said. The man did not look up at them as they passed, even though they were close enough for May to see that his brow was sweating.

Outside, the palms shimmered in the light above them.

At the trolley stop, Lily counted change, her hand open. "I'm dreadfully nervous about Dora."

"She could be holed up somewhere with a Henry."

Lily laughed. "Could be."

"She'll turn up."

"There are women in Cleveland too. The same way."

"In Cleveland? That's far from here." May could see the bright red trolley in the distance.

"Oh, you know how the newspapers exaggerate. It was probably just some husband who came home and found out his wife had a secret boyfriend. A crime of passion. That happens all the time." Lily stepped onto the trolley ahead of May. "Someone should do something about these men. No one ever does." She turned a little as she said it.

"That's for sure."

"Claude wants us all to come over and see if we can figure out together where Dora is. You don't have to come."

"I think I'd like to—"

"Maybe if we all put our heads together—"

May pictured them in Claude's living room, headless, sitting in a circle, each holding another's head. They cradled the heads, and then put the heads together, reaching forward to join them. May shut her eyes, squeezing, trying to make the image vanish.

"Are you all right?" Lily touched her arm. May looked down and saw her friend's white-gloved hand resting there on her arm like a small pale bird.

"Just hot." May smiled. She hadn't fixed her teeth that morning, but Lily seemed not to notice.

When the trolley began to move, the wind felt nice, like a cool cloth on her skin. She took out a compact. She opened it and peered into the little round mirror. She blotted her face with a tissue, delicately, the way she'd read about in magazines, careful around the eyes. She could see a black car driving behind the trolley, and she watched it for a while, until Lily said, "What are you doing?" and May clicked the compact shut and put it back in her bag. But it had been curious—the way the car stopped at every corner, staying behind the trolley rather than pulling around it.

They got off downtown, and May looked around for the car, expecting to see it still behind the trolley, but she didn't. They walked to Robinson's. May could see their reflections in the black polished granite of the department store as they passed, two pale ghosts. "Oh, look at that!" Lily pointed, and for a moment, May was sure Lily had spotted the car, but when May looked, Lily was pointing to the display window. The dress was a black crepe, cut slim through the hip with a keyhole neckline. "I'd wear that for an evening party," Lily said.

"Me too. How did you meet Claude?"

"Through Ray. I used to work in Ray's club. Before I knew you." She turned to May. "I got into trouble. He got me out. He knew someone. A doctor."

There were creams and jellies, the thick rubber cap, but she had a name in her address book—just in case. Everyone did. The girls passed names around the way they had once passed notes to each other in school, furtively, nodding and whispering. They told each other when one was bad too—if he took the money and left the baby, or if a girl had to go to the hospital after. The name that May kept in her address book wasn't that of a doctor, but of someone who knew the doctor. It was the name one used to make the connection, to get a girl from point A to B. It was all done in the dark, in secret, or it was done early in the morning—just as it got light, before everyone went to work or left their houses—in the gray dawn. To get to the doctor, a girl had to wear a blindfold, passing from one car to the next. Everyone got paid. And it wasn't cheap. The boy had to help, but sometimes he refused, saying it wasn't his fault, that the girl was with someone else—yelling it was someone else's. If there wasn't enough money for a doctor, a girl tried other things: pills and falls. Jumping up and down. Dancing all night—anything to jolt it loose from its blood-infused nest. There was more than one story about a girl who tried it her-self—nicked something inside and bled all the life away—the baby's and her own.

For a while, a girl called Judy had roomed next door to May and Lily. Judy made a big deal about waiting for marriage. Judy would look at them askance when they talked about needing a Henry. May and Lily called Judy the Enforcer behind her back. Lily said Judy prayed every night in the bathroom for their eternal salvation, but May said no, that was wrong. Judy prayed all night for their eternal *damnation*. "If it's only Judy and the Enforcers in heaven, imagine how boring it is," May said. When Judy got engaged, May was happy when she saw that the fellow was dopey looking. He had big ears and was already losing his hair in the front. May thought it was proba-bly good that Judy never wanted much to do with Henry. She whispered that to Lily after Judy packed her bags and left, and Lily laughed. "Serves her right for being such a stupid nun," she said.

Once, May thought she was pregnant, but it turned out she only had a stomach flu. She didn't know if it was sickness or relief, but lying in bed, the blood finally coming as the illness ebbed, she felt like the clean edge of a newly washed sheet whipping away in the wind.

"Ray was the fellow?" May asked

Lily nodded. "I can't barely stand to be near him. If he touches me, I feel like I'm going to vomit. Don't ever let your-self be alone with him."

May knew what that meant. And it was true she couldn't

imagine Lily with a man like Ray. "Is that why you said you didn't know them that night at the bar?"

"I didn't want to get into the whole thing. Sometimes I pretend it didn't happen."

"I see." But she didn't, not really. Lily could have left that part out, but May didn't accuse her of lying. After all, May lied. She told lies about the life she was supposed to have: Richard, the baby, spooling it out, and then listened to herself take it all away again, yank it back. Richard died in a plane crash. The baby died of fever, the luck drying up like bones in the desert sun. Once or twice she'd added the detail of finding a dog on a day they drove out to the country, but she couldn't decide what had happened to the dog in the end, so she stopped telling that part. She forgot it too, if she added it, and when someone said, "What happened to that cute little puppy? Do you still have it?" for a moment, she didn't know what they meant, and backtracked, buying herself time by pretending she misunderstood. She carried the lies. She carried the stories, always trying to remember which version she'd told.

Perhaps if she remembered, she'd say the dog ran away one day after the baby died, or that it was hit by a car. It was sad, but she needed endings so that she could present herself as having a beginning.

"You could have left that part out." May said it quietly, but Lily was looking at her and she heard it.

"I know. It's just—"

"What?"

"Claude wanted to meet you, but you're really too sweet for that group. I told him I wouldn't bring you."

"They're not bad." It was true that she didn't like Ray—but she liked Claude. She liked his hand on her arm, the way he smiled at her. She recalled the well-lit hallway, the tall vases in the entryway filled with purple larkspur, the gleam of the piano's surface, and the fountain in the courtyard—that statuary, that woman with leaved hands—caught, incomplete—one leg rooted, the other free.

She would ask Claude about the statue when she saw him again. What did it mean? Yes, she would see him again. He might fall in love with her—and perhaps he already was!

It was something to be in a room that was so well tended to, so clean and fortunate, and to meet Claude, who sounded awfully like a radio announcer, and even though his face was a bit narrow, he was still handsome, a presence, the sort of man who lifted his hat if he passed a woman on a staircase.

It was hard to believe what Dora had said—and anyway, Lily said it wasn't true.

"But they *are* bad," Lily said.

"Like what Dora—"

Lily brought her fingers to her temples and rubbed as if she had a headache. "Not like what Dora said. That was nonsense. They're *awfully* worried about Dora—" May waited, but Lily didn't say anything else.

"Did you know Joan very well?" May asked.

"Only from a party or two. But all of Hollywood shows up at those parties. Or all the girls do, anyway. Claude knows people in the business. And the girls come hoping—" But she didn't finish. "Let's try that dress on." Lily took May by the hand. "If you like it, I'll buy it for you."

"You can't buy that dress for me, Lily."

"Oh, can't I? I have a surprise for you—a good one."

"What is it?"

"I got the part."

May hung the black dress in the closet. She pushed her other dresses to the side and gave it some space, as if it needed to breathe. She touched the fabric. A bit of luxury, and black kept the best. In the dress department at Robinson's, she'd asked the saleswoman if she knew Hazel. "She told me to come and apply for a job," May had said. "She said I should talk to a certain man." The saleswoman looked at May as if she were telling a fib, but she told her how to get to the offices anyway. The hiring office was in the basement, and she'd have to go find the man there. After all that, Lily hadn't had time to stay, and May had decided she didn't want to go without her. She thought the basement of Robinson's might be low-ceilinged and damp. Lately she hadn't liked going places that were closed or dark. She liked to get out as quickly as she could, to be in the sunshine, the sky blue and open all around her.

"You can have my tan coat too," Lily said. She hung it on the back of the door.

"Won't you need it?"

"I have a new one. Cashmere—" She turned to face May, smiling. "I don't know much about the part yet, but they're being awfully nice. I think it's a sort of mystery. Only—"

"What?"

"It's hard to be excited about my personal good fortune when Dora's missing."

"How do they know she's really gone? I mean, are her things gone too?"

"She hasn't been back. She hasn't called anyone. I didn't ask Lorelei anything about Dora's things." Lily didn't look at May. She was folding her clothes, but May studied her profile. She took in her downturned mouth, the crease at the center of her forehead. She tried to think about what Agnes might ask Lily.

"Dora doesn't have a secret fellow, does she? Maybe a married man, or a—"

"No, not that I know of. A what?"

"I don't know. Someone she gets things from. A man who buys things for her."

"Dora's not like that. And she doesn't need it."

May lay on her back and looked at the ceiling. People were always leaving. Lily was leaving just now! May had gone away once without telling anyone—with Richard, of course. May rolled onto her stomach and watched Lily pack. "Could she be in the hospital? She was awfully screwy the other night. She was talking about that book—"

"It could be." Lily nodded, cutting May off.

"What was that book that she wanted?"

But Lily only shook her head.

May plucked at a loose thread on the bedspread. The truth was never really one thing. A fact was one thing, but the truth could be many things. Maybe she could be a detective, like Adams. Or a news gal, like Agnes. Or she would fall in love. Disappear into one of the new bungalows. "I wish you didn't have to go." May's throat closed up when she said it.

"I paid your rent for the week." Lily didn't look at May when she said it.

"You didn't have to—" But she did. May didn't have any money. She would go back to Robinson's after Lily left. She got up and looked in the mirror, touching her hair. Where *was* Dora anyway? She'd turn up. She was rich. She could go anywhere at any time.

"It's a going away present. Say—" Lily reached into the closet and pulled something from the top shelf. "I can't forget this." It was the mask Lily had had to wear when she'd filled in for Joan—an enormous mouse's head. They'd given Joan's part to another woman because Lily couldn't take it. She had the movie role. If May could dance like that, maybe they would have given it to her. She should have asked Lily. "It was for the show at the Palace," she said. "The Circus. I should give it back." She put it on and stood there with her hands on her hips.

May laughed, but the mask was ugly. "It's horrid," May said. "Who made it?"

Lily shrugged and then took it off. "Someone who hates dancers. It's so heavy."

Downstairs, May helped Lily load her suitcases into the trunk of a taxi. "You be good, kid," Lily said, hugging her. "I'll let you know if I hear anything about Dora."

When Lily pulled away, May waved, standing on the corner in the late afternoon sun. She waved until she couldn't see the taxi anymore, and then she stood for a moment wondering if it were too late in the day to set out for Robinson's.

"Why if it isn't the famous hat model."

She turned and saw Adams standing there. "Oh, hello."

"You stood me up."

"I didn't."

"Have dinner with me tonight."

"All right."

"I thought you were at the Edmonton."

"I am."

"But you came out of the Hamilton."

"I did?"

"You did."

"You're a fine detective. Have you been following me?"

"No. I have a friend who lives nearby."

"Where's that?"

"Just down the street."

"Oh." May looked around as if she might see where he meant.

"Have dinner with me tonight," he repeated.

"Of course I will."

"I'll pick you up at eight."

"I'll be ready."

"Should I come to the Edmonton or to the Hamilton?"

She looked down. "The Hamilton."

"See you then." He laughed. "I *knew* I'd see you again!" He snapped his fingers. "What luck."

She watched him walk down the street, nodding at people as he passed.

She did something then that she'd tried to break herself of doing. It was silly, something she'd started to do in grammar school. She imagined that Adams was her husband. It was so brief, a glimpse of what it might be: the mornings of coffee and toast and the hope of a baby. Orange juice and a soft-boiled egg. "Did we kill the rabbit?" She imagined him saying, leaning over his newspaper, his face fuller from the dinners she made, softer from the possibility of fatherhood, the pitterpat of bare feet. "Yes," she whispered. "It's dead as a doornail." The morning light that came through the red-and-white-checked kitchen curtains turned everything rosy and warm, but then she realized it wasn't Adams she was imagining, but Richard.

AGNES

They kidded her in the office. They called her a *lady writer* and swiveled in their chairs, their neck ties loosened and wagging over their shoulders, their jackets hitched behind them. The windows were opened to let in the air, the fans rotated, the cigarette smoke swirled and settled above them. In the late morning, they lowered the blinds halfway, and sunlight lay in stripes across her desk. "It's today," Max said.

"Tonight," she corrected. Her first piece would be in the evening edition. She wanted to be somewhere alone, eating steak and drinking a glass of wine when it came out. She didn't want anyone to see her when she saw her name in print for the first time.

In the meantime, she labeled.

Mrs. Edward Grimes, Mrs. George Collins. Married. Engaged. Divided. Tied. United. Bound. Divided. Divorced. Separated. Severed. Stabbed. Strangled.

Tent Church, 1946, Downtown Los Angeles.

She kept a loupe in the drawer of her desk. She took it out and studied the photograph. She looked at the crowd of people outside the tent, waiting to go in. None of the faces looked familiar. This back was turned or someone's face was blurred with motion. A hat obscured a profile. And she didn't know what she was looking for—not yet, anyway.

Black crosses were painted on the tent's white flaps. The earth around the tent was compact, flattened, an empty space to fill with parishioners' parked cars. Wooden signs had been erected at the mouth of the tent: Salvation. *Here.* Miracles. *Here.* Inside, she could make out scattered wooden chairs—the sort they used at the circus or for picnics that folded.

Will we see you in heaven, Brother? Jesus with his miracles.

What was a miracle in a place like that but a magic trick? A sleight of hand. The dead risen. The blind man seeing.

Have you heard about the witches yet? Hazel hadn't laughed when she said it, rocking back a bit, her hair curling down her back, and yet—Agnes couldn't say it, let alone write it. Who *didn't* stumble and laugh over the word *witches*? A coven in sunny Los Angeles! They were all well out of those woods now, weren't they? Man could split an atom, become god himself. There was penicillin, even. The mysteries would be solved with science. No more work for witches. She pictured a witch looking at the want ads, no luck. All Agnes knew of witches was what she'd seen in films: cartoon witches in black pointed caps sweeping across the spotlight of a full moon on broomsticks. Or Salem's witches—a fevered figment.

But one of Hazel's roommates had admonished her for repeating the witch rumor. It occurred to her, as she sat working, her hand steady, that it didn't matter if it were real—just that someone could use it as an excuse to do something awful. Everyone sits for a palmist now and then, hands sweaty in anticipation, secretly hoping there are answers—the lover will arrive, the pot of gold will be discovered. A step further, and those same people went to tent churches, spoke in tongues, exorcised themselves—prostrate, sweating, crying.

Witches. Miracles. Atoms. She shook her head and kept working.

Danny startled her when he knocked on the corner of her desk. "Lunch?" he asked. "We should celebrate."

"Again?" She gave him a half-smile. "And that's not how a *gentleman* asks."

"Would you have lunch with me?" He bowed a little. His shirt was slightly wrinkled. He'd left his tie somewhere. He looked like a college boy.

She leaned back in her chair. She gestured at her stacks of photographs. "They keep coming."

He sat down on the corner of her desk and leaned over the pile. "We could go for a run tonight—"

"I can't," she said. She pointed to the photographs. She thought she might track down Hazel at Robinson's, and she couldn't have him along for that. He would distract her, flirt. Maybe he'd bring out his camera. The glare of his flash would startle the customers, draw attention to them.

When he left, she looked back at the photograph of the church's parishioners. She found a woman's face in the crowd. She put her loupe back on and looked at the woman. She was grimacing. Her mouth stretched into a broad frown, her neck muscles taut. She looked straight into the camera. Her hands grasped the lapels of her coat, and she pulled as if she wanted to rip it open. Once Agnes had seen her face, she couldn't look at anyone else in the photograph. Soon she turned the photograph over, face down on her desk. But that wasn't enough. She put the photograph in the drawer of her desk, but still she couldn't get the woman's strangled expression out of her mind. What had led to that rictus? Wasn't it odd—what Agnes felt? She tried to name it. She felt—what?—not as if Agnes had seen the woman, but as if the woman had seen *her*.

6

MAY

Adams walked into the Hamilton at exactly six. He came up behind May, and then walked around to face her. He stood in front of her, smiling. "You look wonderful," he said. She was wearing the black dress that Lily had gotten for her, and she'd taken time with her teeth, packing the wax firmly, filling the holes. Adams reached for her hand. She thought he was probably a good dancer. If she decided she liked being near him, she might suggest going out later. Her lungs felt clear. She'd taken a nap.

He took her arm.

"The days are already getting shorter," said May once they were outside. It was just getting dark.

"Yes, they are. Do you mind walking?"

"That depends. Where are we going?" She looked down at her shoes. They had belonged to Lily and they were a half size too small for May. Adams followed her gaze.

"I'll never understand why women wear those."

"Wear what—shoes?" She laughed.

"The heels. What if you have to run? You won't get far."

"Why would I have to run? I hope we're not running any place."

Adams smiled at her. "I promise we won't run." He said the name of the restaurant, and May knew it. The waiters wore jackets and told customers about the food in an easy, polite way, standing with their hands behind their backs and leaning slightly forward.

"So how long have you been here?"

"In Los Angeles?"

"Yes."

"Oh, not long." She thought, counting the months. "Not even a year."

He whistled something familiar—a song that was on the radio. "I like that one," she said. "Do you like to dance?"

"I do."

"Maybe we could go—later."

"Your wish—" he said, opening the door to the restaurant for her.

At the table, he ordered two martinis. "You must know a lot of people now. Friends."

"I've met a lot of girlfriends."

"What about boyfriends? Anyone serious?"

She looked down and smiled. She touched the rim of her martini glass and tilted her head to the side. "Would I be sitting here with you if I had a serious fellow?"

He laughed. He put his elbow on the back of his chair and pushed his hand through his hair. She could see the strap of his gun holster then, a black bit of leather at his shoulder. "I adore you," he said. "I want to know everything about you."

She took a sip of her martini. "It's not that interesting," she said.

"Oh, I don't believe that. Hat modeling? Fascinating."

"I don't have any work at the moment. And when I do, it's just that someone puts a hat on my head and says, 'Turn this way. Turn that way. Chin down. Smile.' It's very dull." May knew a girl who was a hat model, and once, May had let a boy take lots of photos of her wearing a hat. It was his idea that she was pretty enough to be a model—though certainly others had said it. The boy said she needed photos, and he would be happy to take them. She stood on the steps of the high school smiling, but the sun was in her eyes, and later, when she saw that she was squinting in the photos, she put them in the bottom of her trunk and left them there. They didn't look professional at all.

"All right, then. Tell me about all the people you've met. Tell me about Lily."

"Lily just got a big movie roll. She knows so many actors now."

"Are they as eccentric as everyone says? I've met a few."

"The most eccentric people I know are not actors, actually." She thought of Claude, of the black berry floating in the flute of champagne. "You're the one who must meet eccentric people."

"You'd be surprised—" He laughed. "Some criminals are quite dull."

She wanted to tell him about Dora, ask about the Raptor, but the waiter came over. "You order," she told him, and he ordered two steaks, only asking how she wanted hers cooked. He called her *Darling*, and again she imagined that domestic scene—an image from a magazine, maybe—of a woman and a man sharing breakfast in their new home, the checked curtains tied back to let in the copious sunshine: an advertisement for someone else's life.

"What's wrong?" he asked when he finished ordering. "You look so sad."

"Do I? I'm quite happy." She smiled at him, a full, open-lipped smile. "Say," she said.

"Yes?"

"Do you ever get frightened?"

"Frightened?"

"By the work you do. You must see the worst things."

"I do see the worst things."

"What's the worst thing you've ever seen?" She leaned toward him.

"Oh—" He brushed his hand through the air as if he were waving away an insect. "I can't tell you that. You'll have nightmares."

"I already have nightmares."

"You? But you're a beautiful hat model. What sort of nightmares could you have?"

"I'm afraid of the Raptor," she said. "That's what."

"Don't go out after dark alone."

"But sometimes a girl can't help it."

"Help it."

"But what if it's an emergency? Or I know a lot of girls who work at night, and they come home alone on the bus or the trolley."

"I'd say a girl isn't safe alone after dark in this city and that's that."

May didn't say anything. She wanted to tell him he didn't know anything about being a girl—that sometimes it was necessary to walk home alone if you didn't care for your date, that you couldn't exactly sit around in a room all night if you ever wanted anything to happen. She would be bored to tears. What a stupid thing, she thought, telling a girl she just has to stay home. She sat for a while looking at the rim of her martini glass, wondering if Dora had turned up yet. "Is there any news?"

"About what?"

"The Raptor."

Adams rested his chin on hand and gazed at her. He seemed sleepy. "Let's not talk about work."

"Are you on the case, then?"

He shook his head. "Tell me about your life. Tell me about all the people you've met." He lifted his hand in the air for the waiter. When the waiter came back over, and Adams ordered two more martinis. When he was gone, Adams smiled at May. "Why did you come to Los Angeles?"

"For my health," she said. "The cold bothers me." It was the dullest of answers but she left it there for him, angry that he wouldn't talk to her about the Raptor. "I'm a little cold right now, actually." She was pouting, she knew. And he wouldn't like it, but she didn't care. Their food hadn't even come yet and she wanted to go home—or to be out with Lily at the bar, dancing with a boy like James.

Adams swung around to her side of the booth and slid in. He put his arm around her. "Hey," he said. "We can't have you cold."

She inched away, surprised.

"Do you want my jacket?" He was taking it off, clumsily maneuvering in the booth.

"No," she said. "Don't." And then she laughed. The whole thing was ridiculous. Their martinis came then.

"Cheers," he said, touching her glass. "To sunshine and warmth."

"To sunshine," she echoed.

"Can I stay on this side of the booth?"

"For a moment."

"I'll tell you about the Raptor," he said. "But not tonight. It's a mess. I need a break, okay?"

"That's fine."

"I just like looking at you. You're swell. You're the kind of girl a fellow wants to make smile."

AGNES

She wanted her work to be above the fold, but the main desk deemed it *of human interest*, so Agnes's story would appear on the third page, near the bottom. And it *was* only the evening edition—but still! She didn't mind. She imagined men and women reading after dinner, their plates pushed aside, the night creeping in. They'd close the windows, peer over each other's shoulders, say, "Well, I'll be—" when they read about Joan's movie, about Beverly's money. She walked back to the Edmonton from the office, leaving the unlabeled photographs abandoned on her desk.

Did the newsstands have the evening edition yet? They would have had it by four, and it was past six already. Of course they had it. But her palms were sweating. She stopped at one near the Edmonton. She took off her gloves so they wouldn't get newsprint on them. Agnes turned to the page—there was her name—first and last—*Agnes Crandall*—the only woman's name in byline. Well, I'll be.

She'd get there.

She'd get bulldog.

There it was. She passed a man money for three copies, and stood in front of him, reading.

No one is from here—neither the girl I'm talking to about her friend's murder nor the murdered girl herself. Hazel is from Ohio. Joan was from Minnesota. Two girls with big dreams. Hazel tells me about the war veterans, the wanderers, and the girls like her—like Joan, the Raptor's latest victim—they all need a place to live.

"That's me," she said to the man behind the newsstand. "I'm Agnes Crandall."

He took the paper and read. "Are you pulling my leg? This is you?"

"It sure is."

"That's a mean business."

"It sure is." She smiled at him, but he didn't smile back, and she realized he was talking about the Raptor—not the newspaper business. She straightened her face. "It sure is," she said again.

She walked to a diner around the corner. She would get a steak and read her work again. Afterward, a drink in the bar down the street. She'd keep a paper folded underneath her arm. Wasn't it something to be in print! She might tell someone and she might not. Was Danny reading it? She pictured him getting a copy and sitting on the hood of his car on Mount Hollywood.

She was halfway down the column when she felt a hand on her arm. "Why, I know you—" Agnes turned to see who had spoken—a woman in a gray jacket, a scarf covering her hair. It was Dora, the girl from the Mary T. "Remember me?" she said, smiling.

"Of course." Agnes shifted her papers. "It's Dora. What a surprise." And it was. When she tried to imagine Dora's life after the Mary T., she thought of her as one of those ladies who lived in a spare room at Mother and Father's—some big estate with her own wing. She'd spend half her life that way, everyone looking after her, watching her, but here she was, her cheeks flushed, her hair pin curled and parted down the side.

Not the girl she'd seen before—the nutshell—ashen, unkempt in a sweater with holes that she'd refused to change.

Dora pointed at the papers. "I read that just about four o'clock when it came out. To tell you the truth, I was coming to find you."

"You were?"

Dora sat down across from Agnes. "I'm in hiding," she said. "I have some information for you."

"Is everything all right?" Agnes thought of Dora's mother—the way she'd gazed down at Agnes even though they were eye-to-eye. "Dora's fine—" her mother had said to Agnes as they sat in the visiting room together. "It's *growing pains* for god's sake. She doesn't need an operation."

"The Mary T. was a long time ago, wasn't it?" Dora smiled at her. "I've been on my own for ever so long now. I'm fine. Cross my heart." She drew an X on the lapel of her jacket and laughed.

"How did you know where I was staying?"

"A friend of mine knows that woman you wrote about—Hazel. Hazel told her and she told me. We all live in these hotels, you see." She gestured vaguely out the window. "And, well, we talk." Her eyes large and black. "You'll see that I'm not imagining things. In a moment, when I tell you what I know, you'll think I'm still mad, but soon enough you'll find that I'm not."

"I won't."

"You will. But that's all right. Someone is trying to kill me. I know things. I know—" She stopped.

"What do you know?"

"I know who the Raptor is."

7

MAY

In the morning, May had a fever. It was raining, the sky a flat gray. Lily was gone. Richard was dead. Dora was missing. She looked at her shoes in the corner. The sole was coming off, peeled back and wagging like an animal's thick black tongue.

Back home, the leaves would be changing.

She had always been glad when the big crimson maple near the library shed its leaves—when she could see it naked and empty in the snow. In the summer, she did not like to pass beneath it, when its leaves turned a red so deep, so shadowed and dark that they blotted all the light. It was when she thought of the roots—how far they went, how deep, how if she went down into the ground to look, they might wrap at her ankles, pull her down. Grab at her the way Mr. Perry had, who said, "It's true that even my name is sweet. Perry means *pear*. I had to open a candy shop." He offered her a jawbreaker from the glass jar, turning away.

"There are none left," she told him.

"No?" He peered into the glass jar, and when he tilted his chin, she saw the round spot on his head where his hair whiskered away. "I have some in the back." He looked up, smiling. "You can come around the counter and look with me." He put his hand on top of her head, and she worried he would muss her bow, which she'd gotten just right.

"Up there," he told her. "I'll lift you up."

It was dark in the backroom. There were boxes piled as tall as men standing against shadowed doorways. A little higher, he kept saying, and when finally she found them and took them in her hands he lifted her down and squeezed her to him, as if she were his very own daughter and she felt the husk of his stubble chin press into the side of her neck.

He gave her three jawbreakers and licorice. *For free*, she thought, but he called it a trade. "You can always see me for a trade," he told her. She liked to put a jawbreaker in her tea and watch it dissolve, but by the time she got out of the store and into the sunlight, she didn't want any of it. It tasted sour and made her throat close up. It was then that she saw the tree: standing there in front of the library like an enormous black-coated sentinel.

This was the *Mr. Perry*. The trade. The *Mr. Perry* involved nothing physical. To think of him made her feel she'd swallowed soured fruit. It fermented in her gut, made the back of her throat hot, made her want to hit, to throw, to tear something from the world—to rend the branch of the crimson maple itself, to wield and hook and destroy.

But she could reverse it. Take what she needed.

That was the sort of man Hazel meant—the one at Robinson's who decided about the dress models. He was a Mr. Perry. Hands, Hazel had said. You know the kind. But he'll buy you lunch if you're sweet.

Be sweet.

She could not—

But she could not let her feet get wet! She could *not* get cold. Cold meant sick. She must have new shoes.

She dressed carefully for Robinson's. She chose the rose dress and the black bolero, her makeup heavier, her lips fuller; her eyelids darkened with the oily black stick. When she looked in the mirror, she saw another girl. Another May.

She couldn't—

She stood in the doorway, her hand on the knob.

It wouldn't be that bad. Maybe it was just a hand on the waist. A hand traveling down her back. Maybe that was all.

But the man wasn't there. "Certainly not for a girl like you," the saleswoman said, looking May up and down. May stared at the woman, and then tried to walk around her, into the offices.

What did she mean, a girl like *you*. She called the woman a name. A name she wasn't supposed to say aloud, but of course, when she was with Lily, they said it. She'd tell Lily about this woman, who wouldn't let her see about a job. "Who do you think you are?" May said. "You don't know what sort of girl I am." Her chin up, she turned on her heel. She would come back later. The store was big enough. There were others to ask.

She walked quickly down the corridor between the jewelry cases, past the perfume girls—all dressed in simple cottons of lilac and mint. All with pink lips and rouged cheeks.

May had been ready. Had made herself. It had started to rain already. Already. And now she had nowhere to go. She pushed through the door and stood on the sidewalk, feeling the damp seep through the soles of her shoes.

She walked, quickly, dodging beneath the shop awnings, and then found a diner. Inside, she ordered a cocoa. A shoe store was across the street. She watched for a while. There were so few customers. She could just go in and look.

In the shop, she asked for a pair of shoes, and then watched her reflection in the long mirror that stood by the cash register: a woman perched on the small white satin couch, leaning more on the right hip than the left, accentuating the curve. When the salesman—stooped, a bare left ring finger—brought the shoes, she tried them, slipping her feet in and out, letting him notice her fine ankles, the firmness of her calf. This one touched her like she was china, like a slim breakable champagne glass, a finger expertly dipping behind the heel to set the shoe on her foot. She walked back and forth in front of him, letting him watch her, turning her feet this way and that, asking him what he thought.

"Do you like them?"

"I do. I think they suit you."

"Watch me as I walk down here. How do I walk in them?"

"Very well."

She heard the stifled pleasure in his reply. She sat back down, pretending to pout. "They *are* dear. I could never afford them."

"I can hold them for you. Perhaps you can pay in install-ments?"

She was halfway there. She leaned over, undoing the small ankle buckle, letting him gaze at the shadowy space between her breasts, and when she knew he was looking, she straight-ened just enough so she could see his eyes. "Do you like what you see?"

The shoe salesman blushed, but she waited until he lost his first embarrassment and arrived in wonder, until he became Mr. Perry, waiting impatiently in the storeroom with his candy. Then he disgusted her, but not enough to end it.

She'd learned what needed to be done.

Once, she'd gotten to this point and walked out into the street still wearing the new shoes. The salesman had stared after her, but she could only do it if a man were alone in the store, and this one wasn't. There was another man—a fat man with a radish-colored nose—and she knew he was the kind who would be rough with her, who would leave a bruise on her wrist when he chased her down. He was the kind who took something for free. She couldn't risk it.

Out of habit, she looked for an escape.

If she took the shoe salesman into the canyons, she could get two or three pairs of new shoes. She would just let this one, lean and harmless, look at her in a car, after dark, alone in the canyons. She could lift her skirt for him, bare her breasts, and let him pleasure himself in the dark, and she didn't even have to watch him do it. She could look past him, into the darkness of that nothing of open sky. She could imagine William's tunnels below them.

Or she could think of Richard in his airplane flying high above.

She told the men about Richard, about the baby. She told them when she sensed they were on the cusp of asking for more, of wanting to touch her as they looked. She did not want them to touch her. You couldn't even put a name to it, what they did in the car in the canyons or at the pier, in an alleyway behind a shop. "The pregnancy was complicated," she'd say afterward, if they asked her for a late meal or a coffee. "I can't be with a man." She might touch their hand across the table. "This is all I can offer." The shopping bag with the shoes inside was under the table, touching her ankle. She brought a handkerchief to her face and turned away.

"There, there," the shoe salesman said. "It hardly matters."

And she managed a smile, because afterward, she thought of the men as her friends. She'd seen them open and vulnerable. She always felt sorry for them in that moment of pleasure, so twisted in agony and shame they seemed. She tried not to look.

AGNES

In Agnes's room, Dora stood at the window. "Look," she said, lifting a the lace curtain away with one finger. "There's a man outside—on the corner."

"Do you know him?" She looked from the window to Dora.

When the curtain fell, Dora grabbed Agnes's arm. "They're going to *kill* me." She was pale, her small face framed by the dark of the room.

"Who's trying to kill you, Dora?"

"Claude Borel."

Agnes knew his name from labeling photographs, but even if she hadn't had a job at the *Daily*, she'd recognize the name. The entire city knew who Borel was. He'd made a fortune buying and selling land just before the war. He bought it for cheap, all around the city, and then sold it off, parcel by parcel, for higher amounts to real estate developers. "The society man?" she asked. She remembered Dora in the Mary T.—how she'd sat on the veranda, an unlit cigarette between her trembling fingers because the nurses would not give her matches.

"Claude Borel is the Raptor. And Claude Borel is a warlock."

Agnes lifted her eyebrows. "Claude Borel?" Dora sat down on the bed with her back to Dora. In the near-dark, in the mirror, she watched herself try to stifle a laugh. She watched her jaw tighten, felt her throat close. She thought of the woman's face in the photograph—the one in the crowd at the tent church. She hadn't been able to stop thinking of it, actually—that lock-jawed grimace.

"You don't have to believe me. I know what it sounds like. I told you—"

"A warlock, Dora?" She'd been excited in the diner by Dora's words. Of course it was something foolish. Nothing was that easy. No one simply walked in and said, "I know who the Raptor is." Folly, Agnes thought, chiding herself for thinking the girl might have something.

"Just listen to me. Start poking around. Right now it doesn't matter if you believe me. You'll get there soon enough." She reached into her handbag and brought out a cigarette. "Just look into it." She struck a match, and the flame illuminated her face. Agnes reached to turn the bedside light on, but Dora stopped her. "Don't," she said. "Not yet. Look and see if he's still there."

Agnes would humor her. It would make a good story for Danny—and for Ben too, she thought, remembering that Ben had read what she'd written about the Mary T.—how good he thought it was. Agnes rose and went to the window. Indeed. The man was still there, just under the street light, his hat low on his face. Dora stood behind her. She could feel her breath on her neck when she exhaled.

"They're everywhere," Dora said. "And they can be. They can do anything. Borel's a very important financier—"

Agnes turned away. "All right—" She went to her bag and took out her pen and notepad. She turned the overhead light on in the closet and left the door open a crack. Dora nodded, understanding, seeing that Agnes took her seriously. "I'll look into it." *Claude Borel,* she wrote. But she couldn't write *warlock.* She tried to write *financier* instead.

"He manipulates people. I learned so much in the Mary T. about personalities, you know. And he is what they used to call a man with syndromes. Ever so many. I didn't see at first, but that's part of it. He's brilliant—" But Agnes was barely listening, she was looking at her own reflection in the darkened mirror. One half of her face was illuminated by the light cast from the closet, and the other half was dark. Her eyes were playing tricks on her. The darkened half—it was too strange! It didn't look like her—she blinked.

She gripped the pen, her fingers cold. It was foolish, oh, but she thought she saw the woman from the photograph—the taut neck muscles, the jutting chin—"What does he finance?" she almost shouted, thinking her voice would break the illusion, but Dora didn't seem notice. She was still standing at the window, her back to Agnes.

"You mean *who*. He finances his friends, and—and all sorts of other things. He's on the board of everything. Art museums, the observatory—" She turned from the window and sat across from Agnes. "He buys people. Collects them so they don't tattle. And they have séances—he and that man Aimsley. Ray and some of the others. A girl called Lily. It's *black magic*."

Agnes rubbed her hands together. She would not write *black magic*. In a small act of defiance, she rose and went to the light, turning it on. She would bring the conversation back to the world of the room: the bed with the golden coverlet, the yellowed cigarette-stained ceiling, a nightstand that held a black shining telephone, the hook perched in the cradle. "Is Lily a dancer at the Palace?" Everything was as it should be. The bed, the side table, the chairs, and herself, there, in the mirror. Her wide plain face. The red of her hair brighter than she remembered.

Dora looked quickly at the window to see that the curtain was closed, and then back at Agnes. "Lily's an actress. Lily's not a terrible person but she does anything they ask of her—the Palace. That's Ray's club. Yes, she filled in for Joan when Joan went—" She stopped and stubbed her cigarette out. "Do you see? They all know each other. Ray's always around Claude. He's a sort of fix-it man. And that's just it, isn't it? The rumors are so strange that everyone assumes they can't possibly be true. Who would believe it? A cabal in sunny Los Angeles?" She laughed, lifting her chin. "It sounds ridiculous to me, even, and I—well, I know it's true."

"It can't be—" Agnes hadn't seen Dora in at least three years, she counted, and now they were in a room in a hotel on the boulevard—her stories as fantastic as ever. But stories, Agnes thought, were not quite Dora's game. She hadn't told stories at the Mary T. That was left to others. Dora had just been, well, sad—and outside of herself, frightened of the possibilities, her nails bitten down. This woman, this Dora, she was different.

Agnes could hear the sound of the traffic beyond the window. The walls of the room were plaster, papered with stripes and brown flocked bouquets, the *Ranunculaceae*, the crow's foot. Cloying in its banality. Dora fidgeted. Beneath the lapel of Dora's coat, Agnes could see the glint of a hat pin— that discreet weapon of survival. "You carry this?" she asked, motioning to the lapel of her coat.

Dora glanced down. "Ah, the hat pin. Everyone does these days." Agnes could feel Dora studying her. "You ought to get one." When Agnes didn't answer, she went on. "You think I'm mad. It's like something from a Boris Karloff film."

"Why did you keep going to the house? Weren't you frightened?"

"I didn't believe it! I was like everyone else! I heard rumors. I knew they all got up to a lot of nonsense, but who doesn't? It was after what happened with Joan, you see. After Joan died, I started nosing around." She rose and paced around the room. "I went the other night when Claude was having people over. I went back to find a book they use. They write everything in it. I really liked Joanie. I really did." She took a crumpled hand-kerchief out of her coat pocket and wiped her eyes. "Oh, it's horrible, horrible." She put her face in her hands. "You have to do something," she said, looking back at Agnes. "You must get the book. It's in the basement. They caught me looking. Ray did—and I ran. I got out of there. I didn't even go back to my hotel." Dora took Agnes's hand. "They've been trying to manifest something—a demon."

Agnes shook her head. "I don't understand—"

"The man with horns and wings."

"The devil?" Agnes stopped writing again and looked up at Dora.

"Maybe not quite the devil—but how do you know what will happen when you start that business? Oh, I wish I'd never met them." Dora paced the room.

"The devil doesn't exist, Dora."

Dora waited for a moment before answering. "Are you so sure?" she said. "What do you think you're writing about? Who do you think the Raptor is? I mean, what if whomever calls himself the devil knows that *we* exist. Does it matter if we believe it? It only matters that he believes it."

"The Raptor is a man—just a man. Turn out the light." Agnes went to the window and looked out at the street. She could make out a figure on the corner, waiting. She stepped away.

"Is he still there?" Dora asked. "I told you," Dora said. "They'll be after you now too."

"*They* don't know who I am." She pulled the window shade down.

"They'll find you. I found you. I'm getting out of here—there's a ship that leaves for South America in a little over a week. Or maybe I'll take a train across the country and go to Europe. I've got to get myself sorted out. And I wanted to tell you this story. Let me stay for a few days. I'll tell you everything. Someone has to know. You can do something."

"If you know who the Raptor is, shouldn't you call the police?"

"Claude practically pays their salaries. He owns them. Besides, they'd just say I was crazy. I wanted to put you on it. You're smart. You've got a clean reputation. You weren't locked up in the Mary T. With me, everyone can point to the Mary T. I know it. And they'll talk about the things I did for fun—the parties."

Agnes looked around the room. It was too small for both of them. She thought of her little house in Pasadena. If they went back, Dora could sleep on the couch. Agnes would draw the story out, find all the truth in it. If nothing else, Dora knew the players. She knew their friends. She would tell them to talk to Agnes. There could be something there. After all, she reasoned, if Dora knew Hazel—maybe there *was* something to her story—perhaps there was no devil, but a clue, a key, some buried verity.

"Do you know someone called Marty? Maybe Martin?" Agnes asked, but Dora looked at her blankly. Agnes watched as she mouthed the name *Martin*.

"No," she said. "No, I don't."

8

MAY

Back at the Hamilton, May sat on the edge of her bed and took her shoes off. She stretched her toes, clicked and cracked her ankles. She picked up each old shoe and threw it to the back of the closet. A rap came from the other side of the wall. "Keep it down in there," a voice called. She smiled. It wasn't even that late. It was still early enough to go out.

The new shoes were nestled inside of a soft cloth bag. Inside the bag, they were wrapped in clean white tissue paper. She unwrapped them carefully, anticipating the moment when the shoes would be free of their enclosures. When they were, she put them on and got up and walked around, looking down at her feet. It was still early enough to go out.

There were plenty of other ways to get things, sure, but there was this way, too—if she were in a jam—and no one was worse off for it. Not really.

May watched the girls who went to work at regular jobs. Some of them lived in the Hamilton. They got up early and left the building in plain gray suits, in shapeless coats, and in hats that had gone out of fashion during the war. She imagined them walking into the tall pale buildings downtown, their faces turned to the sidewalk. It was almost too much to bear, thinking of it. What if May got sick in the middle of the day? What if she had one of her spells and had to lie down? What would she tell them all, standing there in the middle of the office, her fingers too sore to hold a pencil and pad?

May's handwriting was pretty—though what rotten short-hand she had. She always got lost in the little arcs and dips, trying for "to have" when she meant "and if." Soon enough the whole endeavor was lost, and her typing wasn't much either. She'd liked to talk in class, to lean over the typewriter and ask another girl about the way she set her hair.

Her sister Ann had worked in a factory during the war, and May tried to imagine wearing overalls, carrying a lunch pail with her name on it the way her sister had, standing over a bit of metal at her workstation, holding a drill, her hair tucked beneath a kerchief. She would have liked a nice pair of coveralls, a sturdy pair of loafers to dance in—something she could get scuffed doing a cradle wheel or a pretzel. Ann had left that job when the war ended. May wondered what had become of the coveralls with the crossed back and the worn loafers.

It was too late to go out. It was midnight. She thought of turning up at Claude's. Maybe if she did everything just so he would let her stay there, in the maid's room. She wouldn't mind. The rent money would run out. She sat down again and soon she was too tired to get up.

May changed into her pajamas. She put the shoes back on and walked around in them again, and then she went to the bathroom to wash the makeup from her face, the zinc white pancake turning her soapy hands pale. She saw herself there, in the mirror—the in-between May, angry May—grimacing, her face streaked with black tears, her skin mottled, wet with a claylike slip of still clinging makeup, her lips pale and purpled against the last bit of dark lipstick.

She dreamed she was in the tunnels. The walls were cool and wet. She touched a tree's roots. She knew where it grew. It was a crimson maple, its branches casting shadows over Mr. Perry's candy shop back East. She made herself into a bundle and wedged her body into the roots. Soon she realized she was nestled with animals—a fox or a rabbit—the soft fur against her cheek, but then the fur turned to feathers, and she was there with a bird—enormous, somnolent—and she its little hatched egg.

In the morning, she was as stiff as if she'd slept inside of a wooden box.

AGNES

Evil existed—there was proof enough of that. It took up residence in the soul, that shadow stitch running beneath the hem, hidden by law and obligation. The devil himself was a shortcut, a caricature. A way to explain the mystery of the human heart. The man with horns and wings! Red and cloven, breathing fire. She almost laughed, but Dora would ask, "What's so funny?"—and Agnes was not in the mood for invention.

In the morning, they checked out of the Hamilton, or Agnes did while Dora waited in another part of the lobby, emerging when Agnes was finished. They took a taxi to Pasadena, and all day, Dora told her stories. She talked until she fell asleep on Agnes's couch. Beverly Dean had been a part of the group. Dora had seen her a few nights before she died. She'd been out with Claude. And Claude's secretary—a woman called Ruth. She'd been a drug addict, surely, but always careful. And then dead. Another person who might talk. "Like me," she said, drawing a finger across her throat. Dead. How Lily brought girls in. How she'd brought Dora in. And then another woman named May. She brought her too.

Dora could talk forever. And Agnes wrote it all down for Elgin, crafting and shortening as Dora slept. Agnes couldn't include the bits about witchcraft, though. She couldn't risk it. She imagined Max laughing, his big jowl shaking. *Magic.* She wrote about the desire to make life grander—with music, with movement. Like hurling a wine glass against a stone wall. I'm here. I'm alive. Struck through with light. Her article was cautionary. It was about survival. She swept taboo to the side. She was as plain as anyone would allow her to be. She quoted Dora, unnamed, *Sometimes a girl gets outside of the lines*—she said. She didn't like feeling like a finger-wagging aunt, but she'd use the space of one article to warn.

She left Dora asleep on the couch and went into the *Daily's* office early. She wanted to find photographs of the people that

Dora talked about—to track their movements across the city—
to see the intersections of lives over time.

In the archives, she found mention of Claude in other men's
files. She found him in their photographs. Here he was at the
mayor's honorary ball at the Biltmore. There he was at the police commissioner's son's baptism. He took an interest in the
city's architectural plans. He'd invested heavily in the expansion
of the observatory. There was a photograph of him pointing to
the heavens. A photograph of an upcoming gala at the observatory, his name in small print. He was everywhere—his name in
the land records, in property deeds—and yet he was nowhere.
He often went unnamed in photographs, but appeared in them
nonetheless—in the background or at a separate dinner table
from the main participants—the city's leaders. And he knew
her boss, apparently, though Elgin had never said it. There they
were at a tree lighting—just last year—with the paper's owner.

She found him twice in photographs from the Palace, with
her loupe, and always felt triumphant in her identifications. She
began to recognize the tilt of his head, the slope of his shoulder. He dressed plainly, so as not to be noticed, she imagined, so
he could be misidentified—she thought. He was a man forever
in disguise. She took out the drawing of the Raptor—the one
sighting—and compared it to Claude's face. She carried her
loupe on an eyeglass chain. She squinted at Claude's features. It
was no use—but there was something—in the shape of the jaw,
maybe, or in the size of the eyes.

She brought the photographs to Dora. She showed her the
photograph of the woman at the tent church, the one that
haunted her dreams, the grimace that she caught sight of in
mirrors as she passed, only glimpsed. "Do you know that woman?" She passed Dora her loupe.

Dora leaned over the photograph and scanned it. "Which
woman?"

"The one with the face."

"The face? They all have faces."

"The one *making* a face."

"I'm sorry, I don't know what you mean." Dora looked up, letting the loupe fall into her palm.

Agnes sighed. She took the loupe from Dora and looked. Now she saw the mistake. It was the wrong photograph. In this, the same woman was in profile. She wasn't looking at the camera at all. "Not this picture. I'll find it." She went through her satchel, but there was no other photograph. She put her hand to her forehead. This was the only picture she'd left in her desk drawer. Where was the woman? She was in profile, her expression serene, even, as if she were looking at a line of hills in the distance.

"Let me see the photograph again," Dora said. She tapped the picture. "That's Ruth. That's Claude's secretary." She pointed to the woman. "Did you know that? But she's not making a face."

9

May

The shoe salesman had given her two dollars. It was dry out again, so May wore her old shoes. She chose a brown dress and went to the drugstore for breakfast. Breakfast cost three cents and they served two whole eggs, and because of that, it was always crowded. She bought a paper from a different newspaper boy and saw that Agnes had written another article.

Agnes interviewed an unnamed woman. She quoted the woman as saying, *Sometimes a girl gets outside of the lines—*

May stopped reading. She ran her finger beneath the words. "Sometimes a girl gets outside of the lines—" she said it aloud, and a man who was waiting for a spot at the counter looked over at her.

Dora. Of course. Agnes must know what had become of Dora.

In the closeness of the drugstore, May could tell that her dress needed to be cleaned. She got a seat at the counter and looked absently at a bit of oil swirling at the center of her coffee. She did not get up to call Lily or anyone else. No one knew that Dora was thick with Agnes—did they?

She'd never heard it said, and anyway, they wouldn't know the unnamed woman was Dora unless she'd used the very same words—

Dora liked to talk, sure, but maybe Claude and Lily and all weren't even reading Agnes's articles. Maybe they didn't care, and even if they were reading, and even if Dora *had* said the very same thing to them, how carefully had they listened?

The two dollars in May's bag would be gone in a week, and it certainly wasn't enough to pay rent. Adams would take her to dinner. And so would William and Alice, but even if she went to William and Alice's house every night, she'd still have to pay for her room. She could find another girl to split the rent with, but it was better to be alone— especially if you needed to work out a plan.

AGNES

"They pay girls to come," Dora said, sitting cross-legged on the sofa that Agnes had made up as a temporary bed for her guest. She had a blanket wrapped around her shoulders.

"What do you mean?"

"They *pay girls*—" She looked at Agnes, waiting for her to figure it out. "And boys. They pay them too."

"Who pays them?"

Dora shrugged. "I guess Claude, but maybe the old men who show up too. They always seemed important—the men— the kind who like to be in charge of things. I was only there a few times. But you hear rumors too. Those parties are different from the ones I went to. There are the parties for the men who pay girls, and then there are the parties for people who pretend that doesn't happen."

She wrote into the night. In the daytime, she told herself she didn't believe in witches. She reminded herself that she needed the facts. She drilled Dora. "How do they find the girls?" she asked.

"Ruth did sometimes. Beverly. And when they died, it was Lily—they like girls who don't have any money. You know, so they can *pay* them." Dora stared at Agnes. "Do you understand me? Lily was one of the girls they paid, and then they put her in charge of finding new girls."

"But who put her in charge?"

"Claude, of course, and then I guess Ruth—since she was at the top by then. And Ray probably suggested girls from his club, and sometimes they gave the lowest rung girls jobs there."

Agnes nodded. "I understand, I do—" At night, she turned the stories over. They pay girls. They *pay*. They promise. Then—

then what happens? And Dora's placid expression—how she waited for Agnes to put the pieces together. How many girls? Ten? One-hundred? "Everyone knows," Dora said. "Everyone knows about what happens in that house. Didn't Hazel tell you?"

No. But Hazel had talked about magic too.

Ben called her all the time. It was like he was reaching for her hands as she slipped out of a boat and into a lake, but she *wanted* to be in the lake. She made Ben promises. She was working. She would see him that weekend—or the next. She had to let Dora finish her story.

Lily had introduced Dora to Claude. Lily must have mistaken Dora for someone they could pay—but Dora wouldn't have anything to do with it. "Who was Ruth?" Agnes asked again. "What was her role?" She'd stopped seeing the rigored woman briefly in reflection, and she often returned to the photograph of Ruth at the tent church, but her face was never frozen in the same way. She was a woman glancing off to the side, thinking of nothing in particular.

"Ruth was at the top—and so is Lily. They're the main women. And then there are the ones who don't care—Lorelei, for instance. She was the one I shared a place with. I tried to talk to her about all this, and she got angry at me. She said I was being foolish. She said everyone got paid for their trouble, and that was the end of the story. I told her, *You can't pay a dead woman enough*, but that didn't mean a thing to her. She doesn't think they have anything to do with the murders."

"And the others? The ones they pay?"

"Oh, everyone gets paid in one way or another, but you mean the lowest rung girls. They call them the *showgirls*. You see them once and then they're gone. They come from the nightclubs. You can always tell. They come to the parties in dresses cut for someone else. They're excited to be there—like it's a lucky break. Whatever it is, it's *not* lucky, but if you're poor and you leave with twenty dollars, well. That might feel like luck."

"Did you ever see any of those girls again?"

"No—come to think of it. No. I didn't ever see anyone twice—but like I said, I wasn't at those sorts of parties. Only once or twice. And I didn't stay."

She couldn't hand off this story to Elgin. She would need more corroboration, proof. "Who did you see at those parties—I mean the men. Did you see anyone important?"

"*I* don't know who's important, do I?" Dora raised her eyebrows at Agnes. "I wonder what they want May for. She's a little like the showgirls, but she's Lily's friend. And Lily doesn't seem to want her to come around. Now that she's got a part in a film, she doesn't need them anymore. But they need her. They won't let her go. Or maybe they want May as a new main girl? Or a new Joan, a new Lily. I don't know. Someone to help with the man with horns and wings."

"Someone should warn her."

"I *tried.* Lily acted like I was crazy. Now they'll know they can't trust me. I'll end up like Beverly. You talk and you're dead."

Agnes paused over her notes. *Dead.* She wrote, the loop of the lower case *d* caught halfway, the silver pen from Argentina pressing into paper.

"*Dead,* that's right." Dora watched Agnes. "Joan. Beverly. Ruth. Do *you* have another theory? You really should find that book I wanted at Claude's. I don't know how, but—"

"What was the name of the book?"

"Oh, it's got a Latin name—sounds like…goats, I think—a magic book. Beverly called it a key. Beverly said it has terrific power. Claude keeps a record of everything in the book, Beverly said. It gives me chills just thinking about it. Art of something—goats?"

The Art of Goats? They laughed. It couldn't be. Not really. But Dora grew serious. "Oh, it's awful," she said. "It's full of drawings of ugly little creatures."

"I'd like to see it," Agnes said.

10

MAY

At Claude's, Lily was radiant in a red dress, her hair swept over one shoulder. When she leaned forward so that Ray could light her cigarette, he gazed at her. "You look like a million bucks," he told her.

"Thanks," Lily said, sitting back, exhaling.

"Things are really working out for you," he said.

May looked at her friend's face, but it was empty of expression. She was as distant as a photograph inside of a closed album. May crossed her ankles and hoped someone would notice her shoes. She was rewarded when Lily gestured at them. "Those are pretty. Are they new?"

Would Lily think she'd spent money rashly? "They were a gift," May said, pleased when she looked down at them.

"You'll have to tell me about the fellow, then." Lily's voice was soft. She wasn't angry.

"He's a shoe salesman."

"Well, that makes sense."

A big blond woman came in and sat down next to Ray. He put his arm around her but she pushed him away. "This is Lorelei," Ray said.

"Paws," Lorelei said.

"She's the bee's knees." Ray put his hand on Lorelei's knee as he spoke. "She's a big humming bee's knee."

"Oh, go on." Lorelei winked at May. "He knows a thing or two."

"Lorelei's known Dora for a long time," Ray said. "Haven't you, sweetheart?"

"As a matter of fact, I'm her roommate." Lorelei drank something clear from a tall glass. She fished a lime out and brought it to her pink lips. "We share a room at Ray's. She didn't come home after that party you had. I'm dead worried."

"Where do you think Dora would go?" Claude asked. "Say she just wanted to get away for a little while and didn't want anyone to know—where would she go? It's been over a week and no one's heard from her."

"Who knows? That kid goes where she likes. But I'm all ripped up about it. It's not like her to just disappear on me. No note."

"Don't say that—" It was Karl, from that first night she came to the house. She had not heard him speak before. He had a German accent, and he was small and round and leaned one elbow against the mantel of the fireplace. He stood next to a slight man, dressed in a black sweater and dark slacks. The slight man had a mustache. He smoked a brown cigarette.

"Don't say what?" Lorelei asked.

"*Ripped up*—" the man in the black sweater said.

"Don't say 'ripped up,' I said." The German smiled a little. "I was thinking of the Raptor."

"Oh, you're a funny one." Lorelei rolled her eyes.

"Come on, Karl. It's not a joke." Claude was playing the piano, something idling and invented, with unexpected breaks and pace changes.

"Apologies." Karl shrugged. "I am also worried. I like Dora."

"I'm not," the mustached man said. "I think she's just gone away with a lover and everyone's making a big deal out of nothing."

"Do you know something we don't, Aimsley?"

"How would I know anything? She stopped talking to me."

Lorelei leaned forward. "See? She does what she wants. She stopped talking to Aimsley. She decided he was a witch." Lorelei laughed. "She thinks he does some kind of black magic."

Aimsley smiled. "I have no idea what she was on about. The last time I saw Dora, she accused me of witchcraft. She said, 'I know what you do,' and I thought, 'Oh dear,' because I do get up to a lot of nonsense—just nothing so dangerous."

"Don't let him fool you." Lorelei turned to May and Lily. "He's as dangerous as they come."

Aimsley's voice rose. "Come on, Lorelei. You know how Dora is. She said, 'I saw you. I *saw* you,' but she wouldn't tell me where or when, and after that, well, after that she'd leave the room whenever I came in."

"She had all kinds of crazy ideas," Lorelei said. She leaned forward and touched May on the knee. Her eyes were green, the iris a pinprick of miotic black. "Did she say anything to you—the other night? At the party?"

May thought of Dora's small face, her large, watery eyes. *She said Claude killed his secretary,* May imagined saying, but she only shook her head. "No, but she was upset."

"She thought someone was following her," Lorelei said. "She kept seeing a black car."

"A black car?" May leaned forward a little. "What sort?"

"A sedan. You can't go outside without almost getting hit by a black sedan. She had a wild imagination."

"Has," Lily said. "She *has* a wild imagination." Lily looked like all the color in her whole body had bled into the red of the dress, leaving her pale and strange. "If any of you have done something to her—"

"Why would you say something like that?" Claude paused over the keys. "We just want to find her. Does Dora have family? I never asked." He was looking at May. "She liked you," he said to her. "She told me."

"She *likes* May," Lily corrected. "Oh, it's dreadful to worry like this." Lily stood and walked to the doorway that led out into the courtyard. She took a cigarette from a silver box atop the piano and stepped out into the courtyard.

"Honeys disappear all the time," Ray said. "They get up and find a man and before you know it they call you from New York City and tell you they're married. Don't do that to me, huh?" He put his arm around Lorelei. "We're just setting out in the world."

"Why do you want to find her so badly?" May said. "Has

she done something?" No one answered her. They turned their faces to her one by one in a kind of wonder.

"We're all simply *worried*, darling," Karl said, but he was smiling at her, as if she'd figured something out.

Claude rose and went to the record player. The slow bang of the drum began.

"We've got to *enjoy* life," Aimsley called. He moved his hips to the music. "Raptor be damned."

"Easy for you to say. You're a man." Lorelei was looking at May when she said it.

"Dance with me, Lorelei," Karl said, and she stood. Lorelei was as tall as Claude, and Karl was small. He reminded May of a little turtle, his chin tucked, his cheek at Lorelei's breast. "Aren't we fancy?" he called out.

"Oh, you." She pushed him away with one hand.

"I promise I'll be a gentleman." And they danced to the drum and the trumpet, moving across the room. When they broke, Lorelei walked around the room, examining Claude's collections of photographs and sculptures.

"Where's this?" she asked, pointing to a photo of Claude and an unknown man. They were standing in the sand, in front of a pyramid.

"Egypt, of course," Claude said.

"Who's this with you?"

But Claude didn't answer. He was talking to Ray. May watched Ray and Claude talk, their heads close together. Claude looked over at May and nodded.

"Well, look at me," Lorelei called out. Her voice was muffled. May turned. Lorelei had put on a mask—an enormous papier maché rabbit's head. "Where'd you get this gorgeous mask, Claude?"

"Ray gave it to me. It's from 'The Circus.'" He smiled as he watched Lorelei, who kept her hands out at her sides for balance as she danced.

"Can you see?" Karl called out.

"Just!" She danced, turning this way and that. The ears stood straight up, the creature's eyes were open in wide surprise, his cheeks puffed and pink.

Ray went to Lorelei and danced. He moved around her so that she couldn't see him, and she stumbled a little.

Claude leaned toward May. "How are you? Do you need anything?"

"You should sit here." She touched the sofa next to her. "I really can't hear you." She ran her tongue over her teeth, testing the wax.

Claude sat down next to her and ran a finger across her cheek. "You're lovely," he said. "I wanted to meet you on the first night—the first time I saw you, but Lily—she wouldn't do it, so I had Ray come around and kidnap you the next night. I do apologize."

"That was very rude. I had a date."

"But don't you like it here?"

"I'd like it better if Dora were here."

"Dora—" he began.

"I'm *worried* about Dora. She was in the hospital—I mean, what if someone takes advantage?"

Claude leaned back. "I put a man on it."

"What man? You don't need a man. If I had the money, I'd spend all my time trying to find her. A man poking around will only frighten her. Maybe he's not so good—your man."

Lorelei had lost a shoe. She passed Claude and May, falling into them, pressing on their knees to find her way around the room. "Take the mask off, Lorelei," Lily called out as she came back in from the courtyard. "You'll kill yourself." But everyone liked the show, and Lorelei entertained them. Soon they were asking her to find things in the room for them. "Get that picture from the mantel," and though it took her some time, she did find it, and dropped it in May's lap. May looked down, examining the image. Two men in black suits standing in the sand in front of a sphinx. They were hatless, and the man standing to the left and slightly behind Claude was large, a pipe in his mouth, his eyes small and unreadable.

"Who is this?" May asked, pointing.

"Oh, he's a remarkable man," Claude said. "I was lucky to meet him when I was in Egypt."

"How is he remarkable?"

Claude watched Lorelei. He was laughing. He held his thumb and index finger to the bridge of his nose.

May leaned back and looked at the photograph. The remarkable man was wearing a necklace, a round medallion of some sort. "What's this?" she asked Claude, pointing.

He squinted at it. "Sometime I'll tell you about it—" He took the photo from May's hand and stared at her for a moment.

Ray asked Lorelei to get a bottle of wine from the basement.

"I can do that—" Lorelei said, and they all followed her into the kitchen. She felt for the door.

"I don't think this is a good idea—" Claude tried.

"She might—" May was going to say *fall*, but the sound that followed stopped them all. May hunched her shoulders. Lily grabbed her arm. Aimsley gasped. Lorelei tumbled down the steps, and in the silence that followed, they all looked at each other.

"Lorelei?" Ray called out.

They stood at the basement door. "She didn't even turn the light on," Karl said.

"Where's the light?" Lily called, feeling for a switch.

They went down behind Lily, and even with the clatter of their shoes on the wooden steps, the shape at the bottom did not move. Lily knelt and pulled Lorelei's dress back down over her thighs. They crowded around to have a look.

"Is she dead?" Karl asked as Claude squatted to pull the rabbit mask from Lorelei's head.

"No," Claude answered, bringing two fingers to her neck. "She's unconscious."

"Well," Karl said, folding his arms. "She's going to wake up with one hell of a headache."

Claude snapped his fingers in front of her face. "Lorelei!" he yelled, but still she didn't move.

Ray went up the steps and came back down with a glass of water. "I'm going to pour a little of this on her face," he said.

"That doesn't seem right," Aimsley said. May could feel his breath on her neck as he peered over her shoulder. May looked around. The basement was unfinished, full of dirt and stone. At the far end, there was a small wooden door. She wondered where it led.

Ray let the water trickle over Lorelei's face, and Claude continued to call her name. She began to blink, her lids quivering. Her mouth opened, a black hollow, and out came a scream. Soon she couldn't stop. Claude held her shoulders down.

"Don't move," he said. "Don't move. You're all right."

"No!" she yelled. "Get off of me! I know what's going on." She seemed delirious. "I know what you do!"

"She's gone mad!" Aimsley cried, and when May looked over at him, she realized he was smiling.

"She'll wake the whole neighborhood," Karl chided.

"Believe me," Claude said. "No one can hear her. This place is sound proof."

Ray put his hands in his pockets and looked around the basement. Lily stepped closer to May. Claude bit his lip. He frowned. He looked up at his friends. "Well—what are you staring at? Someone go call an ambulance."

AGNES

Agnes and Danny stood near the reflecting pool off of Flower, in front of the library. The weather had cooled, and she liked standing near him in the shadow of the cypress trees, where the wind picked up along the corridor. She was talking about Dora—about the girls who were paid to come to Claude's.

"Why do you suppose she trusts you?" Danny asked.

"I have a farmer's face."

He laughed. "A farmer's face? Whatever do you mean?" His eyes wandered her face.

"Look," she said.

"Should I imagine you in overalls?"

"If it helps." Could he see it? When she gazed at her own face, she saw that it was flat and open—the skin freckled from the sun, the eyes round and wide-set, the watery gray of an overdeveloped photograph. A small, thin-lipped mouth—one that might remain shut, she imagined a talker might assume. It was her face, that was all. It wasn't anything she did or didn't do. Her face was open, waiting to be changed, like a field in late summer.

She explained it to him, and while she talked, he looked. He had the expression of someone being told a joke. When she was finished, he smiled at her. "I see," he said. He looked away. "Look at my profile," he said. She could tell he was trying not to laugh. "I have the profile of an insurance salesman."

"You don't."

"I do."

"I don't know what an insurance salesman looks like."

"Yes, you do."

"Go on."

"I will." He turned back to her, the expression still in his eyes. "I will," he said again.

"Well," she said before they separated. "Good luck with the goats." In the library, they'd searched for Dora's book, asking in the archives, and though the librarian had some idea of what they meant, in the end, he shook his head, saying, "It's not my specialty," and passed them the names of rare book dealers

Danny tipped his hat. "You will surely find the goats first. After all—being a farmer, I mean—"

She'd never mentioned her farmer's face to anyone—and out loud, she didn't like the way it sounded—it sounded as if she counted her own well-honed talents as some bit of accidental good fortune. Of course it wasn't simply her face. She'd gotten good at reaching for what she wanted, asking the right questions, and then listening—not just to answers, but for hesitations, for the silences—the lengths of the silences—knowing when to wait and when to say, "Just one more thing—" or fit a proposal into a pause. "If I put it to you this way—" she might say.

If I put it to you like this, or this. If I say it's my face but it's really my voice. If it's not my voice but my words. Or the order of them, or the way I lean across a table to ask. It's the rhythm and the silence.

Tell me. Tell me. Tell me all the secrets.

There were tensions. Spaces that asked to be filled. The frisson of strangers. And in an empty room, the sense that another had just left.

Dora said she had felt that at Claude's, that there was something invisible, some power, and she *wanted* it. "I have feelings," Dora had told her the night she'd talked about the book. "About possibilities. I was curious—" And so she'd continued on at Claude's, stepping into the shadows, sitting in the big white room when they turned off all the lights and joined their hands and chanted. And Beverly had told her one night after that that she'd get a part in a film soon—the spirits had said so—and when it happened, over drinks with Lily and Lorelei, Lily was jealous, and Beverly took her hands and said, "Don't worry—" It was kind, the way she noticed and pulled her in, saying, "Keep going to Claude's and you'll see—" Beverly had worn a bracelet, coiled like a snake that ran around her wrist, and the light had caught in such a way that it made it look like it moved—

Ridiculous, Agnes thought, but as she walked in the long afternoon shadows of the boulevard, she felt a tug of dread, remembering the other night, and how, cleaning up the kitchen, washing the dishes—Dora snug on the sofa, the house quiet but for the clink of glass against plate in her soapy hands—she'd felt someone standing behind her. *Right behind her.*

She'd turned, gripping the edge of the counter, edging her way down the hall, her breath short. A heart attack? She was too young. A stroke? She opened the door of the coat closet and went in. She turned on the light and leaned against the wall, one hand to her chest. Her voice had left her, or maybe she'd call out for help—she only watched the string from the overhead light swing in front of her like a hypnotist's watch, slowing her breath with its movement, until her wits returned.

She began to laugh. And then she laughed so hard that she began to cry, thinking of Dora finding her laughing in the closet—wouldn't she be worried! It made her laugh harder. What was happening? She dried her eyes and opened the door.

There was nothing in her house, just as there was no one now on the street waiting in the shadows.

At the corner, she stood watching the traffic. Across the street, a woman was laughing with a man, and she smiled, but then the woman looked right at Agnes, and made the face that Ruth had made in the photograph. Agnes looked down at the sidewalk, her heart racing. She couldn't have seen that. It couldn't be—she looked up and the man and the woman were gone. The light had changed and she crossed the street, and all the while, she felt as if something—something as indefinable but definite as smoke were two paces behind her, catching at her ankles, curled and ready.

11

MAY

She could not get out of it. She'd promised William that she would go shopping for Edith's birthday present with him. He took May to Clifton's for lunch. While they ate, he talked about the tunnels. Soon she lost track of what William was saying, felt guilty, and looked up at him, nodding, and said, "Yes. I'd like to see the tunnels. Could you take me?" She hadn't meant that moment—that day—but William was excited.

"Well, let's go," he said.

"Right now? We have to find Edith a present."

"Yes, but we can do that afterward."

"May I finish my chicken?"

"By all means."

"I didn't know we would go today. I don't think I'm dressed for it."

"We don't have to go in."

"No?"

"I'll just show you where one is."

"All right." She ate slowly, wondering if she could get out of it.

In the car on the way there, William hummed and thrummed the steering wheel with his fingers. "Oh, this is something," he said. They drove to the spot where Edith's church tent stood, and then a little farther. William turned off the road and pulled up to a dirt lot. It was open and flat, and the sun was high and hot.

"Here?" May said, as they got out of the car.

"I know it doesn't look like much," William answered. "Someday, Edith's church will be here. It will be enormous. Two blocks at least."

"Two blocks, huh?"

"It's all being negotiated just now with the man who owns this land. Borel. Have you heard of him?"

She hesitated, and it seemed that William assumed she did not, because he kept talking, explaining all the things he knew about the church, wondering aloud what would happen to the tunnels. "I'll be sorry if we can't get in them anymore," he said.

"We?"

They stood in the sunshine together. The land didn't look like anything. It was a vacant lot, cut and crossed in preparation for construction. Nearby, a few dump trucks, full of gravel and debris, sat empty of drivers. At the other end of the lot, May could see Edith's church tent, but the tent was empty at this time of day. May had imagined something different: a clean dip into darkness, a path to follow—not a construction site in an empty lot.

"Come on," William said. He held his hand out to her. May hesitated, looking down at the broken beer bottles, wondering about her shoes, already stiffening with dirt. The brown glass bottles glistened in the sun. "It's all right. Come on," he repeated.

"But it's so dark." She peered into the mouth of the tunnel. She had to lean down to see it. It was bigger than the door in Claude's basement but smaller than a space you could easily slip into. She'd left her hat and gloves in the car. She wouldn't have to crawl, but she would have to duck, to narrow her frame. "My dress," she said.

"We'll get you another." William held up his flashlight. "It's an adventure. I've never been in this one. We'll just go a little way to see it. From here, we can get into the tunnel of one of the trolleys they've stopped running."

She was still full from the chicken and potatoes she'd eaten, and in the sun, staring at the mouth of the tunnel, she felt a little nauseous. Her dress was tight at the waistband, her breathing shallow. "How did you find it?" she asked.

"A man told me about it. It's boarded up, but someone's made a hole here. See?" He swept his hand through the air as if he were presenting a prize. His shirt was dark beneath his arms; a triangle of sweat showed between his shoulder blades. He'd left his jacket in the car.

"What man?"

"I met him at church one night. He said he was trying to piece all the tunnels together, like I was, and he showed this to me. We came walking over here after the sermon. He knows about so many of the tunnels."

"Did Edith come too?"

"Of course not. She's not like you."

It was true. Edith wasn't like her—not at all.

"Should we go in and see it?" William seemed impatient.

May made a calculation. She could ruin her shoes and dress and please William, and in the end, she'd have a pair of new shoes and a dress as a reward. "All right," she said. "Turn that thing on first." She pointed to the flashlight. It was the sort army men carried, brown with a crooked neck.

His face lit up. "You won't be sorry." He ducked into the mouth of the tunnel. He turned the flashlight on. "See?" he said. "Just like home." He held it high and she could see ahead, to where the tunnel widened and she'd have room to stand.

"Is it paved down there?"

"Yes. It's perfectly fine. It's going to be a lot of fun. Come on."

She took his hand. It wasn't strange, not at first, being inside the city. The sides of the tunnel didn't touch her, but she could sense them there, and the farther they went the more her eyes adjusted to the single beam of light. There were noises buffered by earth and stone and dirt. Shifts from above. Unidentifiable echoes. Soon their voices bounced across the cavern of the empty station. May could make out the long wooden benches where passengers had waited for trains. William moved the light across the ceiling, which seemed uneven and organic. "Are those bats do you think?" he said idly. The entrance, when May turned, was a white pinprick of light.

"I hope not." She caught the smell of urine, of the ground's coldness below that, and when she put a hand to her mouth, William shone the light on her and she was blinded.

"Are you scared?"

She tried to shield her eyes from the light, holding up one hand. "No."

"Does it bother you to be in the light?"

"Yes. Turn it away, please."

He did. He shone the light on the opposite wall. Others came here. There were drawings and scattered writing on the tunnel's walls. Symbols. May couldn't make anything out. "Look at that," William said. It was a drawing in the shape of a bird with wide-spanning wings and a sharp beak. William let the beam of light linger over it. "How very strange," he said, moving the light over the wall. Behind the bird, as if in its wake, was a picture of a woman lying face down. He turned the flashlight off. They stood together in the darkness. "Are you frightened?" William asked.

"Yes."

"There's nothing to be frightened of. The city is so full of light. I like to come down here and think. It's cool, you see. I know it's not pleasant in the way most people think, but it's cool and dark."

"But that drawing—" she said. "It's like the Raptor."

"It's all anyone thinks about these days," he laughed out. "The Raptor. There were birds and women before the Raptor." He turned the light on again. "They'll be birds and women after."

Certainly that was true. She didn't like the drawing, but searched for it in the dim light as if she should keep watch on it. "What do you think about then—when you're here?" May wished she had her own flashlight. Her palms were sweating. It was plain. She shouldn't have come.

"All sorts of things. The war."

"Does Edith know?"

"Somewhat. Marvin showed this tunnel to me, said it connects with others. One leads underneath City Hall, even."

"Who's Marvin?"

"The man who told me about this tunnel."

William's answers always led back into themselves. He didn't answer, anyway, in a normal fashion. He seemed obstinate in the dark, like someone else. "Marvin seems to know an awful lot about the tunnels—" May tried. "And you too. It's like a secret club."

"It *is* a club of sorts—" he cried out, and then, more quietly, he said, "We've started meeting for a drink once a month."

"Oh. Does Edith know?"

"Does Edith know?" William mimicked. He swept the light around. "She doesn't need to know everything."

"I suppose not."

William was quiet. He turned the light off again. "I've seen the way people look at you," he said.

"What do you mean?"

"They stare. Does it bother you?"

"Yes." She said it hesitantly. *Yes.* But it was easy to say it in the darkness. She had the sense she was talking to herself, as if William's voice were her own voice, the voice of her thoughts. She could hear William breathing in the dark. It sounded as if he were having trouble. She coughed, as if it might help him breathe if she were the one to clear her throat. "The air is sour here," she said. "It's bad." She coughed again. "You know my lungs." She wished she could see his face. In the pitch black of the tunnel, she felt as if she were falling through the center of the earth. "They're no good." She didn't know how long they stood like that. In the dark, a person lost track of time. "William?" she said, and he didn't answer. "William, can you please turn the light on?"

He flashed it on and off several times. "Oh no, the batteries must be going."

"Stop it," she said. "Don't be a child. Turn the light on." But he didn't. She closed her eyes. It seemed easier to be in the dark that way, she thought, and if she didn't say anything else, William would come to his senses.

"Did you know that some people are born with all of their organs on the other side of the body?" he said. "It's like they're a mirror image of someone else—a replica from the looking glass." May curled her toes. She kept her eyes closed and didn't say anything. "Yes—" William went on. "It's like a mirror image of you or me. The condition has a rather long name: *dextrocardia situs inversus totalis.* I'd love to see it one day."

"See it?"

"Why yes—in a photograph, of course. But it's quite rare. Leonardo discovered it. There's something interesting."

"Who?"

"Leonardo da Vinci. The painter."

"Oh."

"He was an anatomist—most artists are in some way."

The body was full of its own tunnels—veins and the hollows of bones, the pump of the aorta, the ventricles in the heart. The darkness had begun to take on dimension. She could not make out any single object, or even say where a wall might be, but the darkness was not as still and thick or impenetrable as it had been before. It was shadow cast upon shadow. The ceiling was alive with bats. "I really didn't come here for an art lecture." Her voice was louder than she'd imagined it would be. "I'd like to leave."

"I was only saying— What if there are copies of us walking around somewhere, only they're backward?"

She turned toward the white dot. She thought of the small door in Claude's basement, rounded and low, like the squat cartoon doorways in *Snow White.*

"I do apologize, May." William turned the light on. He swept it across the empty tracks and one way and then the other. "I'm sorry, May. I get carried away."

"It's all right." He was farther away from her than he had been before. She hadn't heard him move, and she wondered how he'd done it, gotten so far away without making a noise. He flared the light around the station, letting it fall on the image of the bird again. "That's a strange thing to find painted on a wall." The bird might have been an eagle. It could have been a raven. It was some sort of raptor. He held the flashlight on the image. "What do you think of that?" His voice was full of wonder. "Marvin said he's seen these drawings all over. He told me about it the other night when we met."

May imagined William sitting in a diner with a man whose face she couldn't see. The man drew a black bird on a napkin, and turned it toward William. She turned and started to walk, moving slowly, her hands out in front of her in case she fell.

"Hey," William said. He sounded like himself again. He came close to her. He took her by the arm. "Hey, May, let's go, yes." He tightened his grip on her arm. She tried to shake him off, but he held her arm tightly. He turned her toward him and turned the flashlight off. "Shh," he said, when she protested. "Do you hear that?"

"Hear what?" She didn't hear anything. His hands were around her waist. "William—" she began, trying to push him away.

"Shh—it sounds like wings. All the bats have woken up."

"Stop." She broke free of him and staggered ahead.

"May, wait. May, I'm sorry. I shouldn't have. I'm sorry. I'm just teasing. I didn't mean it."

"Stay away from me."

He was holding the light out in front of her so that she could see. "I'm sorry," he said again. "It was stupid."

They'd reached the mouth of the tunnel. "It *was* stupid," she said, squinting in the sunshine. "It was terribly stupid." She brushed her dress off. Her hands were dirty. "You shouldn't do that."

She brought her hand to her chest and kept it there until her heart began to slow, until it returned to its normal tempo. She imagined her body reversed, another body. If she were in that body, all that had happened might have happened differently. In that other body, Richard would still be alive. She would only know William and Edith as her sister's friends. She would believe they were as lucky as she was.

AGNES

By the time she got to the third book shop, her feet were sore from walking. The last dealer had sent her to this place, buried down a little side street, saying they had some *unusual* books. That dealer hadn't heard of anything like *The Art of Goats*. Something magical. *Goats*. If she had to say it again, she would laugh. The dealers had laughed with her. No, no, they'd said, I would remember! But this one—the third dealer, stood in front of her and only smiled. His hair was perfectly black. He wore a checked woolen jacket and held a book. He was neat, but his fingernails, she noticed, were long, unclipped, and then she became fixated on his hands, which seemed impossibly smooth and white. "Ah yes, the *Ars Goetia*. I can see you're not entirely familiar with it. Come—" He turned away from her and took her toward the back of the shop. "Karl," he called, and another man appeared on a balconied second floor. The man put his hands on a golden railing and looked down at Agnes. She blinked up at him, the sunlight from the windows striking his glasses. "This woman is searching for a certain *grimoire*."

"What wonderful news, Aimsley," Karl said. He had an accent—German, Agnes thought. "We haven't see you before I don't think—"

"No, this is my first visit." She turned away from Karl and back toward Aimsley. He touched her arm. "Just here," he said, lifting a heavy black curtain. "We keep the special books here." He smiled at her. "They dislike the sunshine." He held the curtain for her. She passed into a small room where wooden bookcases with glass doors were built into the walls. He touched the books' spines, and he turned to her, his eyes fixed on her own. "Do you know which version you want?"

"One with drawings, I think."

"Ah." He turned toward the bookcase. "Perhaps this one. It's very popular at the moment." He opened the bookcase with a small silver key and took down a slim volume. "There are other books in this collection, but this is quite a conversation starter."

The book was gray, hardbound. A bright red three-by-three windowpane pattern scored the cover. He put the grimoire down on a wooden desk that was stacked with books in states of ill-repair—tied together with string or fastened with rubber bands—and made enough space so he could open it for her. When he moved the book, she noticed that he did so with gentleness, as if he were soothing a frightened animal. He turned the pages, smoothing each with a fingernail as he did so. Here were etchings of magical creatures: a dog with three heads, an owl with a stork's legs. Horrible creatures, grotesque, distorted.

"It's from a small press—an art press—and the edition number is limited, so if you were after this particular *Ars Goetia*—is this the book you are after?" he asked.

"These illustrations," Agnes said.

"Beautiful," he murmured.

"What are these creatures supposed to represent?"

"Demons—" He smiled at her when he said it. He had small yellowed teeth. "You don't know anything about it?"

"Not a great deal."

"The book has a complicated history. No one knows who wrote the original *Ars Goetia*—Solomon, of course, but that may be folklore. The first *known* printing dates back to the 1300s."

"My—" She turned the pages. "This one looks quite menacing." She tapped a page that showed a winged man, his head affixed with antlers. He crouched in tall grass, his black eyes opaque with ink. "A man with wings and horns—" she said to herself.

"People often come for these books with a story to tell—" Aimsley offered, "about why they've come looking. What is it that sent you?"

She straightened. Was he too inquisitive—what did she sense? He was steering her, she thought, steering her along, and while he steered, he watched. She mentioned the other two booksellers, to which he said, *Of course,* but when she finished with that, he continued to look at her, finally bringing out, "Nothing else? But why did you want this book?"

"I'm a reporter," she said. "For the *Daily.* Agnes Crandall." She put her hand out. "It's a story I'm doing about the occult in Los Angeles."

"Aimsley Preston." He took her hand. "Charmed. You're a reporter. *Well.* The story must be astonishing."

"I think so, but, Mr. Pres—"

"Aimsley."

"*Aimsley.* Might I speak to you on the record? For the story? About this shop—your customers." Hadn't Dora mentioned an Aimsley? It wasn't a common name. "You must know—" She paused. "Magicians. Warlocks, even."

"Ah." He looked around as if someone else might be in the room with them—someone he did not want to overhear. "I think *not.* My customers, you see, the ones who are interested in the books in this room are, well, private about their passions. If I were to begin talking to a newspaper, no one would come to me."

"I see. If you change your mind—" she began.

"Would you like me to wrap the book for you?"

"Oh, I'm afraid I can't buy it today. It must cost quite a lot."

"Not as much as you'd think. There won't be a great many of these printed in the future, and I keep them in this room because they bother some of my regulars—the collectors, you know, if it's history books or, say, *bird* folios they're after—" They looked at each other. The corners of his mouth went up.

She could show the book to Dora.

He turned and held the black velvet curtain open again for her, and the room outside seemed brighter. She looked up but did not see Karl. He took the book to the counter, and she watched his slim white hands fold and press the brown paper around the book. She wanted to ask if he knew Claude Borel. "Do you know—" she began, and when she said *Claude Borel,* he stopped what he was doing, which was pressing a sharp fold into the paper with his long fingernail. He kept his face down.

"No," he said. "That name doesn't sound the least familiar."

He passed her the parcel, smiling. "Be careful with that," he said. "You want to take care. It can be dangerous if you don't know what you're doing."

"What might happen?" she asked, leaning forward.

But he only shook his head at her. "The strongest books are the ones we make for ourselves. Those books can't be duplicated. This," he said, "is a beginner's book, an art object, but it still has power."

She told him she would be careful, and that if she had questions, she might be back. He nodded pleasantly, accompanying her to the door, and even if she'd turned when she crossed the street and looked back, she would not see what he did next. When she was gone, he picked up the telephone.

Back in Pasadena, she said the name to Dora. *Aimsley.* Dora's eyes fluttered. She'd washed her hair, and was pinning it into place. She was sitting at the kitchen table with postcards. She'd started one to her mother. *Don't worry about me, Mother*—it said. "Dear me, yes. Did he have very long fingernails?"

There was no mistake.

Agnes put the book down on the kitchen table. "Is this the book?" she asked.

Dora stood and leaned over it. "It's similar." She took the book and opened it. "It's like Claude's—I think. I only saw it once. Claude's is full of notes, though, and hand-drawn maps."

"Maps? What sort of maps?"

"I really don't know. Lots of black lines." She pressed the pages down. "Dreadful. I must get out of here—does he know who you are?"

"Yes, but—the book won't connect you to me."

"Who do you suppose would've told you about the book?"

She didn't have an answer.

Ben took them to dinner. He let Agnes drive. She took the curved roads slowly. They drove up and into the mountains, to a place surrounded by tall pines. A resort. They ate in front of a fireplace. "I've got to get out of here," Dora said. "I look at everyone and wonder if they want to kill me"

"Where will you go?" Ben asked.

"Abroad. I'll take the train to New York. Then I'll go to the south of France and lie in the sun and not talk to anyone."

"It will be cold in France," Ben said. "Too cold to lie in the sun."

"Then I'll go to Paris and wait for it to get warm. Or I'll go to Argentina. Maybe I could get a ship straight there from the port. I could do that. I'll hop from summertime to summertime." She took a sip of her wine.

That's what it is to have money, Agnes thought—never waiting, never yearning for the sunshine. Always having it at her fingertips, even in the depth of winter.

12

MAY

Claude gave May money—after they'd taken Lorelei away, after the shot that had calmed her, the long needle passing into her arm. Lorelei's eyes tipped back, her jaw slackened, and though she'd been screaming a moment before, she managed a small smile. "What are you all staring at?" she muttered.

"What's *in* that shot?" Ray asked.

Claude held two fingers against Lorelei's neck. "Morphine, of course. She'll be comfortable now."

Upstairs, Claude brought the money to May in a long white envelope; she wanted to grab it. She took it gingerly and opened it, counting the crisp bills. "I might need more," she said, and he smiled and turned his back to her and went back to the locked drawer that May imagined was like a bank teller's—stacked with crisp twenties and tens. She turned away, looking at herself in a long mirror, fixing her hair, putting on lipstick.

She wanted to touch Claude, to bring a hand to the side of his neck, as he had with Lorelei when he felt for her pulse. When he turned away, she noted the inverted black triangle of his hair at the nape of his neck, the set of his shoulders. "Why would she run away?" May said. "Why was she so scared?"

Claude looked at May in the mirror, a half-smile on his face. "She was scared? What did she say to you?"

"Nothing. Nothing really. I guess something frightened her."

They stood looking at each other. He had one hand in his pocket. "Let me take you out tonight."

"It's late."

"The whole world is late."

He took her out to an elegant club where a woman stood

beneath a white spotlight, her arms reaching, singing an extended note as the room fell into darkness around her. May sat close
to him at a little round table, her elbow pressed against his, and
she knew he wasn't watching the singer, but her. The set ended,
and a man from the audience carried a bouquet of bright red
roses up to the woman. When May looked at them together,
she thought the man had the same expression on his face that
Richard had sometimes had when he'd looked at her.

It was a cheat to be in the world without him.

On the way back to Claude's car, he pressed her into an alley.
"See here," he said, when she struggled. "Don't you want what
Lily has?" He kept one hand at her throat. She told him he must
stop, but he continued to press, and soon a kind of inertia took
her over, and her mind slipped away, and she wondered if she
was who she thought she was, and from a great distance, she
heard him say: "You really must learn that we are all absolutely
up to no good." He didn't kiss her. He kept his cheek next to
hers, pressing his hand against her dress, between her thighs,
and all the while he continued to tell her he was up to no good.

Back in the car, she looked out at the dark street, putting a
hand to her still flushed cheek. She wondered if her dress was
torn. She didn't understand the way the time had slipped away
from her. It was as if she'd become another May there in the
alley, and the real May had left and turned her back on the affair,
waiting for it to be over before slipping back into her own skin.
It had started as one thing and ended as another. He would
have seen that he could do that to her by the way she looked at
him in his study. She bit down on her lip, hard, until she tasted
blood in her mouth and her jaw ached.

And maybe now she was the mirrored May—herself reversed—as William had spoken of in the tunnel. She put her
hand over her heart and was relieved to hear its beat.

AGNES

Ben wore a gray suit, a light blue summer shirt. It was afternoon, the sunshine white, the shadows short. Agnes drove the car, taking the serpentine road to the observatory, thinking of the view from above—of Danny's photographs—light racing over the road, the black night of film.

She wanted to see what Ben thought of what she'd written. Danny liked everything too much, and it made her suspicious. She would show it to Ben, who was more critical, his thoughts more linear. She would give him no more than ten pages. The pages were in her satchel, in the backseat, and they were like a live thing for her—the tremble of paper like a cicada's dormant wing; the black of the ink, the eye of the beetle. She'd cleaned and oiled her typewriter, changed the ribbon.

Begin.

"I'm getting good at this," Agnes said when she parked at the observatory. "Soon I'll be driving all over the place."

"Where will you go?"

"Down to San Diego—to Baja after."

"We could go together. A vacation. When did you plan it?"

"Just now." She smiled. They could drive south along the coast until they reached their destination, pass through the dusty little towns. It would get warmer as they went, and soon they would find a place to stay, the sun orange on the horizon, the days short but beguiling and warm and stretching over the afternoon hours as long bands of light coming through a window—from which, she thought—they might see the farmers' flower fields in bloom—the colored stripes that lay across the earth like ribbons, the air heady with their scent.

She and Ben walked along the promenade where she could look out at the white tops of the San Gabriel Mountains set against the pale blue sky. They made their way around, and on another terrace, beyond the rooftops of the city, she saw the sea.

They sat on a low wall. Agnes passed Ben the pages she'd typed up. She worried they'd blow away. She made him give her back each page when he'd finished reading, and she smoothed and re-smoothed the pages on her lap before putting them one by one into the satchel again. She understood that she shouldn't be nervous, but it didn't matter. She was. It didn't matter that he knew her work, that he thought she was a brilliant writer. It didn't matter. Her mouth was dry.

He was the only one who'd read her work about the Mary T., and he was the only one who'd seen her afterward, when nothing had come of it, and she stayed in bed with the curtains closed. Like that manuscript, this one was also bound, typed, with one-inch margins—as if she were going to do something with it. "Dora talks a lot, and the things she says—" Her voice trailed off as she watched his eyes move over the page. "You'll see."

When he finished, he whistled. He folded his arms. "What do you think of Dora?" he asked.

"What do *you* think of Dora?"

"I think she's prone to invention." He didn't look at her when he said it. He was still holding the last page of the manuscript, and she reached over and took it from him.

"Do you think I'm a fool for listening to her?" she wanted to know.

He took her hand. "You?" he said. "Never."

"Yes, but—" she tried. He was right. Of course Dora was prone to invention, but that didn't mean that what she said was false.

"Have you shown this to anyone else?"

Agnes shook her head. "I need more sources. I can't hand it off like this. It's a fairy tale. It's a story about witches."

"But do you believe it?"

"In a way—" She reached for her satchel and took out the envelope that held the photographs she'd collected of Claude. She pointed. "*There*," she said. It was Claude with Ray in the background, and Joan among the women who danced at the Palace. "And there, again," she said, holding out another photograph.

"But these are people who know each other—" he began. He said it so softly. He said it in a way that made her think of a

flower's petal falling away. "Of course they're together in photographs." In the distance, the sun struck the water. He didn't
believe her. "He has no history of crime, does he? Borel? Why
would he risk everything like this?"

"You don't believe me." She tucked the photographs away.

"It's not *you* I don't believe." He touched her back. "It's all
right," he said.

She took out a cigarette. Her hand was shaking. "I believe
her—"

Ben felt his jacket for matches. "It could be, I suppose. It
could be true."

She smoked, her profile set against him. She squinted at the
sea. Ben would be glad when Dora left—when they could go
back to the way things were. But how were things before? Agnes
tried to decide. She remembered her scraps of paper: Always
look ahead, never behind; keep moving. And it had worked.
After she'd been at the *Daily* for a few months, she'd started to
feel better about her drafts about the operation, about the Mary
T. She'd started to think she could get a job writing for *City
Life*—something for women, maybe. She could do that. She
could see herself setting out for a fashion show, white-gloved
and quiet as a prayer. She would put the Mary T. and Dora
behind her. Marry Ben.

One night, she'd opened the door to the closet where she
kept her work on the Mary T. She pulled the plain brown manuscript box down, slipped on her shoes and a light sweater, and
walked down to the garage at the corner where they burned
trash. She'd stood in front of the iron drum, throwing four or
five pages in at once, then more, then the box. Then the whole
thing was gone.

She looked at Ben and threw her cigarette on the ground.
She wasn't a fashion reporter, for god's sake. She wasn't white-
gloved and silent. "Let's go see that mural," she said, standing,
like she was shutting a door. He kept looking at her as they
went.

Inside, at the ticket desk, a young man told them about the

upcoming gala. The proceeds would go toward a new wing. "Would you like to go?" Ben asked. He was trying to make her feel better. She wondered what would happen if she turned to the young man and said, "It's so very hard to make me happy, you see, but he thinks a gala might do it."

"Do," she said, and Ben bought tickets. Hadn't she read about the new wing? Wasn't Claude one of the big donors? Surely he would be there. She could watch him from across the room. She might even talk to him—ask him something newsy and bright. And she would watch his eyes as he gave the answer, gauge the way he looked at her—

Ben took her arm.

They walked the wide white hallways, and soon they were standing in the room with the pendulum. The golden ball swung, caught the room upside down: Ben's face, her own. It measured earth's rotation. How strange it was, she thought, watching as it knocked a peg down. They were all in motion, always, whether they knew it or not. Everything was always one moment in the past or just about to happen.

Even that thought. Gone.

13

MAY

She decided what had happened in the alley was different than she'd thought at the time. Sometimes, she told herself, men could be rough, but it was only because they were in love and had so much desire. She told herself this in the bath, as she looked at the bruise Claude had left on her thigh. The bruise was the color of the crimson maple, the black-red of the dried edge of a rose.

Desire, desire, desire, she whispered. She closed her eyes and kept the word in her head, letting it bloom.

Ray came around with the car. She thought it would be just one night but it was three.

They slept in the day, drawing the blinds. They woke in the evening and got ready for the night—she in new clothes— dresses with low backs, smelling of foreign perfumes and smoke from long-ago parties. They'd been his wife's dresses, he said. "Where is she?" May asked, but Claude only shrugged. "I have no idea."

He sent Ray back to the Hamilton to pay for May's room. She thought of her gray cardboard suitcase sitting at the back of the closet, the wooden floor scuffed, her old shoes with the slipped tongue. The drip of the faucet and the flash of the sign. Open.

At night, Ray pulled the gleaming black car around. He drove them to restaurants where she and Claude ate alone in private dining rooms papered in red twisting roses set against black, mirrored walls. Fantasy rooms. She did not talk to him, nor did he talk to her. Ray left the keys with Claude and went off to one of his clubs. Claude drove them back to his house, never asking if she wanted instead to return to the Hamilton.

She imagined she could wrest love from him, rip it back. He would give her all the things she wanted—he'd promised that, hadn't he? The promise was the thick envelope filled with crisp bills. She liked the feel of the money, and ran her thumb over the surface of a twenty. He said when she came back with Dora he would buy her acting lessons—that he would hire a photographer to take professional pictures of her—nothing like the ones she kept in her trunk. No. He would have some-one come over. A real photographer, and when the pictures came back, he would choose which ones were best, and she would finally see herself. He would *make* her see herself. The photographer would likely put those photographs of May in his show book—he would do it if Claude told him to—and soon enough, everyone would be asking about her. Does she sing, can she act? Oh yes. Oh, she certainly can. Claude looked at her sideways, implying something. Wasn't she sly, he seemed to be saying. "Don't you want what Lily has?" he asked her again, and this time, she answered: "Doesn't everybody?"

Didn't everybody want what Lily had? Beauty, the promise of fame.

Luck.

He turned her around, roping her hair with his hand, and later, asked her to lie still as he went to her handbag and found her lipstick. It was the new one with the case that looked like onyx, the tube red. He drew a shape on her body, across her torso. "Now you're mine," he said.

She'd seen a film about a man who rises from a grave in the dead of night, called by a magician. The magician said the same thing when the man arrived on his doorstep. *Now you're mine*— only the magician threw his head back and laughed. Claude didn't laugh. He lay down next to her. She listened to his breath, the way it slowed. She thought he was asleep but he said, "We'll do it right this time," his back to her, his face to the window. She didn't answer. Her own breath felt shallow and short.

She dreamed of wandering the house, going into the basement, finding that door, low in the shadows, the scrape of her shoe against the unfinished floor—shut, then opening—where did it go? A narrow tunnel, perhaps, that led to deeper tunnels—the ones William investigated. She might crawl through that door, find herself naked in a room of strangers. Claude might take her there, past the walls of her life, far beyond the white canvas of Edith's church, gasping and flapping in perpetual sunshine.

She woke in the small hours and went into the bathroom to look at the drawing on her torso in the mirror. A red spiral— the sort she'd drawn as a girl in imitation of a rose—but the makeup had smeared unpleasantly across her skin, up her side. She scrubbed at it with soap and a cloth until it faded and got back into bed.

On the third night, she took a flashlight and went down into the basement. She wanted to open the small door, to see what was on the other side, but when she found it, she sat on her knees and pressed her ear to the door instead, too afraid to open it. The longer she stayed in the dark, the more she could hear. She heard the echo of wind, the scratching of animals. She knew there was space beyond the door, a path—and though she knew it couldn't be—she imagined a copse of crimson maples beyond, their black leaves crackling in a hot wind.

On her way up, she caught sight of something shining beneath the steps. It was the syringe case that Claude had brought out for Lorelei. The case was made of silver, hinged, similar to something for eyeglasses. Inside, there was a single hypodermic syringe, cotton gauze, and three needles in fogged glass holders. The vial of liquid—that was the morphine. She uncorked the vial. It smelled rich and sweet, like chocolate. She closed everything up and turned the case over in her hands. She liked silver, the smoothness, the way it tarnished and then glowed when polished. She kept the case, and carried it back upstairs. She slipped it into the black handbag she'd left on the floor of the living room.

She looked out at the fountain, at the marble woman, caught aglow in a single light, her reaching, leafy hands, her tilted, up-turned chin, her open mouth, and the water that made her cold skin shine in the night.

When May woke up in the morning, Claude asked her why her knees were dirty. "I was in the courtyard," she answered. "I couldn't sleep."

"What were you doing in the yard?"

"I couldn't sleep," she said again. She didn't have to tell him anything. "I'm leaving today."

"Oh?" He got up and stretched. It was nothing to him. He went to a mirror and admired himself. They watched each other's faces in the reflection.

"Give me some money," she said. "I need more money." She would take all the money and disappear. Florida, she thought. Go there. Or to an island off the coast—but the money would run out. If she brought Dora back, there would be more money. An apartment, maybe, a reward. Fame. Her photograph in a magazine.

"When you find Dora, don't tell her I have anything to do with this. She's afraid of me."

"Why?"

"She thinks we're all witches."

"Are you?"

"Of course we are." He laughed. "Just get her back here."

"Maybe I won't find her."

"You will." He left the room and when he came back, he had more money. "When you come back," he said, "I want you to meet some friends of mine. They'll like you."

"Will I like them?"

He didn't seem to hear her. "We'll have to get your teeth fixed first, I imagine."

AGNES

With Danny, she didn't ask if what she'd written was real. She didn't wonder if she were somewhat of a fool for listening to Dora. She kept a pair of old loafers in the trunk of Danny's car. It was hard to drive a car in heels, she realized, just as it had once been hard to walk in them. She still hit the brake too hard when she had to stop.

Pull at one thread, she'd said to Danny. Pull it and see how it unravels.

The tent was downtown, where the streetcar used to run. "Should we go in?" Danny asked when they stopped in front of the church. It seemed less dramatic than it had in photographs. The sides of the tent were muddy, not crisp and white as they'd appeared. The crosses were faded from sunlight. The church sunk toward the earth, an elephant that was in need of rest.

"Let's get out and have a look around," Agnes said, but neither of them moved. They watched three men in the distance. The men stood in the lot, which had a shallow dip and was big enough to fit a new hotel. The ground was dry and dusty. The men kept their hands in their pockets, and their hats were pulled low over their foreheads. They had their backs to the tent.

One of the men pointed. He pointed away from the church tent, toward a wall where trash was piled.

"They look like prospectors," Danny said. He brought the Graflex out and rolled the window down.

"They've seen us. Look sharp." Agnes watched the men as they began to come toward the car. She got out. "It's a beautiful day, brothers," she called to them, lifting her hand.

"I wouldn't say that." Only one of the men came forward. The other two hung back, watchful. He was broad and handsome in a brown work jacket. He wore boots, and his trousers were dirty to the knees as if he'd been walking in mud.

"Every day with Jesus is a beautiful day." She smiled. It was windy. She put her hand to her hair. "Have you seen the preacher? We're doing a story for *Salvation Weekly*," she lied. She spoke quickly. "We've driven all the way from Topeka." She shouldn't have said that, she thought, because he was looking at Danny's license plate.

"Topeka?" he said. One corner of his mouth went up. He saw the lie.

"Our car broke down just as we got here," she said. "We had to borrow my cousin's today." She affected breeziness. She was a chatty woman, she could see him thinking. That would probably annoy him. It was plain. "Have you seen the preacher today?"

He nodded, looking from her face to Danny's. "The preacher? You can usually find him here. Unless he's somewhere else." Danny got out of the car with his camera. Agnes knew what Danny was doing: he could leave the camera hanging at his waist, and still take photographs. She could tell by the way he kept one hand in his jacket pocket that he'd attached the shutter release cable. He reached out with his other hand. "Brother," he called the man.

She talked over the noise the release might make— What a miracle that they got there at all, what with the steam pouring from the engine, the awful rattle. "God wanted us to make it," she said.

He smiled, laughed, nodded. "Sure he did."

She began to insist. She told him about *Salvation Weekly*, and soon he cut her off with a curt goodbye. She smiled, still, waving at him and his friends as they walked across the lot and disappeared.

"*Salvation Weekly?*" Danny laughed.

"Did you get their pictures?"

"I sure did."

14

MAY

At Robinson's, in the dark and cool of the fur salon, May touched the coats, letting her fingers slide down the mink as the sales girl stood by, watchful but polite, telling her the qualities of each kind of fur: all were warm, but the mink was warmest. The sable shone. The Persian lamb was short-haired—pretty with May's delicate features—the girl remarked. "Or you could try the fox, the marmot." She helped May into the coats, and May let the weight of the animal skin settle onto her shoulders.

"This one," she said when she put on the mink. She took the envelope full of money out.

When the girl took the coat and went to have it packaged and wrapped, May closed her eyes. It seemed to her that the bloodless hides still held the smell of something warm and rich—corporeal. A smell like wet earth.

She would find a hotel near the *Daily* building. Something a little nicer. A week in a good room. Hotel Nightingale would do, where the walls were freshly papered, where there was a telephone on a shining wooden table and a private bath with packaged soaps. A window to watch for Agnes. She could wait. She would wait for Agnes, and Agnes would take her to Dora.

You must come with me, May might say, taking Dora's hand. And maybe she'd lead her back to Claude's through some underground maze, she in her mink coat, Dora chattering next to her, her voice bouncing off the walls as they made their way. She'd carry a lantern—or a flashlight like William's—the light skipping around as they went, and soon enough they'd find the little door that led to Claude's house, and just then Dora might gasp and protest, but it would be too late.

At Christmastime, she would arrive in Boston, stepping off

the train, the porter holding one gloved hand. She would let Ann wear the coat if she asked, and she would drape it over her mother's shoulders if there were a draft. Holding her coat out like—she thought—like Claude and the woman she'd seen at the club that night. Claude and—and *Beverly Dean.*

AGNES

"Joan sang in the choir," the preacher said. "Of course I knew her. She was a beautiful soul." He was wearing a peach-colored shirt, and his fair hair was cut short, like an army man's. His cheeks were as rosy as if he'd been standing on a hill in a sharp wind or had been slapped by a woman. He'd come right out to meet them, nodding and smiling, stepping down from a stage at the front of the tent.

"We're from the *Daily*," Agnes explained when he reached them. He brought them to the back of the tent, where they sat in wooden folding chairs. He sat cross-legged, his Bible balanced on one knee, one hand on top of it, as if he were taking an oath.

"We all miss Joan's spirit," he said. He talked about Joan's voice, about her skill as a singer, and Agnes wondered, watching his face, if he said the same things about everyone. He was reflexively bright, as if admiring his reflection in a mirror. Agnes returned a carefully constructed expression—one that gleaned information—she affecting a candid pleasantness that people talked into, at, and around.

"Do you know a man named Marty or Martin?" she finally asked, breezily interrupting him.

"There are men named Martin here. Plenty. But do you have anything else? Do you have a last name?"

"No. But one of Joan's friends said she met him here, and that they were seeing each other."

"I'd like to help you find him. I can ask the other singers. They might know."

"Did you see her talking to anyone? Anyone in particular?"

"No. I don't recall anything like that. I will ask though. How can I get in touch with you?" Agnes wrote her name and number down and gave it to him.

"One more thing—" she said. "Do you know Claude Borel? Has he ever been here?"

"Borel? The society man? Oh no. Not that I know of. I would be happy if he did, though. He lives the life of the body, not the life of the soul."

"What have you heard about him?"

"What everyone knows—the parties, the money. It's hard to live in this town and not hear his name mentioned. It's funny you should ask, though."

"Why is that?"

"Joan knew him. She told me once. She said she wanted to confess something to me, and she asked me if I knew him, and I said, as I just did to you, that I've only heard of him."

"Did she say what that was?"

"No. She was going to tell me that week."

"Did she?"

"That was the Sunday before she died."

15

MAY

On a windy Saturday afternoon, May went to church with Edith. The walls of the tent flapped, the canvas catching the air, sucking and pulling. When the choir began to sing, Edith clutched at the neckline of her dress and then lifted her fists into the air. She shut her eyes. May tried to decide if—as the choir insisted—it would be better to have Jesus than gold. Possibly not. Definitely not. Jesus would march her back to Medford.

Gold would set her free.

She laughed a little, imagining unearthing a gleaming pot in one of William's tunnels. She would be smart and take the gold. Likely the sweating and swaying and calling-out crowd would too. Given the opportunity. It was harder to fool a poor person. A rich person got the pot of gold *and* a translucent Jesus hovering above the pot of gold, blessing it, smiling benevolently, his hand raised as if he were waving. It was true that Jesus preferred rich people. It didn't say so anywhere; in fact, everyone said just the opposite, but wasn't it clear?

May's family had never gone to church regularly. The church was at the end of the block, and the best thing about going was the dress she wore. It was blue and stiff with pin tucks around the neckline. She and her mother had made it together, her mother ironing the brown paper for the pattern, showing her how to trace a seam.

May grew bored at church, her neck itching from the starch. It was more interesting in the winter, when the women who sat in front of her took off their coats with fur collars, and May would reach forward to touch them, as soft as a kitten's back. She stroked. The other mothers looked at May, but her mother didn't seem to mind. "Oh, she's just a child," May heard her mother say after the service. "She's not hurting anything." Mr. Perry was there, his eyes following May when she went up for communion. Once he stood behind her in the communion line, and she could feel him there like a ghost on her skin. When Mr. Perry finally got sick and died, church was more bearable. Even the crimson maple stopped frightening her. They went to Mr. Perry's funeral, and May looked at the other girls' faces, their eyes blank, their mouths shut.

Edith was too much sometimes, May thought, looking at her. Her face was wet, her skin shining with sweat. "I want a baby," she said, turning to May. She said it in a way that made May feel accused of something. Edith looked like she had a fever. "I want a baby," she said again, and this time, May pulled her close to her and put her arms around her. The back of Edith's dress was damp, her skin hot.

"Jesus will bring you one," May said, and she imagined Jesus sailing through the air, his white robes billowing. He carried a swaddled baby in his arms and headed straight for Edith, who waited on the hard, dry earth of the lot with her arms outstretched.

"He won't."

"He will, now. You just see."

"No," Edith said. "*He* won't," and then May understood that she meant William.

"William doesn't want a baby?" But Edith only put her face in her white-gloved hands. "Let's pray," May said, thinking it would comfort Edith, but Edith was already pushing her way down the aisle, just as the service was ending, while everyone was turning to their neighbor with the compressed smiles of painted dolls. Edith was not even bothering to say excuse me. She reached the end of the row and stepped out through a gap in the tent's fabric, and when the wind blew, May caught a glimpse of her crying outside in the sunshine.

She tried to follow, but the crowd was breaking up, and just as she thought she'd be able to pass through the gap in the tent's fabric, a man blocked her way. "Is that the famous hat model? Hello, stranger," he said.

"Adams—" Wasn't he always turning up? Oh, he was a bother. He was in parks or on street corners, and he was blocking her way to Edith.

"You don't seem happy to see me."

"My friend—" she began, reaching for the tent flap, but he took her arm and turned her toward the table where the women from the choir were setting out cake and lemonade.

He whistled. "Look at that," he said, and she did. She could smell the sugar, almost taste the sweet of the icing. She looked back at the gap in the tent but didn't see Edith.

May would have to make an excuse and find her, but first, she would have a slice of the cake.

AGNES

"I don't trust him," Agnes said when they were back in the car. "Something doesn't feel right. Who owns this land? What are they going to do with it? They can't keep a tent here forever."

"This land is worth a lot," Danny said. He took out a notepad and wrote the women's names down: *Beverly, Joan.* He wrote *CB,* and then *people to photograph.* He turned the radio on. *Land?* They went to a drive-in and ordered hamburgers and listened to the ten-oh codes, eating together in silence.

She thought of Ben, how they'd gone to dinner together after the observatory, and on the way, he'd kept his hand on the small of her back as they walked, looking down at her as they passed beneath the shadow of a long slant of an awning. *I'm fine,* she wanted to say. Stubborn, insistent. But she hadn't been. She'd sat across the table from him and watched as he reached into the breast pocket of his jacket. She began to panic, thinking that he might be about to propose. She was relieved when he brought his hand out again and there was nothing in it.

"What's on your mind, case cracker?" Danny was smiling at her. "You look like the end of the world."

"I do?" She touched her hair, pretending vanity. "That's something a girl wants to look nice for."

He laughed. He kept looking at her.

"What?" she finally said, but he only shook his head. She reached forward and turned the radio up. They listened for a while, idling, her hand on the steering wheel, her elbow on the open window.

A man's body had washed ashore on the beach in Cabrillo.

"I'll drive this time," she said.

By the time they got there, two officers were already squatting over the body. It had rained earlier, and the beach was empty, the sand dark and wet beneath her loafers. Danny ran out ahead of Agnes with his camera. The wind whipped in from the ocean, blowing her hair straight back. When she caught up to them, she was breathing hard. She looked down at the man. His eyes were missing, his black hair matted across his forehead. She did not recognize him until she saw his hands—and the fingernails—long and articulated, blue, now. "I know who that is," she said to the detectives. "That's a man called Aimsley Preston."

She went down to the station with them and answered their questions. No, she did not know him well. No, she did not know anything other than that. He had a rare book shop and she'd gone in not long ago. She remembered Karl leaning over the balcony, the dark room where she'd bought the grimoire, and Aimsely's pale fingers as he'd smoothed the fold in the brown book wrapping paper.

16

MAY

December was changeable in a way that made May feel feverish. Hot one day, colder the next, but always too warm for the mink. May checked into the Hotel Nightingale. The room was chilly, and at night, May slept beneath the mink, curled into it on her still-made bed. In the daytime, she wore Lily's cast-off woolen coat and sat in the diner across the street from the *Daily* building. She'd watched the building for two whole days. She knew habits: lunch, late lunch. Stay late. Leave early.

What did Agnes look like? May imagined her as one of the teachers back in Medford—colorless in a gray dress, no girdle, big black shoes from the last century, hair pulled into a crooked bun—but was she the woman in the navy-blue coat? Red-haired, quick-moving? Agnes was younger than May had imagined, with better posture. Watching her, May sat up straighter.

The woman in the blue coat with red hair couldn't be anyone other than Agnes, May decided. There *was* no other woman who left the building with the men, who walked among them with a sense of purpose. She seemed central, centered, sometimes even in the lead, pushing through the glass doors, a handbag in the crook of her elbow, her chin up.

That was Agnes. May drank the rest of her tea and stood, waiting, and when they came out of the *Daily* building, she left a nickel on the saucer.

She tagged well behind the group. Agnes laughed at something and mimicked hitting a baseball. "Out of the park!" a man yelled, pretending to watch the baseball, his hand shielding his eyes from the sun. Agnes whistled.

They turned a corner, but when May reached the same corner a moment later, she stopped. They'd vanished. She looked up and down the street, turning around in a circle. Then she saw the bar. There was no sign—just a name painted on a door in small green letters. *Frank's*. She smelled beer—that sweetly fetid stink of spoiled apples.

Inside, she sat at the bar with her back to their table and watched them in the mirror. One Coca-Cola, two, she counted. Soon a man got up and came toward her, raising his arm for the bartender. Another man called out: "Don't be all night, Danny." Danny looked at May's legs sideways as he ordered for the table.

"What's your drink, miss?" he said to May when the bartender came over, nodding at him. "It's on me."

"Something that looks like sunshine."

She watched his profile as he ordered. He was nice to look at—a wide soft mouth, a heavy brow. She checked his hand for a ring as he took a money clip from his pocket. He did not have one, and she smiled when he said, "See if you like it." He put his elbow on the bar and turned toward her. "I'm Danny."

"I'm May." He'd ordered the same drink for himself, and she touched his glass to his. The color was the perfect orange of autumn. "Cheers," she said, taking a sip. "What is that?"

"It's called an *old pal*. That color's from Campari. I asked them to get a bottle in here," he said. "Are you meeting someone?"

"I'm killing time," she said. "I'll give you a moment, I guess."

"Then why don't you kill some time with us?" He nodded in the direction of his friends. He took her arm as they walked toward the table. "This is May," he said. He pulled up a chair for her and she sat down next to him, nodding at everyone. "We're in the newspaper business," he said. "A bunch of hacks."

"I read all the papers," May said. She looked at Agnes and smiled, trying to decide if she thought she was pretty or not. No, May decided. Not especially. Her face was too serious. Her eyes were too small. "I always wanted to be a writer," she lied.

They went around the table saying their names, and when they finished, they all looked at May at once. "What do you do, then, if you're not a writer yet?"

"I'm a hat model."

"But it's much better to be a hat model than a writer," Agnes said. She said it as if she were winking. As if it were a joke. She looked at May for too long. Did she know who she was? May wondered. What would Dora say about her? May's the one who's fiancé died, she might say. Or, May's the one who doesn't know anything.

"Well, it's not much to stand around wearing a hat," May said. "You do something important. You'll help catch the Raptor."

At the mention of the murderer, they began to talk all at once. Anything from the cops today? New leads? They dissected details, time frames, the man walking away, a car seen speeding away. May's stomach hurt. She swallowed. Her teeth ached. "Do the police have a suspect?" she asked. She felt far away, on the other side of the room.

"You want another?" Danny watched her. "Hey," Danny said to the table. "Simmer down," he said to the table. "This one will think we're all ghouls."

"We are," said a man in a gray suit and checked tie. He lifted a beer stein and smiled.

"If you want to be a writer—" Agnes said. She wore a dark green sweater. Her face was partly in shadow, her eyes ringed with circles. Her lips were painted the same red as the leather bar stools behind her. Agnes shrugged. "This is what we do."

"Doesn't it keep you up at night?" May pressed her jaw with her index finger. She winced at the pain, but it put her back in the room with them.

"We're immune," the man in the gray suit said. "We have to sell papers. You know what people want?"

"What do people want, Max?" Danny was back with May's drink. He brought her a ginger ale in one glass and a scotch in a shorter glass. He turned to her. "I thought you might change your mind. You look like you need it."

"Blood. Heads rolling. The bloodier the better. Especially if it's a pretty girl or a kid."

"Oh, stop or I'll start to think *you're* the Raptor." Agnes

laughed. She ran a hand through her thick hair, pushing it behind her ear. "See? No one cares about a girl when she's alive.
No one knows anything about these women."

"You do," May said. "I've read your articles."

Agnes lifted her glass to May.

"I think it's a gang." Max lit a cigarette. The smoke rose, and
May wondered if it was dark out yet.

"A murder gang. Now that's terrifying." Danny took out his
notepad.

"Hobbies," Agnes said, looking into her drink. "Everyone
needs one."

"You've heard of stranger things," Max said.

"That's the truth."

"This city is dangerous."

"Every place is dangerous," May said. She watched Danny
write in his notepad. What did it say? "Lots of girls—" She
stopped, uncertain of where she was going. "A girl should always look around her on the street at night."

"Is it safe where you're staying?" Agnes asked.

"Oh yes. The Hotel Nightingale is quite nice."

"Isn't that the truth." Agnes nodded. "It's getting late,"
she said. "I should skedaddle, boys, but first—" She took out
change for the cigarette machine.

"Me, too," May said, and followed her. She stood next to her
at the cigarette machine. "I have something to ask you." May
watched Agnes's expression as she dropped coins into the slot.

"What's that? Do you want to know if Danny's married?
He's not."

"No. Nothing like that. I'm looking for Dora."

Agnes gazed at her with a blank expression. "Who?" she said.

"Dora. You know her. She told me."

"I don't know anyone named Dora. Oh, unless you mean my
aunt. *Her* name is Dora."

"Yes—you do."

"I don't know where you get your ideas, dear, but I don't
know anyone named Dora."

May had seen liars. Good ones. And she didn't think Agnes was lying. "I was sure—" she began, but then it occurred to her that *Dora* could have been lying. She reflexively apologized. "I thought—"

"Why are you looking for her?"

"She's my friend—" May started. "And no one knows where she is. With everything that's happening—"

"What's happening?" Agnes turned to her.

"The Raptor—"

"Ah, well, I hope you find her." Agnes pulled the silver lever on the machine.

When they got back to the table, May sat down again, but Agnes folded her purse beneath her arm, pulled on her navy-blue coat, and downed the rest of her drink. She banged the glass down. "To life—" she said. "May it be long."

"Long and prosperous—" Danny said, but Agnes was already out the door. May watched her go. How unlikeable that woman was! How rude. She looked at the table. Had anyone else noticed? She turned to Danny and smiled. "I'm hungry," May said. "Would you take me to dinner?"

"That's a forward one," Max said, standing and putting on his coat.

Danny turned his chair to face May's. "I know a place," he said. "We can walk." But they stayed for a while, and when the jukebox got too loud, he leaned close to her and spoke into her ear—closer than he needed, maybe. He didn't seem to know who she was, anyway. It was a fool's errand, trying to find Dora, but May had a nice room and an envelope full of money, and maybe it was fate, after all. To be here. They got up and he held out her coat for her.

Out on the street, he kept looking over at her and smiling and it felt like a kiss on the cheek, like sunshine. There were a few people on the street, and when they passed, May imagined they thought she and Danny were newly in love.

She thought of Lily's laughter. She saw her friend sitting on the edge of her bed in the Hamilton, letting her hands drop into her lap, leaning slightly forward and shaking her head, saying: "He doesn't know it—but he asked you to dinner, and you're already picking out your wedding dress."

It was true. She'd done it with Adams. She did it with Danny. May pretended love because if she didn't try it out, she wouldn't know, and so she wrote it in letters to boys she met at parties, on the backs of photos with the men she danced with. *I'll always treasure the moments we shared. Yours always*— It was a lie, of course. A week later, she couldn't remember their names. But love started with a lie, didn't it?

Just a small one.

Sometimes she closed her eyes and tried to envision love as a thing—as a person or a place that she could bring to herself—and once she imagined a white horse galloping through a bright snowy field. She saw herself open her arms to the horse, knowing it was a sign, an omen. She held out her hands to it, whispering, *Come.*

AGNES

She walked around the block two times, wondering if she should go back into the bar, confront May. What do you know about Claude Borel? she could say, leaning forward like a detective interviewing a suspect. Did he send you? What do you know about Aimsley Preston's death? It was disconcerting for her to show up. Clearly she'd followed them there. And that said something about her, didn't it? She was crafty. What a pretty woman she was, Agnes thought. Like Disney's Snow White with her black hair and blue eyes. But her skin was rough, chapped or raw, and Agnes could see the way she'd tried to hide the bad skin—with pale makeup. And how could she afford the Nightingale? Dora had said that May didn't have any money. She was a poor girl with a pretty face. She was the city's pastime, its bread and butter.

Danny didn't seem to care. And why was Danny so interested? His head turned at the first pretty face. First Hazel, now May. Some gentleman he was. She was glad Dora hadn't come—not that she would have, it was a work drink, but still. Dora had gone to fetch her car. It was parked in a garage near the Biltmore. She thought of calling her, asking her to come pick her up, but instead she walked around the block again, and then stood on a corner waiting for the streetcar.

Her shoulder ached from the weight of the satchel. She'd spent part of the day gathering photographs to show to Dora. Aimsley was in some of them. He turned up at art exhibits, at parties for the affluent. She looked at the men in their suits and the women in the pretty dresses, smiling, coifed, elegant, all of them. A head thrown back in laughter, a drink lifted. Agnes looked for some indication that these faces were masks, but found none.

With each linked name, her circle of suspects widened. It would be impossible to prove, if there was anything to prove, that there existed some vast conspiracy of depravity. She wondered where the money came from, who paid whom. She was trying to keep a record of all the links, of the spider web spinning out in front of her, but it moved like mist.

The coroner had ruled Aimsley's death a suicide, which these days, wasn't unusual. Men did it all the time—and sometimes women, too, but mostly men. It was the war, of course. Battle fatigue, shell shock. Sometimes the whole thing got to be too much and a man took a long walk into the sea. That was the euphemism—*a long walk into the sea*. Was it called that everywhere, or was it geographic? Were there long walks into the mountains? Into fields? A man took off his shoes, trousers, jacket, shirt. Everything. He set a silver-faced watch set atop a small pile of clothing. A worn wallet weighting a note that began *Dearest*—

Aimsley's note was one line, and when the detective showed it to Agnes, he'd laughed, saying, *Haven't we all?* because the note only read: We've done it wrong.

When she told Dora what the note had said, Dora opened her eyes so wide that Agnes could see white all around the iris.

"Did *what* wrong?" she said.

It was cold outside. It felt like midnight.

Aimsley had scrapes on his shoulders, deep gouges, and bruising across his throat. The coroner said it was from the rocks. The corner said it was from the waves. Who was she to second-guess the coroner? But Danny had said something about it too. He took photographs of the marks—and of Aimsley's swollen features, the sockets that had contained eyes—"The fish," the detective explained, pointing. "Nothing unusual about that."

Still. She didn't like to think of it. She wasn't, as Max had said in the bar, immune. She doubted the detective was immune—or anyone at the paper. It wasn't something gotten used to.

When the streetcar arrived, it was nearly empty. She took a seat and looked out the window, and as it pulled away, she saw Danny and May walking arm in arm. *A hat model.* Agnes shook her head. A hat model, for god's sake. Is that what sort of woman Danny liked? Though admittedly—there must be something more to May. She'd found Agnes, after all, and she'd found Dora, even if she didn't yet know it.

"Someone's come looking for you," she called when she closed the door, and Dora appeared out of the darkness of the hallway, one hand on her chest, a thin trail of cigarette smoke lingering in the air behind her.

"Who?"

"May."

"*May?* What's she up to? It's a good thing I'm leaving tomorrow. I knew they'd find me."

"I thought you liked May."

"I do, but they could have gotten to her by now. She could be working for Claude. He gets them, you know. He offers them jobs, money, education. And she needs all those things— but how?" She studied Agnes, her brows drawn together. "I must have told her I know you," Dora said vaguely. She'd been packing her suitcase in the living room, and she went back to it, talking to Agnes as she went. "What did you say?"

"That I don't know you. I never heard of you."

Dora straightened, nodding, her hands smoothing and folding a sweater. "I wonder—"

"I put her off your trail anyway." Agnes dropped her satchel and went into the kitchen for a glass of water. She came back out. "Oh, I wanted to ask you—" She went to her satchel and took a photograph out. "Is this Lily?"

The picture was from a few years ago, and showed the dancers at the Palace. Dora came over and looked. She nodded. "That's Lily all right. I guess that's how she met Ray. Can I see?" Agnes handed her the photograph. "And there's Joan." She tapped the photo. "See?" She handed it back to Agnes. Sure enough, Joan was in the line of dancers too. "Lily can't pretend she doesn't know her. Of course she does. Geez, I wonder if it was Lily who brought Joan to Claude. And now Joan's dead—" She paused and looked around the room. "Claude, Ray, Lily, Joan—" She said the names as if she were counting them on her fingers. "Claude, Ray, Lily, Joan—May. I should warn May."

"She's staying at the Nightingale," Agnes said. "Bring her here if she'll come."

17

MAY

May kissed Danny in front of the hotel. She pulled him toward her. She gave him a long kiss, a distracting kiss, and put her hand inside his jacket pocket. When he stepped away, she had his notepad tucked into the sleeve of her coat. "I'll see you soon," he said.

"You will." She watched him walk away. His step was light. His legs were long. He reminded her of boys who played basketball in high school—his reaching hands, his narrow hips, his bounding legs. He was the kind of boy who brought flowers, who sat patiently on the sofa in his good suit while a girl's mother asked him about his father's work—or he had been, once.

Cities changed people in a way that made them stop believing in time, but someone was always reminding May that time existed. Girls laughed, saying, "We won't be young and beautiful forever," to each other in the mirror, lined up, putting on lipstick, fixing straps or hemlines. There was only a certain amount of currency allotted.

In the Nightingale's lobby, the porter handed her a white envelope. *May*, it said, in black ink. Three small letters. She opened it. The note was from Dora. Dora hadn't been lying after all. She did know Agnes. In the bar, it was Agnes who had lied. Dora wanted to see May. Dora said May would find her at the midnight show at the theater down the street. *I'll find you*, the note read. *Wait in the balcony.*

AGNES

At night, the Palace seemed more elaborate—the faux balcony

lit from below, its shallowness obscured by shadow, and the painted columns were bright with white spotlights. A red rug ran from sidewalk to entry, where two potted palms stood. In the daytime, it felt haphazard—decorative elements tacked on to a warehouse—but at night, standing outside, a person could feel lucky. She glanced at the men and women around her. They smoked and laughed, careless in their good outfits.

Inside, a waitress showed her to a table, which was set for two—why not call Ben, or Danny, even?—but she'd passed the telephone closet in the lobby without stopping. She didn't want to see Ben, and Danny might be with May. If that were true, she'd rather not know.

Agnes sat with her back to the wall, and when the waitress left, she moved her chair a little so that she could watch the evening unfold without being noticed. She ordered a drink and bought two cigarettes from the girl when she came around. "What time does the show start?" she asked the cigarette girl.

"Oh, not long now. As soon as everyone has their dinner plate. There's a singer first. Here she is—" The girl put the cigarettes in a clean ashtray and placed the ashtray on the white tablecloth. "Enjoy the show," she said. A woman came out on to the stage. The lights behind her turned the blue of a summer night. She wore a pale evening dress and reached her gloved hands toward the audience as she sang. When the lights changed color, so did the dress. Agnes was glad when the song was over. Music made her mind wander. It made her think of love. First Ben, and the way she'd danced with him on the night the war ended, her eyes closed, wet with tears—then Danny and May walking arm in arm.

The lights went up again briefly, and Agnes thought she saw Ray standing offstage, his hands in his pockets, watching the singer, watching Agnes—but then he was gone.

The plot of "The Circus" was simple: a tiger escaped from her cage; the ringmaster had to capture her. He chased her through the audience, and the tiger—a woman in a paper mask and striped leotard—danced in the spaces between patrons.

She ducked behind onlookers—which made everyone laugh—
and the ringmaster made a show of not being able to find her.
Back onstage, the animals circled the tiger, protecting her, and
distracted the ringmaster with tricks: a mouse and an elephant
waltzed. A lion performed pirouettes. At the end of the number, the ringmaster broke free of the circle and caught the tiger.
He placed her in a golden cage, but just as he was disappearing
behind the curtain, the other creatures unlocked the cage and
lifted the tiger out.

Agnes looked at the laughing patrons, their empty dinner
plates in front of them.

It didn't matter what happened between Danny and May,
not really.

After the show ended, the lights came up, and a band took
the stage. Couples rose to dance, and soon the room was full
of sound and motion. Agnes made her way to the stage's side
entrance. She found Ginger in the back. "You came," Ginger
said, taking her hand. "What did you think of our show?" She
took her into the dressing room and shut the door. The tiger's
mask was sitting on the counter in front of the mirror.

"I thought it was fantastic," Agnes said. "But how do you
spin in that mask?"

Ginger laughed. "Carefully." She sat down and rubbed her
neck. She reached for a jar of cream and began to massage it
into the skin where the mask had sat. The marks looked just
like the striations Aimsley was found with. It wasn't the rocks.
It wasn't the waves.

"Did you know Aimsley Preston?" Agnes asked quickly,
looking at the marks.

Ginger stopped what she was doing. Her mouth fell open.
Her eyes grew wide. It took her a moment to recover, but finally she said, "Who?"

18

MAY

The cinema's seats were worn, the velvet coming away from the armrests, and the patterned carpet was faded in spots, as if someone had scrubbed at a stain and brought the dye away. May kept her coat on, sinking down into it as she sat in the left wing of the balcony, just as Agnes had instructed. She did not look around, but waited for the lights to go down. She imagined Dora standing somewhere off to the side, perhaps hidden in folds of the dark red curtains, watching to make sure May wasn't followed.

No one else was in the balcony. The movie began; in it, a man was driving to Mexico. A woman sat beside him. He kept his arm around her. There were gunshots, the car veered, and then Dora sat down next to May. "I'm leaving tomorrow," she said. "I wanted to warn you about Claude."

"Where will you go?"

"No place anyone can find me."

May turned to her. "Why did you disappear?"

Dora was watching the movie, her eyes moving back and forth between the woman and man, but then she turned to May, as if she were angry. "Claude was going to kill me. Don't you see that? He's the Raptor. He killed Ruth. He killed Joan. Beverly. Take your pick." There were more gunshots in the movie, and Dora turned back to the screen.

"How do you know?"

"I walked in on them with Joan. I told Ruth what I'd seen. And the next day, Ruth was dead. And then Joan was dead too." Dora looked at May for a long moment. The light from the film made shapes on Dora's face, shadows and abrupt hard angles.

"And if I don't get out of here, I'll be dead too. And now that you know—"

"I want to get out of here. I don't want anything to do with this."

"You did want to know. You *listened* to me that night at Claude's. I could tell."

Her eyes were as black as the darkest shadows in the film. "I was *there*. I walked into the room when Claude and the others were after Joan. I saw it. They were after her. Later they said it was a game, that she was aware of what was happening, but I don't think that's true. She looked knocked out."

May remembered the black berries floating in her drink.

"And I bet you're being followed. They'll wait for you to find me and then that's it." She drew a finger across her throat.

May thought of Lily. *Dora's crazy,* she heard her say. *Oh, she exaggerates everything, you know.* "No one's followed me. No one knows where I am."

"That's what you think. They're using you."

In the film, the car veered off the road. From the wreckage in the next shot, a woman began to pull herself free. The expression on the actress's face reminded May of the way her face felt in the alley when Claude had pressed himself into her. She was trapped inside the car.

"Talk to Agnes. Tell her whatever you know. She can put the pieces together. I have to leave, May."

"Where will you go?"

"Someplace where no one knows me—"

Dora began to stand, but May grabbed her hand. "I'm so far outside of the lines—" she said. It was as if she were pleading with Dora, with herself. *I'm my mirror self,* she wanted to say. *I'm backward now.*

Dora pulled her hand away and gazed at May. "You should stay outside of them. It's better for you. Listen—" She sat down again. "Be very clever. Like Agnes. Don't let on that you know anything."

Clever.

She had an envelope full of money. She'd found Dora when no one else could. She was clever, wasn't she?

"You stay and be clever. Don't do what I did. I went to the police about Ruth, only they didn't do anything because everyone's in Claude's pockets. All they did was tell him that I said it. And then—and you know about the—about the *magic*, don't you?" In the movie, a woman screamed. A door slammed. *Witches*, Dora whispered. The theater went black for a moment. Night. A darkened room.

There were only witch costumes. And Halloween witches. There were witches under the bed. There were witches in her dreams—the black humped shape of them in the trees back East. And Mr. Perry, with his black-tinged fingernails, feeding her licorice. He was the one who'd rotted her teeth—he was the one.

Dora said that Lily was—"She's a *witch*," Dora said, and that Claude knew how to get rid of people. He was the Raptor. He was a witch. He was hiding under the seat, or in the curtains— would be downstairs, in her room when she went back. "You have to believe me. I've told Agnes everything. She knows all about it. If she can prove it, she'll go to the police. She'll write about it. They wouldn't dare touch her. She's too important." Dora rose. "I have to go. But, May—"

The woman in the film was hiding in a copse of trees not far from the car. A man in an overcoat got out of the car that had been chasing hers and looked around. He ran up one hill, calling the woman's name, but she did not move.

"We're not important to them. Remember that. We're all the same girl."

"But we're not the same girl." And Lily wasn't a witch, either. Dora was getting up. Dora was leaving. Dora had probably been calling Lily a name, surely—it was like saying, *Lily's mean*—or *Lily's like all the others*.

Dora's face was fractured with light and shadow. "It doesn't matter." She took May's hand briefly and squeezed it. "I have to leave now. Wait twenty minutes or so before you go." She turned once. "Stay safe," she called, and then turned her coat collar up and left.

Stay safe. May sank into her coat.

In the movie, the man who was chasing the woman finally got in his car and left, and when he was gone, the woman ran to the road and waved down a truck.

Lily's not a witch.

The truck and the road faded out, and then an hourglass appeared on the screen. It was empty, as if all the sand had run through, but in the next shot it was turned again.

What did Dora know about Lily?

The screen filled with white light, washing the hourglass away, and the story began again on a spring day in a village that looked like it was in New England.

AGNES

In the kitchen, Dora sat across from Agnes. She drew a map of Claude's house. She put an X where the service gate led out to the street, and another at the side of the house.

"Are there windows or doors he might leave unlocked?" she asked.

Dora looked up from the paper, her mouth open. "Is that what we're planning? Breaking and entering?"

"It's not breaking if a door's unlocked." She didn't know what she meant to do yet—but Dora kept drawing. She showed her where the basement door was, where the book would be hidden. She slid the paper across the table to Agnes, who folded it twice, and then turned it in her hands. Thinking of Aimsley's long fingers, she smoothed the paper.

Agnes and Ben drove Dora to the port. Dora sat in the back seat, looking out the window. She didn't say much on the way over, but after a while, she leaned forward and touched Agnes on the shoulder. "I'm sorry I can't tell you where I'm going—you've been so good to me," she said.

"When it's all over, you can call me and tell me where you are—or send me a telegram."

"It will never be *all* over I'm afraid."

Agnes glanced at Ben, but he didn't look back at her. She'd started to assume he thought the whole thing was made-up. She couldn't explain to him the way the world had shifted—the way the shadows seemed denser, the lines of long black sedans parked along the pier seemed ominous, like a warning. She couldn't tell him about the way she glimpsed Ruth—or a woman with Ruth's distorted face—in the plain sunshine of street corners, or in the black windows of nighttime shops when she passed.

At the terminal, Dora reached into her handbag. "Here," she said. She pressed the key to her car into Agnes's hand. "I don't know when I'll be back. We can sort it then—but you must keep it for now. Consider it yours."

"You can't give me your car, Dora."

"I can, and I did. You need it. You just have to register it in your name. It's easy. I got the papers for you—the day I went to the bank. See?" She reached into her handbag and took out an envelope. "That's everything you need," she said. She picked up her suitcase and walked backward for a while, waving at them. "Thank you for believing me—" she called out before she turned around.

Agnes and Ben stood on the pier, the wind in their hair, watching Dora as she disappeared into the central terminal. They walked back to Ben's car. Agnes had the key to Dora's car in her pocket. She squeezed it.

"Did you?" Ben asked.

"Did I what?"

"Believe her."

"Yes."

When they reached his car, she slid in next to him. He began speaking in a low voice. "You cannot go forward with this—" he began, and after that, with each word, she stiffened. This was her break. This was her lucky break. A story. A car. Finally, he was shouting, and so was she. She cried out, "But what if I solve it?"

"But what if you end up *murdered*?" he responded. "What if whoever this is—this Raptor—what if he finds out what you're doing and comes after you? And what if it's all a lie—if that girl is simply as mad as she was when you first met her? And you come off as some enormous joke—and there's a libel case to manage? What then?"

"Joke?" she repeated. *Joke?*

"She says there are *demons* for god's sake. You and I both know that cannot be true."

"What if—"

"What?"

"What if it doesn't matter if it's true or not—I mean whether it's true that they can manifest something? What matters is that they might be trying, and in trying they are doing horrible things?"

"They?"

"Well, this can't be just Borel. This is bigger than Borel."

He shook his head. "I can't watch you do this to yourself," he said. "Again."

"Again?"

"The Mary T. came to nothing—and you have no proof of anything. You have *nothing*."

Maybe *this* is the ending to that story, Agnes thought, and maybe I *do* have the proof. She knew who she had to talk to—Lily, certainly. And May. She got out of the car and slammed the door. She would walk back to the city if she had to. The air smelled of seawater and the sky was bright blue. The wind struck right through her thin jacket. She could hear Ben yelling her name, but she did not turn around. *Joke*, she thought. The word went round and round.

Joke.

She would not keep silent.

19

May

It was almost funny: those chattering skeletons, their bones clacking like wooden drumsticks when they moved, but then she was inside of a house without windows and someone was coming—a creature in the shape of a shadow, lengthening out and then shortening, passing through walls at will—and she hid in a closet with the undertaker's suit jacket, pressed and ready. The shadow was blacker than the sky above the ocean at night. Bloodied handprints trailed pale walls, descended to the baseboard, disappeared. There were animals: quartered and drained. She could hear men laughing in an adjoining room as she crawled along the floor, searching for a way out.

Her own screams woke her.

Claude couldn't have. He couldn't have done it. Dora made the whole thing up. But then she thought of Miss Beverly Dean. *Agnes* trusted Dora—

She shook her head.

No.

Claude was *not* the Raptor.

She lay still—afraid of the chair, afraid of the shadow, afraid of sleep. She put the coat on over her slip and turned the light on, and then she remembered: the notepad she'd taken from Danny's pocket.

It was small, the size of a cigarette case or a flask. A black cover. White pages with blue lines. She opened it, noting the way the pages were sometimes stained with coffee or food oil, leaving a stray thumbprint behind, a thickened corner. Danny's handwriting was neat and boxy. He wrote in squat capitals. On one page, there were two columns: the left column carried the initials of the murdered women. In the right column, there were just two sets of initials. *MA, CB*, she read, a black circle drawn twice around the letters. She did not know who MA might be, but CB. *Claude Borel.*

She folded the page down at the binding, running a fingernail over the crease to make it sharp, and then she tore the page from the notepad. She had to run. She had to disappear, but first, she had to warn Lily.

AGNES

She told Danny about going to see "The Circus," the marks on Ginger's neck. "It's the mask—something about the *mask*—" and then, "I can't piece this together," she said.

"You can."

They were in the automat. Agnes was staring into her teacup. She hadn't talked to Ben in days. He'd called and she did not answer. He came to her door. She did not open it.

"I've been doing some research," Danny said. "A little investigating. Following a few people around. I think I might know who this Marty is."

Agnes looked up from her teacup. "Tell me."

"It's a man called Marvin—not Mar*tin. Marvin.*"

"How do you figure?"

"He used to work for Claude's buddy Ray. Ex-military."

She put her hand over her mouth.

"I found him at the church. He was the man who came up to us that day—the first time we went to the church. You said something wasn't right, so I went back. I was watching the place—" And there he was again—Topeka—Topeka is what Agnes had started calling him. Topeka talking to the preacher, hands in pockets.

"And what was he like—the preacher? What did he look like during the conversation?"

"Nothing—head down. Listening. And when Topeka left, I followed him."

"Brilliant—where?"

Danny followed him on foot, wishing he hadn't left his camera in the car. Topeka walked ahead of him, a loose shamble, lifting his hat to women, calling after them sometimes. When that happened, Danny stepped into the shade of a shop's awning or paused in front of a display window.

He followed him to an apartment house in Hollywood, a run-down sort of place with garbage cans out front, children playing a game of cops and robbers, shouting at each other from behind scrappy hedges. Danny watched Topeka, saw the apartment he went into. He looked at his watch. The postman would be along soon. He waited across the street, in a spot where he couldn't be seen. The children incorporated him into their game, calling him mister. He was hiding, too, wasn't he? But he shooed them away, playing the bad guy.

When the postman came, Danny gave him some money and looked at the mail. There you go. He tapped the envelope and handed it back. He walked back to the tent and got his car. "I was going to tell you straight away—" Danny said. "But I decided to see what else Marvin was up to. I didn't have to wait long. That night, someone came to pick him up. Guess where he went?"

"Where?"

"To Claude Borel's house."

Danny brought the photographs out he'd taken that first day at the tent and put them on the table in front of Agnes. "He's our man."

"Why haven't the police figured this out?"

"I'm starting to think they might not care to figure it out."

20

MAY

She sat on the floor for a long time, resting her head on the wall behind her, looking at the initials in the notepad. When the first light came, she rose and packed quietly, dressing in the same clothes she'd worn the day before.

On the streetcar, she opened her purse and took the envelope out that Claude had given to her. The once fat envelope was as thin as if it only contained a utility bill or a short missive. She took the remaining money out, and crumpling the envelope, she let it drop to the floor.

How foolish. *Witches.*

No one in Claude's circle knew William and Edith—she would be safe there, slip into the rhythm of married life: asleep by nine, full from baked potatoes and roasted chicken. Wash her stockings, write a letter to Ann. Maybe she would bake a cake with Edith, the two of them listening to the latest adventure of Helen Trent on the radio. There would be Christmas to consider. She would go to Boston, spend it with her mother and sister.

Never return. Never return to the light, to the silver dash of sea on rocks.

And what about Boston? Ned O'Neil down on one knee in front of the Christmas tree? She might say *yes*—

Yes. They'd have a June wedding, and she'd finally pick out the red curtains for the kitchen in the house that shot straight back through itself—four rooms and a porch. She would remember Claude as a film villain, or he would come back like the treasure buried in William's tunnel—something to think of at night when the lights were out and she could close her eyes

and open her life up like the pages of a book while Ned O'Neil
lay snoring away next to her. When she was tired of him. Wasn't
she already tired of Ned O'Neil? Wasn't she already tired?

And all the while Richard would still be up in the blue sky—
an orange flame, a black cloud of smoke, and Los Angeles
would feel as far away as the moon.

Maybe those initials didn't belong to Claude—

She shook her head. She had to warn Lily. That was all. That
was her only job. And then she'd go away a while to think. Maybe not to Boston. Not yet. Maybe let things sort themselves.
Maybe north to San Francisco, or farther on—to the woods
and the wilds. She laughed at herself. Mrs. Paul Bunyan, then.

She put the last bills in her handbag. In the sunlight, she saw
that the patent leather was smeared with fingerprints, and she
worked over the surface in small circles, cleaning it with the
sleeve of her coat.

Edith was out on the porch airing a rug, and when she saw May,
she put her hands together. "What a surprise!" she called, but
when May came closer, she remarked that May was tired, wasn't
she? Did she want a glass of lemonade?

"Yes," May said. "Yes, I will, thank you."

Edith took her bag and the heavy coat. She paused before
carrying it inside. "Why, would you look at this."

"My friend Lily gave it to me," May said. "She's the actress."

In the narrow room with one sloping attic wall, May un-
packed. She ironed her blue dress until it was smooth. She
stood over the bathroom sink and filled her teeth, melting bits
of wax with matches. May had wanted privacy, but Edith came
in after her and shut the bathroom door. Edith sat down on the
closed toilet and watched May work. "You're too young to have
such bad teeth."

"I know. Mother thinks it's because I ate so much candy
when I was little." She thought of dipping her hands into the
jars in Mr. Perry's shop, her pockets filled with Mary Janes. She
stole while he watched, while the other children watched. "Go

on," she'd told them, looking at Mr. Perry. "Take what you want. He won't stop you." And he didn't—not when May was there.

"Well, I ate candy too."

"I used to steal candy and give it away."

"May!"

May laughed. "It was just candy. And Mr. Perry was a nasty old man. I didn't like him at all. He used to try to kiss me."

"Really?"

But May stopped talking about it. She bit down on her tongue. Edith was still looking at her, so she went on. "I didn't even eat that much candy, honestly. I gave all my candy away. I stole it and then I gave it to a little girl in my neighborhood." The girl lived a few blocks from May. She sat on her front steps with a doll and when May passed, she waved. The girl's hair was a little longer on one side then the other, and May imagined it was because her mother cut it in the kitchen and didn't know how to make the sides even. Her knees were always skinned, and when she smiled, she had two beautiful little dimples. May went up to her and asked her how old she was. "Six," she'd said, and May reached into the pocket of her dress and brought out Mary Janes. "I'll give you a candy every day," she told her. "Just never go into Mr. Perry's candy shop." The girl put her small hands out, her open, pale palms, pink at the center, the fingers still fat, and stared into May's face. "Thank you," she'd said.

May smiled at herself in the mirror. "There's nothing I can do about my teeth, but I suppose I should try again with a dentist. They always want to yank things out of my mouth, and then it's a fortune and I'm swollen up for weeks."

"Sooner or later, you'll have to get the lot pulled."

"I suppose."

"What now?" Edith asked when May finished.

"My face." May took out the panstick and the powder. She dotted beneath her eyes, feathered and dabbed until the dark circles disappeared, until the inflamed skin beneath was concealed.

"It's like magic," Edith said. "I'll remember that."

Magic. That was it—an illusion. Dora was duped, was all.

May stood back and examined herself. Edith was so intent, so watchful. "Is everything all right, Edith?" May asked.

"It's fine. Do you want to come to church tonight—I mean before you meet your friend?"

"I'm afraid I can't, but I will next time."

"What did you say your friend's name was?"

"Lily. She's an actress."

"All right." Edith rubbed her hands together. They made a dry sound. "Don't you ever get scared?"

"Scared?"

"When you go out at night."

"You mean because of the Raptor?"

"That's right."

"Sometimes. I'm careful, though. Do you get scared?"

Edith didn't say anything for a moment. She sat with her chin on her hand. She studied her nails. She bit her nails, May noticed. Down to the quick. Just like May did. "I'm scared of everything," Edith said.

"Why?"

May waited for Edith to answer. She brushed the white powder lightly over her skin, blinking, and then she lined her eyes. She looked like a photograph, a movie still. She lined her mouth, expertly dipping into the cupid's bow of the top lip, remembering the edges. Still Edith didn't say anything. May glanced over at her. She was staring at the wall in front of her, the rose petal pink and black tile. "I'm pregnant," Edith said.

"Oh!" May turned to her. "I'm so happy for you."

But Edith was pale. She looked up at May, her eyes two black circles. She shook her head. "No—"

"What is it?" May set her lipstick down and sat down on the edge of the bathtub. "What is it? It's what you wanted."

"I thought so too. But William—"

"William will be fine. It's just the war. It's done things to people, but they'll get better."

"No. He won't." She shook her head. "I have to leave him."

"What will you do?"

"He's always in the tunnels with that man."

"What man?"

"I can't have this baby. I pray for a solution. Sometimes I pray to lose the baby." Edith began to cry.

"It's all right," May told her. "*Hush*," she whispered. She pulled Edith close, careful not to get makeup on Edith's dress. "I know people," she whispered. "If you don't want it—"

But Edith jerked away, staring. "I'd never do that. What kind of woman—" And then she put her head on May's shoulder. "I wish I were you," she said. "You go where you want and do as you like and everyone loves you. You're so free."

May rocked Edith in her arms. She stroked her hair, which was tangled and held back with bobby pins. "You're going to be such a good mother," she murmured. "We'll all help you with the baby."

She didn't know whom she meant by *we*. She meant herself, of course, and maybe her sister and her mother. And she meant Edith's people. She imagined the two of them getting on a bus and going back to Massachusetts together. On the bus, May would tell Edith the truth about everything. "You have to be terribly clever, now," she'd tell Edith. "You have to be a person of the world. You must live like an artist." She'd say all the things to Edith that Dora had said to her, and then she'd tell her about Claude and Dora. She'd tell her about Danny and Agnes and the drink she had that tasted like black pepper but was as sweet as honey, or the ferns on the walls of her hotel room. She'd tell her all the lies she'd told. Or she wouldn't tell Edith anything. She'd simply hold her hand on the bus. She could write to Danny—*I got mixed up with some things and now I don't know where to go*— She imagined she would say these things to him on the telephone or in a letter. *Though brief, I think our time together meant as much to you as it did to me,* she'd write. May composed the letter as she held Edith, rocking her back and forth.

Wasn't it funny, she thought, and she bit her lip so as not to laugh. May wanted Edith's life and Edith wanted May's life, and both of them felt just about miserable.

Wasn't the world rich?

AGNES

Danny had gone back to the Nightingale to find May, but she'd checked out and hadn't left a note or a forwarding address.

"Do you think she's in on it?" Agnes asked. "Like Lily?"

"That seems doubtful. She struck me as a romantic kind of girl."

Agnes raised her eyebrows. How's that? she wanted to say, but she didn't. They were in the newsroom—the typewriters banging around them, the telephones ringing. He had to lean in so she could hear him. His face was close to hers. He rested his chin on his hand. He was so close that she could smell the starch in his shirt, see that he was about to need a shave.

"What did Dora say?" he asked.

"She seemed to think May doesn't understand what's going on around her. Dora told her to leave Los Angeles—to go back East. Maybe that's what she's done."

Photographs that needed to be labeled by the end of the day sat in front of her. She'd neglected her work, it was true. She reached for a piece of paper.

"Let's do something," she said.

Agnes began to write, listing the women's names who had been killed in a column. She didn't know how many of them were really linked to the Raptor. Agnes traced the first three to the same nightclub. One had even been a regular at the Palace. The last two, Joan and Beverly, could be traced to Claude— Joan through Ray; Beverly through Dora. Beside their names, she wrote *Claude, Ray, Marvin*. She drew lines from each name to another, showing the relationship, making a note. "And then there's Aimsley—" She wrote his name and put a question mark next to it. "I checked to see if Aimsley might have played the part of the ringmaster in 'The Circus' at some point—those marks on his neck—but he didn't. The same man has been playing that part since the beginning."

"You better let me keep this," Danny said, pointing to the paper. "I've misplaced my notepad. I had it all down—it's probably in the car somewhere—"

Agnes slid him the paper. "Even if it's true," she said. "Even if it's Claude and Ray and Marvin—even if it's only one of them—we don't have any proof. We don't have any real proof. We have a bunch of people who know each other."

She thought of Ben saying, *These are just people who know each other.* She'd agreed to meet him for dinner soon. On the telephone, he'd sounded sad. "I imagine we're not going to that party at the observatory," he said. "No," she answered. No, because she had an idea.

"Listen," Agnes said to Danny. "We need proof. We need to get that book that Dora told me about. She said they kept a record of what they'd done in it. Maybe the murders are a part of that. We need to get into Claude's house."

Danny whistled. "Listen to what you just said: break into Claude Borel's house." He shook his head. "Agnes, we—"

"I know just the night." She told him about the gala. "And don't tell me we can't. I'm already mad at Ben for that."

"What did Ben tell you that you couldn't do? Doesn't he know better?"

"Apparently not. He told me to stop trying to figure it out."

"Let's go then. I want to do what Ben said you shouldn't do—even if it means—" and he leaned forward, conspiratorially, whispering into her ear, "breaking into Borel's house."

"We won't take the book. We'll just photograph it. And then if we know it's there and where to find it, the real detectives can show up and finish the job."

"We're the real detectives." Danny laughed. He pointed to Agnes, and then himself. "You and me."

21

MAY

Maybe Lily would want to escape too. She could board the bus with May and Edith, and May would shepherd them both to her mother, back to the little apartment in Medford, where they could have Christmas together, and maybe when the whole thing was over and Claude was in prison, there would be a photo of the three of them in the newspaper sitting at the kitchen table, looking out at the world from the stillness of the past, their eyes fixed on the photographer. Danny would see it, and then May would tell him why she had to lie. Between Lily, Dora, and May, they must know enough to have Claude arrested. She thought of calling Adams, but it was better to play it safe. What if Adams said something to another detective? It would be awful to alert Claude before Lily was safe.

The boulevard was decorated for Christmas. Big silver stars were strewn above the street from telephone poles. The night was bright with electricity. It was too much light. It was a bad omen. May kept her face toward the sidewalk.

When she got to the bar, she looked carefully at the other customers: a woman in a flowered dress; the man in the brown suit with a carnation pinned to his lapel; the two sailors standing over the jukebox; the bartender, a rag thrown over his shoulder. She peered into the shadowed corners where the tables were still empty, the chairs still pushed in, and the candles freshly lit. She sat at one of those tables, away from the light. She pushed herself into the darkest corner.

Lily looked different. It was the salon set of her hair, the big soft shining curls, and the smoothness of her skin. She looked *expensive*. Her coat was cashmere, belted, and brand new. Everyone turned to look at her as she came in, which made May happy, and then nervous. "Are you real? Everyone's staring at you."

"Are they staring?" Lily looked around. "The movie's not out yet. They can't be looking at me. They're probably looking at you." She took off her gloves. They were pearl gray and May fought an impulse to reach over and touch one. "Let's get a little bit drunk," Lily said. "What would you like?"

"An old pal," May said, and Lily raised her hand to the bartender, who came out and gave her a bow.

"Two old pals," Lily said. And then she said it again to May when he left. "Just two old pals."

It was good to see Lily. Her voice was smooth like a radio personality's, and she smelled of powder and something else—cinnamon, maybe. May leaned forward. "I found Dora," she said.

Lily opened her eyes wide. "Where has that kid been?" The bartender put down their drinks, and Lily lay some money on the table.

"Hiding."

"Hiding? Hiding from what?"

"It's who she's hiding from—Claude." May leaned toward her. "She says he's the Raptor, Lily."

Lily gave a big, open-mouthed laugh. "He's not. He's an eccentric. Like all rich men. Just strange." She took a sip of her drink. May was relieved. She didn't want Claude to be the Raptor. Lily didn't think it was true, which meant—what, exactly? Lily smiled at her—a nervous, twitchy thing. It wasn't a real Lily smile at all. Was the laugh an act?

Lily pointed at May. "And don't go around saying that to people." On her wrist, May saw a thick gold bracelet, coiled like a snake.

"Why shouldn't I say it?" May asked. "She said—" *you're a witch*, she wanted to say, but Lily was still smiling. *Ha!* Lily might say, the big red O of her mouth, the white of her beautiful teeth: *Ha! Now I know you're as mad as Dora.*

"Don't tell me anything else she said, please. You could get in trouble for saying such things. Nobody wants a rumor like that on his back. Claude's not the Raptor. And Claude's been good to you. He gave you a lot of money." She didn't look at May as she spoke. She watched the bartender.

How did Lily know what Claude gave her? And then she realized: they all knew she'd be here with Lily. Claude and Ray—they could be outside, leaning against a car, their arms folded. "When did you see Claude?"

"The other night. Listen, everyone's worried about you. *I'm* worried about you. You should come with me."

"Where are you going?"

"To Claude's. He wants to talk to you. Oh, May—he said he knows someone who could get you a role in a film. It's the same way it happened for me."

"You told him you were meeting me?"

"What's the big secret?" Lily opened her hands and looked across the table at May. "Listen, you've got to get yourself together. Don't run around sounding like Dora. Claude's dead worried about Dora." Lily finished her drink quickly and put it down. She lifted her hand to get the bartender's attention. "Another," she said when he came over.

May didn't look at Lily, but at the red arc of lipstick left behind on her glass. "She told me about Joan—about Beverly," May said. "Dora said Claude gave Joan morphine. She said you *know*. She said you know everything."

"Hey—" Lily tried. She reached into her bag and took out a cigarette. Her hand was shaking. "Hey, that's not nice." But her voice sounded like a car that hit a curb. It hitched. "Hey—"

"Beverly Dean was the woman we saw that night when you said you didn't know Claude. She was with him. They found her in her bath. Dead. You should be *dead* worried about yourself, Lily. And look at this." May reached into her handbag and took out the page she'd torn from Danny's notepad.

"What's this?"

"Don't you see? Those are Claude's initials."

"But who are these other people? This could be anything."
Lily smoothed the page out. "I don't know any of these other
initials. Do you? Who wrote this?" Lily tried to take the piece
of paper from May, but May wouldn't let her.

May stared at Lily. It was impossible that Lily didn't see.

"For all you know, this could be about someone's laundry."

"I want to get out of here," May said. "I want to get out of
Los Angeles. For good." Los Angeles wasn't safe. Lily wasn't
safe. May would leave and throw them all off her trail. "I'll go
visit a friend in San Francisco," May said quickly.

"Do you need some money?"

May nodded.

"I can wire it to you. Just give me the address. When's Dora
coming back?"

"She said she's staying away until this all blows over."

"But where is she?"

"She's—" But May couldn't tell her.

"Where will you be in San Francisco? I can write it down
here." She brought her address book out of her bag. "You
shouldn't talk about these things, May. You shouldn't—"

"I'll have to wire you," May said vaguely. "I don't have the
address right here."

"Don't you have your friend's name in your address book?"

"No," May lied. She was thinking of going to Boston. Or to
Chicago. She didn't know.

"Well, what's the neighborhood? Just so I know you're safe."

"I told you I'd wire you." May almost yelled it.

"All right. No need to get bent." Lily sounded angry. "Did
you tell anyone other than me that you think Claude is the Raptor? Just so you know, May, if he goes to jail, so do I."

"What are you talking about?"

"I helped him with the girls."

"What girls?"

"I fouled up, I told you. Before I had this acting job. He paid
me a lot of money to bring around girls. I was starving before
I met Claude."

"What did you do, Lily?"

"I took the girls to him. Party girls. I can't say they were all old enough to be there. I can't say that. If that gets out, I'm finished. No one will ever want me for a movie again. Promise me you'll keep your trap shut. Claude's not the Raptor. I'm sure of it. I've been alone with him so many times. So have you, for that matter."

May understood. That's what they had on Lily. Even if Lily thought that Claude was a murderer, she'd never say a word. Even if they killed Dora or came after May—

They'd made Lily a part of it.

Lily played with the coiled bracelet. "See? Everything's all right. It's just that I got mixed up in it." Lily touched May's arm. "But I'm all right now. I have ever so many offers for films. It's *you* I'm worried about. We all are. I told you. I just want to make sure you're all right. Where are you staying?" Lily put more money on the table. She said it was for the drinks, but it seemed like too much. "I can give you some money now." She held her wallet out to her. May looked. Lily's wallet was fat with bills. She wondered what sort—ones, fives, tens? Twenties, even? "I can give you all of it, May. Just tell me you'll be all right. Tell me where we can find you."

Had she meant to say *I*—tell me where *I* can find you—but she'd slipped? Who wanted to know where May was? Beverly Dean's name had barely registered with Lily. But then May understood: Lily already knew.

Lily *knew*.

May pushed the wallet away and stood. "I want you to—" she began. Her throat was sore, and there was a lightness in the bottoms of her feet, as if she wasn't quite standing. "I want you to leave me alone."

"May!" Lily called after her, running behind her. "I'm trying to save you—"

But May wouldn't turn around. All the way down the boulevard, she could hear Lily calling her name, but she never turned to look to see how near or how far Lily was. She didn't want to know if she were standing there with Ray or even Claude—if they'd been waiting outside while Lily coaxed her back into trusting them.

She wouldn't fall for it.

AGNES

On the night of the observatory's gala, it rained. Agnes imagined Ben standing in a crowd of strangers in front of the pendulum with his hands in his pockets, the rain beating outside, the hills soft and saturated beyond. Had he even gone to the gala? Or maybe—she thought, looking over at Danny as he drove—Ben wasn't alone at all. Maybe he had his arm linked with another woman's—a woman of clipped manners and careful clothing whom he steered around the perimeter of the room, his head lowered, her soft voice in his ear.

If that's what he wanted—

"Park here," Agnes said. "Let's not get any closer." They were near Claude's, where the houses sprawled on plots of land big enough for three or four. They'd dressed in somber colors—the blue of the night, the black of the paved street, the green of the palms. They'd dressed as if they belonged. They could be going to a friend's for dinner, after all, or to a late party. The only understanding was that the good clothes should afford running and climbing. Cleaning and mending would be an afterthought. And Agnes wore her loafers, which were incongruous, but she assumed no one but another woman would notice this.

She got out of the car and put her sunglasses on. Danny looked at her and laughed. "What?" she said.

"You look entirely suspicious."

She took the sunglasses off and put them in her pocket.

He took a flashlight and his camera from the backseat. "Do you have the map?" he asked, and she held it up to him. It was the map Dora had drawn in her kitchen, the pencil's tip dull, the lines thick. There were arrows for entrances, clumsily drawn steps that showed the way to the basement. Agnes refolded the piece of paper and put it in her pocket.

They set out on the dark hill. The rain had ended, but the night was wet and moonless. Water dripped from the big leaves of palms. She'd expected the flash of headlights—or maybe a man with a dog, pausing to watch as they came closer, studying their faces—but there was nothing, and there was no one on the dark road.

When they reached Claude's, she steadied herself and slowed her breath as she ran her hands over the courtyard's wall to find the service entrance, and when she found it: the click, the oiled turn of the knob, the wet brush of a climbing vine. And they were inside, back in the shadows, among the trained ficus trees, their branches arced above them, and the tall, thick-stemmed, cool-weather flowers, their blooms heavy with rainwater.

Agnes was struck by the fountain—the statue—a woman rising out of the black water. Wasn't her face similar to Ruth's? That terror, that shock as her hands and arms were disfigured by metamorphosis, her legs stopped as they became the rooted trunk of a tree.

In the house, a light went out, and they watched a woman in a pale gray shift pass down a glassed hallway—a maid, Agnes guessed, who turned the lights out as she went until she reached the courtyard. She walked right in front of them, but she didn't even look up. She left the way they'd come, and was so close to Danny that Agnes could have reached out and touched her on the shoulder.

Agnes and Danny stayed in the shadows, even after the courtyard's door closed. She looked at the fountain of Daphne, noted the way the leaves of the hair were done, the braided strands, the heaviness of the rope of bay leaf.

They lingered by the wall, waiting and watching, but nothing else happened. The house stayed quiet. "That's it," Agnes said. She touched Danny's shoulder and turned to him in the darkness. "If we're going to do this—"

They traced their way around until they found the door

that Dora had marked. It was open, as she'd said it would be. They passed down a hallway and through a kitchen. Another, and soon it was the wide white steps that Dora had told her about. They descended, and soon found two doors: one that led to a finished room, and another that led to a second set of basement steps, smaller and higher, wooden. This was it. A basement within a basement. This one was unfinished, the floor only packed earth, low-ceilinged. The room felt hollowed-out, claustrophobic, as if it had once been only a crawl space below the house, but the floor had been dug into and emptied out like a grave.

"She said there was a door. A little wooden door like something out of a fairy tale, that's what she said. She said that behind that door, there was a box—a box with a lid. She saw Beverly put the book back once. There—" The beam of the flashlight fell on it. She didn't want to go in. She didn't like the looks of the strange little door—wooden slatted, kept closed with a hook latch.

The door was barely big enough to fit through. She didn't know quite what she'd expected, but down on her hands and knees, she sensed the space's continuation. It wasn't a closet, but a tunnel. Danny came in behind her, and he pulled the door closed behind them. "Shine the light—" she said to Danny. "I can't see—"

Soon she saw the box. It was covered with a heavy red cloth. She could hear Danny breathing. "Are you going to open it?" he said, because she was hesitating, her hands shaking. She did it quickly. The flash of the Graflex caught the moment. She pulled the red cloth back and lifted the box's lid—but there was nothing. The box was empty. Another flash from the Graflex lit up the space around it, and Agnes could see then: it was a tunnel. She could hear the drip of water in the distance, and crawled farther in, trying to get a sense of how far it went.

Nearby—in the house, she thought—somewhere above her—she heard the voices of men. A laugh. She stayed in the tunnel. "Come on—" she whispered to Danny.

"Agnes—" Danny hissed. "You don't know what's down there."

"Who's down there?" a man called. "Who's here?"

Danny had no choice but to follow. He took Agnes's wrist, he brought his finger to his lips and then turned the flashlight off. They moved quietly, crawling in darkness.

The little door opened behind them, but whoever was there—Claude, likely—must not have had a flashlight. They kept still, and when he came in, she could hear him opening the box. He swore when he took the lid off, and it sounded as if he had expected to find something there. At that, he left the tunnel. The door shut.

Agnes and Danny began to crawl again. She could hear the distant echo of city sounds—the rattle of a truck, a far off horn. The space began to open, widen, the walls seemed smoother. "Do you know what this means?" she whispered. "Everything that Dora told me—it's all true." She stood, still ducking, but the ceiling was getting higher. "I think I know what this is," she said. "We're in the train tunnels. The old streetcar—the line that ran underground. That tunnel into Claude's—it must have been for bootlegging."

"Didn't you say that Ray's father was a bootlegger—"

"Yes."

The hard dirt beneath their feet turned to cement, broken apart in places, and then Agnes could see the metal of the tracks, the winding steel path they cut ahead. A tunnel made during Prohibition. Ray would know about that, and Claude—the way the Raptor disappeared into the night. A magic book—the man with horns and wings—Aimsley. The Circus. Ginger. Lily. Dora. May.

They found the exit—a hole that led to an empty lot. When they got close to the exit, the lights were so bright it made Agnes blink. "What is that?" she asked. "What's up there?" But soon enough she saw. It was cars, their headlights on, the white tent church lit in the night, the sides lifted so the congregants could walk in. She and Danny stood at the mouth of the tunnel, their clothes dirty, their faces streaked with mud. A car's lights blinded them, and then a man emerged, holding a woman's hand. "Why, hello," he said to Agnes and Danny. "You look as if you've just come from the war, but I imagine you've been in those tunnels, haven't you?"

Neither of them answered. They felt caught, somehow, blinded, and they stood there blinking—the man's light-colored suit, the woman's pink hat with its little veil.

"What did you find?" The man stepped toward them. He smiled. "Did you find anything? Did you see anything?" It was one of the men who'd hung back when Marvin came up to them that day, one of the prospectors, as Agnes had thought of them. He smiled. "You should be careful. It's dangerous in those old tunnels." He winked at Agnes. "All sorts of things can happen."

The woman in the pink hat looked them up and down. She kept her chin high as she looked—how strange she and Danny must seem! The woman wore a dark dress and a pale coat. "Come on, William," she said to him. "I'm sure they don't want to talk about what they've been up to."

"Coming, Edith," the man called William said. He took her arm and turned away, toward the church, and disappeared into the light.

22

MAY

Damn them. Damn them all. Damn Lily and her fat wallet. Damn her dreams and the safety of being two-faced—one face for May and one for Claude. She thought of Lily's sympathetic gaze. But I'm *worried* about you. It was like watching a close up in a film—the way she shook her head, the dampness of her eyes. She was on the make like everyone else. Film people were grifters. Everyone knew it. The way they were always smiling at parties like it was the best time in the world but looked over your shoulder to see if there was someone else they should be talking to.

So worried.

May wasn't a child, after all. She could work a room too. Maybe better than Lily. Better than all of them.

Dora was right about one thing, anyway. A girl has to be clever. Lily was as bad as Dora had made her out to be. Not a *witch*, of course.

May took one turn and then the next, dodging out of the light when cars passed. She found the trolley. She took it and transferred to a bus, then another, sitting near the driver, watching who got on, who got off. Did they notice her? Did they look for too long?

In Edith and William's neighborhood, the houses were dark and filled with sleep. May turned the knob of their front door, slipping in, and unlike Edith, who suspected no danger from the outside, May locked the door behind her. She went to the kitchen and locked the back door as well. She wondered about the windows, and went to them, flicking the curtains back, scanning the street, pressing the window locks shut. She checked the closets, the basement. She did it all quietly, as quietly as a thief. May slept in a room on the first floor with rose-colored walls and a casketed sewing machine.

When she lay down on the narrow daybed, she closed her eyes. Safety was temporary, like feeling full after a meal. In the morning, she could call Adams. She would tell him she wanted to make an official statement. She didn't care what Lily said. And then she'd go back to—but she didn't know.

But what if Lily got into trouble? What if Lily went to jail?

May turned to her side and shut her eyes. She pressed her hands beneath the pillow, finding the cool spot. She thought of Edith's wedding cake, the long-ago slice beneath her pillow, how worried she'd been about crushing it and the charm not working. Well, maybe that was it. She'd eaten the charm. It was some time after catching the bouquet that she'd gotten sick. Maybe Edith wasn't lucky at all. Maybe Edith was the piece of bad luck that had cast a shadow over May's life. Or maybe William had cast it over Edith's, and May had stood in their shadow for too long, looking up at them—the bride and groom atop the wedding cake looking down at her.

Edith was just like the rest of them, anyway. Her life looked like something else from the outside. It *looked* lucky—like a warm coat or a sturdy house. It looked like flowers blooming in a window box on a bright blue day. It *looked* like being able to buy things in shops without Mr. Perry. But Edith cried in bathrooms too. She cried about getting knocked up. Edith put her face in her hands and became someone else. She was jealous of other girls' lives. She was jealous of the pictures the lives made.

Everybody wanted something else underneath.

In the morning, May had meant to call Adams, but she was cold, and sat near the radiator in the living room and drank coffee instead, talking to Edith. William and his friend Marvin had gone to find Christmas trees.

"I hope they don't go into those awful tunnels," Edith said. "I saw the most peculiar thing last night—a man and a woman leaving the tunnel. It was so very late and they were filthy. They couldn't have been up to any good."

"How odd," May murmured, and then: "Have you met Marvin?"

"No. William always meets him somewhere else. Today it's the tree lot. Sometimes I'm not sure Marvin even exists."

"What do you mean?"

"I've said we should invite Marvin over to dinner several times. It just feels like William would rather I don't meet him. Is that cough of yours all right? You got in late last night. It was so cold and wet."

"I'm fine." May put down her coffee. "I've decided to spend Christmas with a friend in San Francisco," she told Edith. "Will you be all right without me?"

"Of course." Edith was holding a ball of gold yarn. "Do you like this?" She seemed uncertain.

"I do. Is it for—?"

"I haven't told William yet—about the baby."

"You don't have to have it, Edith."

"Stop that." Edith had a look on her face like she was sitting on something sharp. She shifted her weight in the flowered chair.

"I won't say a word about it either way," May said. "I won't say a word to anyone about anything. We could go back to Medford."

"Silly," Edith said. "Why would we go to Medford?"

May sipped her tea and looked at Edith, who had begun casting stitches on to a knitting needle. "You'd be safe there."

"Me? I'm safe here."

"Oh, I just meant—you were so upset yesterday."

"That's what happens. The women at church say it's natural. You'll see when it's your turn."

May watched Edith knit. The needles moved quickly and made a pleasant clicking sound. She didn't see how Edith could be so upset and then act like May had misunderstood. Edith was trying to wedge herself back into luck, to press herself into the corner of the pretty house where no one could see her fear. Edith was making herself into the shape of a lucky woman. She was getting back into the lines. That's what Dora would say.

They sat in silence until William returned with the Christmas tree. He propped it by the back door and then came around the front. "Why is the back door locked?" he asked. William stood between the living room and the dining room. He had his gloves and coat on and he seemed to fill the entire doorframe.

"I get scared."

"Of what?"

"The Raptor, I guess. They haven't caught him yet."

"Is Marvin with you?" Edith asked.

"No. He had to get home to his family. Did something happen—" He was staring at May. "To make you afraid?"

"No." She coughed. Her throat burned. Her limbs were heavy.

Edith protested. "Oh, please," she said. "Let's not talk about horrible things. It's almost Christmas." Edith began to talk about Christmas, and said that May would go to San Francisco, and William volunteered to take her to the station after lunch. She could call Adams from the road. Maybe it was safest not to tell anyone anything. She could keep a secret, and then when everyone knew she hadn't said anything, it would be safe.

William took her to the bus station, and before he leaned over to open the door, he said, "Are you all right? Take this," he said, passing her a few dollars.

"Of course. I'm fine." She should have asked him for more money, she thought later. She could have invented something— cried—though it was harder to lie to William and Edith than to others. So she didn't. She took the money and folded it into her purse. Her hands were shaking. He took her hand and held it hard. "Whatever this is, May—"

"It's nothing. I didn't sleep well. You know my health. I'll be better at my friend's." She turned to him. "Don't go into the tunnels anymore."

"What?"

"Just stop that."

He stared at her. "Why?"

"I don't know. Never mind." She got out of the car and made her way to the station.

"Do you need my help?"

"No, thank you." She turned back, smiling. The day was bright. The sky was blue. It was almost Christmas. "I'm fine."

She did not go to San Francisco. She went south instead. When she reached San Diego, she found the Western Union office. She wrote a telegram to Ned O'Neil: *I'm coming home to you, darling. Short on cash for trip, as usual. Can you spare it? I can't wait to be with you again. Always*—

But she had no more plan to go to Boston than she had to San Francisco. The idea was a thing as present as the memory of a bird's wing in motion. It was nothing. It was the air around the wing. It was the murmuration of starlings leaping into flight, soaring over the flat roads that led away from the mountains, swooping and circling over the yellow grass.

Ned O'Neil had likely never seen such a thing. A man couldn't see life from beneath a car. People who stayed in one place—they saw their faces change in the same mirror over the years. They were the same selves, the same reflections. You could keep changing, keep moving. You could become whatever you wanted as long as the road was in front of you.

Ned O'Neil and whoever his girl was—well—they weren't like May. There was always someone around to *tell* them what to do, and they didn't even bother trying to guess whether it was right or wrong. Ned wanted too little—that was the problem. There were places in Los Angeles where a girl could feel like a queen—even if she only had a nickel to her name. She could meet a date in the Biltmore, walk down the mirrored halls, sit on one of the striped sateen sofas in the lobby and wait for the beginning of something, to let that feeling of luxury and luck linger and take hold. If she had a good dress, no one would be any the wiser. And whatever she had to do after that or before that to survive was no one's business but her own.

Dora had said they weren't important, but Dora was wrong.

AGNES

"Did you recognize him?" Agnes said. They'd left the lot and were making their way back up to the car.

"Yes. We've got a photograph of him. He was one of the men out near the church that day with Topeka—"

"Did he recognize us?"

"Most certainly. Did you see the way he looked at you?"

She swore. "That was unlucky." His eyes—William's eyes—were dark and small. His mouth was pinched in a downturn, and his wife—Edith—reminded her of a crow—a crow in a pink hat!

Agnes did not want to go home—not just yet. She'd gotten used to Dora's chatter, to the lights being on before she arrived. The thought of the empty rooms, the grimoire lying open on the kitchen table—the cold smell of the tunnels still in her hair, on her clothes—well, she didn't want it. What if something were waiting for her there in the shadows? What if Ruth stepped out from behind a curtain, her face rigid in that death smile?

"Don't take me home," she said to the car window, to the night flashing by outside. He had assumed, and was heading toward Pasadena already, but he turned the big car around without saying a word and made his way back to Bunker Hill. He drove to his place—a tall wooden rooming house, a rambling structure. He made her wait outside in the hallway while he cleaned up a bit. She imagined him pulling the covers over an unmade bed, hastily piling clothes in a wardrobe.

But when let her in, she was surprised. It was neater than she'd anticipated. The walls were painted dark green. The wooden floors were swept and covered with a square of Indian carpet. Still—a bachelor's apartment. A rooming house. Two rooms. A hot plate instead of a kitchen. She took a shower in the shared bath down the hall. He gave her pajamas to put on, and she washed her clothes out and he hung them to dry near the radiator that lumbered on once, crashing and hissing as the steam pushed its way up to his floor and through the pipes.

When they were both clean, he poured her a drink, passing it to her in a chipped teacup. "Oh, this is terrible," she commented, lifting the cup and smiling. "But I do feel very ladylike." They sat together at his desk, using it as a table. She picked up the cup with a lifted pinky.

He watched her, his chin resting on his hand. "Well, I would have bought a whole dinner set if I'd known you were coming over." He lifted his glass to her.

She felt far away. The sound of the city outside, a ship's horn in the distance. *The gentleman,* she thought as she watched Danny. She reached across the desk and touched his face. "I think we're in trouble," she said.

"I might agree with that."

23

MAY

May walked down Broadway. It was warmer in San Diego, the air dry and thin, the sky clear. She still felt cold though, but her breathing was better. Worry made people sick. All that constriction in the lungs, like the rough edges of ropes.

Men in uniform passed, giving her sly glances, and she smiled at them with her lips closed. She could stay here, call herself her full name—*Margaret*—or she could shorten it. Peggy. Madge. Gertie. She tried them out one by one, thinking, "I'm Gertie," but she liked May. It was her own invention.

She passed a man and a woman as they got into a car. The man held the door for the woman, who sat awkwardly in the passenger seat. May smiled at the man as she passed, and he nodded. Her hair was probably a mess. She would have to stop and fix herself up.

The city was smaller than Los Angeles, less showy. She wondered about dancing, about the fellows in their uniforms. She had nowhere to go. There was nothing to do. There was no money to pick up. There was no one to meet for dinner. Sometimes she was still fooled into thinking the light would last all day. It was winter here, even though it never seemed like it. She had two dollars and twenty-seven cents. She should have pawned the mink.

She thought of it in Edith's guest room, still and silent as a sleeping fox on the narrow white bed.

The hotel she chose wasn't fancy by any stretch with its plain façade, but someone had put up a Christmas tree in the lobby, and May wished she could go sit on the little couch next to it, curl up. She could say she was waiting for someone, but it didn't occur to her.

"It's four dollars for the night," the clerk said.

May smoothed her hair. "I'll ask my husband what he thinks," she said.

There were girls who would trade something for a room, work a Mr. Perry, and that was their business. May didn't feel like it. Getting into a room with a bed was trickier than getting shoes. The stakes would be higher. If she didn't like the terms of a shoe salesman, she could walk away, leave the store, but once she was in a room with a bed and a locked door, everything changed.

The clerk didn't seem the type to let her work a Mr. Perry anyway. He barely noticed her. Perhaps that part of his life had already departed, lost like the name of a restaurant in another city. He told her the price of the hotel. Men who didn't notice her were interesting problems, but they took up too much time. A man who noticed her always wanted something. A man who didn't—what did he want?

Hunger. What she wanted was food. She hadn't had anything since that morning when William had seen her to the bus. She went to the powder room and fixed her teeth. She combed her hair. She examined her skin. It was greasy from the panstick, and she could see that the rash beneath had turned rough and dry. She'd never get a dinner date looking like that.

She wanted to be May but she also wanted to be Peggy or Gertie or Margaret. She wanted to be May but she wanted to be Edith, too, or Lily. She remembered Claude saying, "Don't you want what Lily's got?" She peered at her face in the mirror. When it was all sorted and cleared up and everybody knew she'd never tell anything about Claude, she would go back to Los Angeles. Maybe Agnes would give her a job. She could type her articles. Or go to the library and do research. Yes. She was good at that. She wasn't a fast reader. When her eyes tired, she still ran her finger beneath the words so she wouldn't skip lines.

The powder room was papered in a muraled forest crowded in verdant fir trees, a blue lake in the distance. She smoothed her dress, turning a shoulder a bit forward, and stood in the posture of a photographed starlet. She imagined herself coming through that forest, wearing the white dress that she'd seen Beverly Dean wear. Did the Raptor come up behind her? Did he spring from behind a tree, or did he wait for her to pass him? Did he put his hands on her throat? She opened her mouth wide, as if she were screaming.

May rinsed her face with cold water. She didn't want to see the things that arrived, unwelcome, into her mind.

Maybe Lily was right. Maybe she chased shadows.

She blotted her skin, examining the dried rash. This was all she had. Her face. Her figure. She'd starve if she didn't have it. If she put on a dark shade of lipstick, it would lighten her skin, make it look less irritated. Fix your face, she thought to herself.

Fix it.

Outside, the street was filled with Christmas shoppers. She looked at them as they passed, noticing their anticipation. What would they think if she told them who the Raptor was? She almost laughed, thinking of it. She imagined telling the man who stood at the corner looking at his wristwatch. He looked up as she passed. *Boo!* she might cry. *The Raptor is after me.*

She ordered the turkey special and coffee. She ate slowly, and every time someone came in, she looked up, wishing that she could have a new face, different colored hair, to crawl into the skin of anyone—the fat man at the cash register or the complaining child—and then pass unseen through the world, moving comfortably in a new body until she transformed again into herself. She'd live for a while in a new body, yes, a body with different grievances. She had a pain behind her eyes and the skin on her cheeks burned. It was a relief to be in a strange city, alone.

She picked up a discarded paper and found the movie listings. The Aztec was just around the corner, and it was open all night. She'd slept in movie theaters before.

Two Action Packed Hits, she read, and hoped the films wouldn't be too loud.

May liked to be clean. She liked to smell good.

She'd seen *Dead or Alive* but not *Alibi*. At seven she crossed the street and went to the theater.

The ticket girl sat in her booth with her chin propped in her hand. "One, please." May slid a quarter and a dime toward her.

"Have you seen *Alibi* yet?" The girl's eyes grew wide and she unspooled a ticket.

"No."

"It's delicious." The ticket girl was young, her hair in a high ponytail. She didn't know anything.

"I've seen the other one already."

"It's a western." The girl shrugged. Her nails were painted red but her lips were pale. Maybe there was a rule about lipstick. "I'm not keen on those."

"Me neither," May admitted. She smiled at the girl. Westerns were flat and felt like little boys' movies. She didn't like chases or ambushes unless they were in cities with shadows and angles and there was at least *some* love interest.

"It's pretty quiet tonight. Go on in." She handed May her ticket.

May passed through the lobby. She stood behind a velvet rope. Nearby, two girls whispered to each other. They chewed gum, and their hair was plaited and pinned. The boys kept their hands in their pockets, lifting their chins at each other. The girls kept looking at the boys, their laughter wild and high. The sound made May feel sick. She was glad when the usher lifted the rope and let them into the theater. She sat as far away from them as she could, by the wall. The first film was *Alibi,* so she stayed awake for that.

She got caught up in the plot. Did the mysterious mind reader Winkler really kill his friend, and would Helene be in danger once she'd figured out how dangerous he was? May wished someone would give her a great deal of money as Winkler did to Helene. She remembered the pleasure of holding the money that Claude had given her, the heaviness of it at the bottom of her purse, the feel of the stiff bills. She was sure Claude was lying about who he was—just as Winkler lied to Helene.

May began to fall asleep, and the film mingled with her
dreams until May became a hostess in a nightclub just like Helene, and it was she who was unwittingly protecting the sinister
Winkler, who looked exactly like Claude in her dream.

When she woke, she went to the movie theater's bathroom
and washed under her arms. She had tea in a diner and waited
for the sun to come up.

At the Western Union window, there was a telegram from
Ned O'Neil and fifty dollars. A fortune. *Happy Christmas, dear
Margaret,* the telegram read. *Come home.* He'd sent her one of
the funny new Santagrams, as if she were just a little girl. She
went shopping. She bought a skirt and two blouses, and then
she looked at the window decorations. White powder glazed a
pair of calfskin gloves. Intricately cut paper snowflakes arced
across windows. A man pulled up in a long blue car. "Hello,
beautiful," he called.

She was afraid to look. Maybe it was Ray. It wasn't Claude.
He'd come at night. He'd wait for her in a room where she
thought she was safe. It could be one of them—any of them.
One she didn't know. "Get lost," she finally said.

"That's no way to talk." The man pulled up to the curb. "Say,
would you like a ride some place?"

"I'm busy," she said. She continued walking, but she looked
over at him this time. He was handsome, broad-shouldered,
with light eyes. He blinked in the sunshine, and when she kept
moving, he drove the car along beside her, pretending to stall it
and then start it again, stepping on the brake too hard—all the
while talking to the car as if it were a horse!

"Would you go to dinner with me? I'm new in town. I don't
know any—"

"I'm new in town too."

"Then we're a perfect match."

"We might be."

"Come on, get in. I'll take you to dinner."

"I really can't." But she'd stopped walking and faced him.

"Those packages look heavy."

"They're not so bad."

"Come on over here. I don't think I've ever seen a prettier girl."

"You're pulling my leg."

"I'd love to." He took his hat off, and May saw that his hair was red. She started walking again, but this time, she walked in the direction that she'd come from. She swung her shopping bag back and forth, glancing at him. "Should I pull over here and park and get out?" he asked.

"That's not necessary. I really don't talk to strange men in cars."

"I'm not strange."

"You might be." But he wasn't. She could tell. He wasn't one of Claude's friends. One of Claude's friends wouldn't drive a blue Chevrolet with dented fins. One of Claude's friends would follow her into a bar or park across the street. "I don't even know your name," she said.

"It's Jack. My name is Jack. I'll show you my driver's license."

She turned and walked over to the car. "Let me see it." She held her palm out to him. If he were from Los Angeles, she'd stop talking to him.

"You should tell me your name."

"Helene."

"Helene," he repeated. He reached into his jacket pocket and took out his wallet. He unfolded a piece of paper and took it out.

"It's from the French."

"Ah."

"Jack from Seattle. What are you doing here?"

"I'm a salesman."

"Is that so?"

"What are you doing tonight?"

It was settled. "Having dinner with you, I suppose."

He parked the car and got out, bowing a little, and then went around to the passenger's side and opened the door. When she came around, he took her bags and put them in the back seat, and she let him hold her hand while she got into the car.

It was early for dinner and so they sat in the nearly empty dining room together at a place on the pier with white tablecloths and drawings of the famous hotel on the island. "We should go see it," May said. She was drinking tea. She'd told him her name wasn't really Helene in the car. "That was a fib," she'd said, lifting his hat off his head to see his red hair again. The tag inside the hat made her think he had a little money—or more than she did, anyway, so she said she'd like him to take her someplace nice, even though she wasn't really dressed for it. For a while, he called her Helene in a teasing way. "No one will notice your dress, Helene, with legs like that."

She could see the mark on his finger from his wedding band. When had he taken it off? Before or after she got into the car? She would have known even without the mark of the ring. He was excited. It was like he'd been given a glass of water on a hot day, and he drank the whole thing quickly and then stood staring at her in astonishment. She'd actually gotten into the car. What sort of good fortune was this?

She liked his astonishment. He had the face of a man in advertisement who'd had a promotion. She laughed at his jokes, even the terrible one about the lady who married the postman. He was a wisecracker who couldn't settle down. A big kid.

"You're slippery like a skating rink," she told him, winking. He liked her, then, too much, she thought—or just enough. She couldn't decide. She let him circle her waist with his arm as they walked back to the car. What was the harm? She wasn't thinking about anything. She wasn't thinking about what she owed Lily or Ned. She wasn't thinking about Claude. She was standing in the sunshine with a man with hair the color of autumn leaves and skin as pale as the inside of her arm.

AGNES

They woke on a Saturday afternoon to the sounds of a day well underway. For a moment, she thought she was with Ben, but then she remembered: Danny. The tunnels. She dressed while he slept, thinking her clothes held the slight smell of sulphur, and when she was almost ready to leave, he woke. He gave her a long slow look. "Why are you leaving?"

"I have a cat," she said.

"You don't have a cat." He laughed. "Come back to bed." She did, but only for a little while. Soon she was up again. He said she was mad, leaving so soon. "It can all wait," he told her. It made her slow and forgetful—this. On her way home, she stopped at a diner and drank two cups of coffee. It was already getting dark. She'd stayed so long!

At home, she took a shower, changed into clean clothes. She wanted to work, but Danny interrupted her thoughts. What have I done? she wondered. She would tell him it was a mistake. She thought of Ben—but no, she was still angry at him. Maybe it was all a mistake. She did not hear the creak of the floorboards. She walked past the opened window once without thinking of it, but then turned. It was too cold for her to have left a window open—and then a light went on behind her.

Lily was sitting on the floor. She had Agnes's papers, the notes, the photographs spread out in front of her. "I want you to come with me." She stood. She wore dark trousers, a black turtlenecked sweater, flat shoes. Agnes looked back at the open window. Lily had broken into her house, slipping in like a shadow.

"What are you doing here?" Agnes said.

"They'll find out about you soon enough—" she said. "You and that photographer. Do you understand? Come with me."

"Where?"

"I'll drive. Give me the key. You're perfectly safe. Safer than if you stay here alone. Come—"

"Where are we going?"

Lily was casual, as if she'd been asked over for a drink or a game of cards. "To the beach, I suppose," she said. "Will you come with me?"

Agnes nodded and gave her the key to Dora's car.

"Let's go quickly now," Lily said.

24

MAY

May wore the pink dress, faded from the wash. She wanted a tin of henna—and a stub of white wax to fill her cavities—matches, so she could melt the wax, let it settle into petals on her fingertips, mold it into place. She needed to be in a garden—the one near the observatory, or farther south. She needed her scuffed shoes for dancing, the tandem, the airplane, to be the flyer, the hand on her waist telling her when. The tautness of the spin. The strain of the trombone; the swiftness—but she needed the small sunlit kitchen too. The house with shutters. She could run away with Jack, to Seattle, but it rained there, and she didn't need that.

If she looked, there were signs: a black dress hanging in an empty closet, Jack pulling up in his car, the surprise of his red hair.

She could fall in love with him. It didn't matter that he was married. Richard had had another girl too.

Once.

She bit her nails, pulling at the pinky until it bled.

Come, all ye faithful. Joyful and— It was already Christmas.

No one would come looking for her, and if they did, well, she wouldn't be found.

Jack took her to the canteen. They danced beneath the arcs of holly, around the big tree. She liked the feel of him when he pulled her in, and later, resting against a column in the hallway, his hand traveled up her thigh and lingered at her hipbone, just his fingers there—a slight pressure. She pulled his face toward hers and kissed him. They left the dance after that, and took a room near the ocean at the first place they came to.

"You know I'm married," he said afterward, drawing a cover over them, lying on his side gazing at her, his head resting on a folded arm.

"I know." Her eyes were half-closed. She rolled toward him. "Where's your ring?"

"In my jacket pocket. But how did you know?"

"It's obvious." She laughed. "Don't lose it. Your wife will be mad as hell."

"I won't. Are you married?"

"I was, once—" She told him about Richard, but this time she called Richard *Dale* instead, and she named the baby Polly. "I'm going to be an actress," she said. "I'm going to be famous. After all, it's what Dale wanted."

"You look like an actress."

She rolled on to her back and looked at the ceiling. The hush and pull of the sea made her sleepy.

"What are you doing down here?" he asked. "You should be in Los Angeles."

"I'm just visiting my friends for a while. Actresses like a change of scenery."

He laughed. "Good one."

She told him about the movie that Lily was in, but she never said the name *Lily*. She called her Rosa instead, though a few times she slipped and said *Lily*, and Jack looked at her in amusement. "Who?" he asked. He lay on his back and smoked a cigarette, one hand behind his head. He locked his jaw and let the smoke roll out. "My wife's pregnant," he said. "She's as big as a house. I'm afraid to touch her."

May thought of doing something to his face then. She thought of taking the cigarette from between his fingers and pressing it into his cheek, but she lay on her stomach looking at him, a small smile on her face. Some people had it all and they pretended they had nothing. It was like they hit a jackpot in a casino and then walked around asking someone to buy them a hamburger.

"Hey," he said. "Where'd you go?"

"I'm sleeping," she lied. "Can't you tell?"

"Sorry to bore you, kid."

"You're not." She sat up. "I'm hungry." But he asked her to lie back down with him. He put his arms around her.

"You've got terrible teeth," he said. "Look at that." He whistled in a way that sounded as if he were impressed.

"Don't look." She closed her mouth.

"Let me see."

She shook her head.

"Let me see."

But she wouldn't, and soon he yawned and rolled away.

"Do you care about my teeth?" she whispered. "Do you think they're ugly?"

"I don't care," he murmured. "No one's perfect. Do you care about my wife?"

She thought about it. She really didn't, but the baby made her sad. "No."

She left Jack asleep and found a telephone in the motel's main office. "I'd like to phone Los Angeles, California," she told the operator. "Reverse charges."

Adams sounded groggy, as if she'd woken him. "Darling!" he cried. "I was worried I'd never hear from you again. Merry Christmas! Tell me what you're doing. Where are you? I went by the Hamilton—"

"I know who the Raptor is."

Adams didn't say anything. She didn't even hear him breathing on the other end of the line. "How's that?" he finally asked.

"I figured it out."

"That doesn't make any sense."

"It's—"

"Oh, come on, now. The police can't even figure it out."

"It's Claude Borel." She waited for him to say something, but there was silence on the other end of the phone. She could hear his breath. "Hello?" she said.

"How do you know that?"

"I figured it out."

"Don't repeat that to anyone, angel."

"Is it true?"

"Listen: Don't repeat that. Don't tell one more person what you've told me."

"I'm going to call the police."

"I am the police, May. We're already on it. We're smack in the middle of Claude Borel. Don't mess things up for us."

"I won't. So you believe me?"

"You're a smart one. Listen. Tell me how you know."

She told him about Danny's notepad. She didn't tell him that she'd been with Danny. He was a reporter friend.

"What else did his notepad say? Did you write it down?"

"It was some initials. No one I recognized. I have it. I ripped it out." She read him the initials over the phone.

"Do you need some money? Where are you? I could come and get you."

She thought of Jack driving her up to Seattle. She thought of disappearing into the fog and the rain. "What's happening, Adams?"

"I can't say. You call me in a few days, but right now, hang up the phone and pretend we didn't talk."

She didn't hang up. He did, and she stood with the telephone at her ear until the operator came on and asked if she would like to place another call. "No, thank you," she said vaguely, but still didn't put the phone back on its hook.

She shouldn't have called Adams. She put her face in her hands. She got up and went out into the motel's small square courtyard and put her hands on her hips and looked into the sky. Blue. Endless blue.

She ran through scenarios. She imagined calling Claude, telling him the whole thing was a misunderstanding. Did he even know she'd said it? Lily probably told him. "I have no idea why I said that!" she would laugh, and he would give her something, chiding her, draping a necklace or a fur. "You know how I get." They'd think she was as crazy as Dora. They probably already did. She could call Ray and feel things out. She could go to her mother, but it would be so cold in Boston, and she didn't feel completely well yet. She would return in the spring, when it was warmer. Maybe she'd marry Ned O'Neil and start a family. She'd sit in on her mother's bridge game, knit an afghan, grow the sort of garden that women kept during the war. She would get dull and fat and listless, and everyone would remember how she used to be, and remark how plain she'd become with the years. And maybe Ned O'Neil would come home dirty and smelling of gasoline and liquor.

She couldn't do it. Dora said that once you got outside of the lines, you didn't want to get back in. It was true.

In the morning, Jack said, "Come with me." They looked at each other in the mirror above the bathroom sink. He was shaving, and she was pinning her hair. "I'm a salesman. I sell tools. I'm going up the coast. Come with me," he repeated.

She sat on the bed and watched as he showed her the display case his tools came in. It was lined with velvet the color of spring grass, and the box itself was maple, stained a deep brown. He told her he'd learned to sell with his hands, teaching himself a flourish in front of a mirror. Palms down meant, *You won't find a better price anywhere*; palms up meant, *Ask, maybe we can reach an agreement*. She laughed. He was funny, showing her. It was like putting on a magic show.

"All right," she said. "You sold me on it. I'll go with you."

Outside, Jack put May's bags in the trunk. She put her hand over her eyes to shield them from the sun. She was wearing a pale cotton dress illustrated with small black birds racing over the surface. The sun shone sideways on her, throwing her shadow into a rose bush.

They made their way slowly up the coast, bumping along the dirt roads. She held the map in her lap and told Jack what turns to take. "If you ever get bored trying to be an actress," Jack said, "you could do this. It keeps the world fresh." He took sips from a silver flask as he drove. "You could sell makeup or anything like that."

"I don't know. I'll keep it in mind."

When he went into the hardware stores, she walked up and down streets, smiling at people and peering into shop windows. Her clothes were city clothes, she could see. Here, everyone wore brighter colors. She stopped at the cobbler's shop and waited while a man cleaned her suede shoes and put caps on them—one at the toe, one on the heel. They were metal and took some getting used to, but soon it was fine. It was like having a brand-new filling. Her mouth never felt like her own if she went to the dentist. She would have to, though, once she got to wherever she was going. Maybe a dentist would take all her haggard teeth and give her a pretty set of new teeth. She could slide the teeth in in the morning and take them out at night. Her teeth would nest in a box like the drill bits Jack had shown her. A notch for each.

I am outside of my life, she thought. She was on the edge of someone else's life—a life that was about to become her own. She had to choose something—that was it. Everyone always imagined a girl took it, her life, swallowed it up like a baby being spoon fed, doing whatever was asked—

Be good, now. Be patient.

What would she choose?

In each town, she tried to imagine herself living there— some of the towns were too small to even merit a main street, but La Jolla was big. She liked the cove, and because they had more than one hardware store, she asked Jack to stay through New Year's. For dinner, they set out to find a restaurant with a view. May said she was cold, so Jack bought her a pink sweater and a round pin that May used to keep the top shut when the wind swept up from the sea.

She looked at him and wanted to feel love. She looked at him and thought how easy it would be to snatch him out of his own life and plant him in hers. He could stand like a great rooted tree and push her feet down into the earth. He could get her pregnant, make her too slow to move. She imagined herself in one of the seaside restaurants, her belly expanding until the pink sweater stretched over it. If he wanted to travel, that would be fine. She wouldn't be lonely. She would have the baby and walk down to the sea every morning to watch the seals sunning themselves on the rocks. She would point at the white birds, lift the baby up in the air. She would fall asleep with the baby on her chest, and at night, Jack would come in. He would not smell of the silver flask, but of the sea and sky. He would smell like Richard. And then, coming back to herself, May would shake her head and wonder where she had been.

AGNES

Lily drove fast, the window rolled down even though it was cold. She drove south, leaving the city, her long hair loose and whipping around her face. She wore a bracelet in the shape of a snake that flashed in the light of oncoming cars. "This?" she said to Agnes, when she saw her eyes on it. "Did Dora tell you about this?" She laughed. "I can't take it off until we're finished."

"Finished?"

"We're not finished yet. We've only just started."

"Where are we going?" Agnes asked. "You better tell me. Is this one of Borel's operations? Am I going to end up at the bottom of the sea?"

Lily laughed, lifting her chin. "Light me a cigarette," she said. "In my bag."

Agnes felt inside Lily's handbag. She fished out Lily's cigarette case, a silver lighter. She took one cigarette for herself and lit them both, passing the other to Lily.

Just beyond San Clemente, Lily turned off the main road, and then she turned again, taking a series of bumpy roads. It was colder near the ocean than it was in the city, and when the car slowed, Agnes could hear the beat of the surf against the rocks. "You better tell me," Agnes said. "What's going on?"

"I think you know."

But she didn't.

Lily stopped the car on a narrow road. She turned to Agnes. "We killed Aimsley."

"What?" Agnes stared at her.

"You didn't guess? We put him in a mask and made him walk out into the ocean. We rather liked that, but the mask must have come off. It made us all sad when he was found without it."

"The note—"

"Oh, that part was all him. I guess he thought he was warning the others. We rather liked that too. It's true, after all. *They* did do it wrong." Lily tapped Agnes's grimoire. "They're trying for a demon, but—" She put her hand on the book and closed her eyes, and then she laughed. "They didn't anticipate us. What did they *think* was going to happen? We'd just keep putting up with it? All these friends being killed—Joan, Beverly, Ruth, and the others—the ones we don't know."

"What's happening?" Agnes asked. "I don't understand this."

"It's simple, silly. The animals turned on their captors."

Was she mad? "I don't—"

"We'll walk from here. Come on." Lily got out of the car and slammed the door. She carried the book beneath her arm. She walked down the sandy road ahead of Agnes, who felt slow and heavy, as if she were walking through the surf, as if the surf were to her knees.

25

May

On New Year's Eve, Jack bought a bottle of champagne and they walked down to the ocean. She took her shoes and stockings off even though it was cold, and he rolled his black socks into a ball and tucked them into his brown shoes. They left their shoes by the path back to the jetty. It was late in the afternoon, and the sun was descending. It was the time of the day when the waves broke farther out, and the light was golden, the long stretch of beach empty. "Were you in the war?" she asked.

"Wasn't everyone?"

There were men who limped or were nearly blind or who had dead wives but living children. They didn't go.

Jack uncorked the champagne, pointing it toward the ocean. He lifted the bottle high in the air and yelled: "Tally ho!" He took a gulp and passed it to her. "Well, I was in the war all right."

"What was it like?"

He shook his head. "Too much noise. Too much fire."

"What did you do in the war?"

"What everyone did."

She took the bottle and drank. She liked the silvery taste of champagne, the stiffness of it. After a few swallows, her jaw stopped aching.

He put his arm around her. "Happy New Year's, darling."

She could hear music coming from one of the restaurants, a big band, the trumpet's pitch soaring above the other instruments. Later, they would go in. They were dressed for it, May in the black dress that Lily had given her, and Jack in a fresh white shirt and dark jacket, a deep green tie knotted at his throat.

Already, couples were beginning to celebrate. She imagined them lifting their glasses high in the air and laughing. The first couple would start dancing, and then the others would follow. She imagined they'd be clumsy at first—too aware of their own pretty clothes, the women not wanting to sweat in silk, the men in their good jackets, recut for the season. They were all distant cousins at a stranger's wedding. They were all waiting. There was so much time before dinner, before dessert, before champagne. There was still so much time before 1947. Hours to go.

She closed her eyes and smelled the sea. She imagined Richard arriving on a boat, stepping over the rim, knee-deep in waves, rushing up the shore. She passed the bottle back to Jack. "Do you miss your wife yet?"

He was staring at the ocean. He put his arm around May.

"Why'd you marry her?"

"It's what you do. Get married. Have a couple. And I guess I thought I'd miss her if I didn't."

"But you don't."

He shook his head.

"We're misfits, then. Both of us."

He stooped and rolled up his trousers. "Come on," he said, grabbing her hand. "Let's go in. We'll just get our feet wet. I want to feel it."

"What do you want to feel?" She held back, thinking of the dress's fabric, its crepe and lace and the way it would shrivel and compress with water.

"I don't know. I bet the water feels good." In the rose light of the sunset, he seemed so alive, not like a salesman, but like a man who'd just won a brand-new car.

She hesitated, but then yes, she did too. She wanted to feel it, too, so she laughed and let him pull her along, saying, *Not too far, not too deep,* as she went.

"Let's live!" he shouted. "I want to live!"

At a gas station on the road, she called Adams. "How does it look?" she asked. "I'm coming home."

"You're in the clear. They've arrested someone."

"Is it anyone I know?"

"I don't know everyone you know, darling, but I don't think so. You should come back here and see me."

She didn't quite believe him. Was it that easy? Everyone merely made a mistake? Dora and Agnes too? Danny? "What about the initials?"

"That could be anything, but I'll take a look at it when you get back."

She looked over at Jack, who was standing by the car. "I feel awfully silly," she told Adams. "Now I'll have to explain to everyone why I've been running everywhere."

"Say you had a sick relative. You can't tell the truth," he said, and his voice sounded restrained, as if she'd sent him on a wild goose chase and needed to be admonished.

"Are you angry with me?"

"How could I ever be angry with you? You're a doll. I want you here where I can look at you."

Jack was leaning against the car with his arms folded. He smiled at her. "Was that your fellow?" he asked.

"Just a friend. A sick uncle, actually." She tried it out.

"What's he got?"

"Got?"

"What's he sick with?"

"Influenza, I guess. He wants me to come back and take care of him." They drove for a while in silence. "He's in Los Angeles," she said.

Jack didn't say anything. She could feel him looking over at her every now and then. After an hour, he said he wanted to stop, to rest, to sleep for a while on the beach. She bought some bread and fruit at the grocer's and found him where he'd set up a blanket. She thought she'd better learn to drive when she got back to Los Angeles. She put her head on his chest one more time and closed her eyes and saw herself driving down a straight road with the sun rising at the end. It was like a movie poster. She might have fallen asleep, but soon Jack began to snore, so she knocked his hat off his face where he had it to shield his eyes from the sun and smiled down at him.

"Was I snoring?" He put his hand behind his head and looked up at her. "Darling you're gorgeous but those teeth—" And they laughed again. She made a face at him and said he was no better.

"You're actually quite funny looking," she teased. "You've got knock knees." He didn't, but she liked the way it sounded. "I'm surprised that they let you in the army."

He rested his head on his arm and looked at her. "I was a terrible soldier."

"Were you?"

"God awful. The worst. I'm surprised they let me anywhere near a gun."

"Because you're cross-eyed?"

He crossed his eyes and stuck out his tongue. "I wish I didn't have to go home."

"You have to."

"Come to Seattle with me. I'll get you a place. We'll get your teeth fixed."

"It's cold there."

"It's cold everywhere sometimes." He lay on his back. "Look at that sky," he said.

And she did. She rolled on to her back and looked up. All the endless blue shooting straight up, and beyond that, the brightest stars. It sure was something, this world. Wild and gorgeous and strange.

At the beginning of the trip, she would have jumped at Jack's offer, but now, according to Adams, the coast was clear in Los Angeles. "Let's not make leaving each other awful, all right? It's very romantic what we've had together." She held his hand. "And your wife wouldn't like your plan much."

He sighed. "I guess you're right. Don't even say goodbye to me. I want to see you again, though."

"Maybe you will. Someday."

"Where will you go?"

"Maybe I'll stay in Los Angeles. Maybe I'll go back East. I like Chicago, all right."

"It's cold there. Will you bring your uncle?"

"Who?"

"You're a fibber, aren't you? Your sick uncle. The one with influenza."

"Oh, him. He's just so dull I forgot him. That's all." She sat up and ate some of the bread and looked out at the sea. "It's cold everywhere but here. I could go to Florida. I liked it there."

"You lived in Florida?"

She nodded. "For a spell."

"Well, when you decide, let me know. I'll come find you."

AGNES

In the light of the moon, Agnes could make out a small house. The house was no more than a shack. Inside, the light was blue and reflective. Lily opened a door that led toward the sea. "Come on," she said.

Down on the beach, Agnes could see a fire—black shapes moving around it. They made their way down. Someone walked toward them. Dora rushed to Agnes, "Hello!" she cried, taking her hands. "I've been waiting for you." She smiled at Agnes. "We've both been kidnapped, but it's perfectly all right. It's so marvelous."

Marvelous—it was a word one used for a museum exhibit or a new restaurant. A vacation word—*We're having the most marvelous time here*—but this was all so strange. A dream. Most of the women were wearing the masks from "The Circus." They stood in a loose half-circle in front of her, the ocean behind them, the firelight in shadow. Dora held her hand, whispering, "It's perfectly all right, really." Dora pulled her forward. Lily put one hand on her shoulder.

"Go on—" Lily said. The women were dressed in coats and trousers instead of lace and feathers and fur. "It's better that you don't know who everyone is," Lily said.

"Why did you bring me here?"

"We need your help. We need you to stay quiet," Dora said.

"Where's May?" Lily asked. "We need May."

"I don't know where she is. Isn't she here?" Agnes looked at the masked women. One of them could be May, after all. But as she looked at them, they shook their oversized heads.

"All right," Lily said. "We have to do this tonight." She looked out at the ocean. "We have to try to save her." She pulled out a book and set it down on the beach. It was Claude's *Ars Goetia*. It was Claude's grimoire.

"Read it," Lily said. "We've all seen it. You and Dora—"

Agnes sat down on the sand. Dora sat next to her. When Dora read, she whispered the words, and soon Agnes gave up trying to read on her own and listened to Dora's whispering.

"Beverly Dean, November, death by strangulation. Has it worked? M. said he saw something in the tunnels—a drawing of a bird—" Dora paused, the light moved around her. "Last night I dreamed that I flew. I had great claws. It is happening—" and "Joan, December. We took her into the tunnels. We took her there and somehow the next day, carrion, she was found in the dunes. It was wonderful that they couldn't identify her. What did we do? No one remembers! We must have all come upon her at once—"

By firelight, Agnes turned the pages. "The maps—" she said.

"These are the tunnels," Dora whispered. "There are tunnels beneath the city. It's mad. They're marking them with these—" Dora turned the pages back to the pictures of animals, half bird, half man. A man with horns and wings. A raptor. A demon. "This is why you never see the Raptor come and go. He's underground. He's in the tunnels."

"Is it a man or a—"

"Lily says they create him with their black hearts. They fashion a man who will do their bidding. They become him, all of them."

"Lily—" Agnes stood. "This is proof."

"Is it?" Lily said. "Is it proof? They will say it's a fiction. And we've already tried—"

The tiger stepped forward. "We called the police. We told them where to find the book." Was it Ginger? Agnes wondered. Or someone else? The voice behind the mask was muffled. The masks weren't made for speaking. The masks were made for show.

"This book is what binds them all," Lily said. "This is where it ends. Only know that you were right. And that now you must be very quiet while we finish it—"

"As quiet as a mouse!" the woman wearing the mouse mask cried.

"Not a peep—" said the elephant. "From either of you."

Lily took the book back. She brought a small blade out and nicked her finger, pressing her bloody imprint to the page. She passed the blade and book to the tiger, who did the same thing, and so on, the mouse, the lion, and so on. A zebra passed the book to Dora, who looked around the circle. "Do it," Lily said, and Dora dragged the blade across her finger. When she finished, she passed the book to Agnes, who, it seemed from some great distance, cut her own finger and pressed it on to the page as well.

26

MAY

They drove with the windows down, sharing the last bottle of beer, saying how good it was even though it was warm. What an adventure!—and it was already over. She looked at Jack's profile. She could see how he would go home to his wife, take off his hat on the doorstep, unlock the big wooden front door, let it swing open to the new living room set, the smell of a roast in the oven, and he would forget about May before he even remembered her again. As he put his ear to his wife's belly and asked her what they'd call him, May would have already slipped into the past—the girl with the terrible teeth and black hair.

"We said we wouldn't have big goodbyes," she told him in front of the Biltmore. "My sister will be here soon." What did it matter if it was her sister or Edith? Her sister or Lily?

"You didn't tell me you were meeting your sister."

"I called from the service station, remember?"

He shook his head at her. "Do you need help with your bags?"

"Oh, that's all right. Most of them are checked at the train station. My sister will help me."

"When will your sister be here?"

"Soon. She has a hair appointment." She smiled at him, keeping her lips closed. She wanted him to go back to where he came from. He didn't belong in her life. He'd slipped in by accident. She'd slip out.

He knew she was lying. She could see the way his eyes changed. "Do you want to go have a drink while you wait?" he asked.

"No. You should go. It's a long drive to Seattle."

"Hours, sure." He tapped at the pockets of his jacket. "I have a pad and paper. Where can I find you?"

They passed through the golden doors of the Biltmore Hotel and into the lobby, where they sat at a small table together and she took out the address book. She opened it and wrote Jack's first and last name and his address in Seattle. "There," she said. "Now when I get settled, I can write to you."

"Promise?"

"I sure will." She didn't look at him. She wanted to wash her face in the ladies' room, to dry it with one of the soft towels, to take out her makeup and line it up on the counter. She wanted to fill her teeth, to wash between her legs, behind her ears, the back of her neck, her hands, her feet if she could manage. She could do it one of the stalls.

She could use one of the phones to call Lily and apologize. How silly she'd been! She thought of Lily's eyes and how soft they were when she told her about Richard. "Oh, that's some bad luck, May," she'd said. And when May saw Lily again, she'd laugh when she told her, "I'm as bad as Dora. Maybe worse."

She looked at Jack, who already had a stranger's face. He would return to wherever he'd come from. "Be safe," he said. He leaned in to kiss her, and she let him, quickly. "I want to see you again—if I'm in town."

"That would be lovely," she lied. She wanted to walk out into the night, to sit at the bar with Lily, the sway of a band or a song on the jukebox, a man waiting. Waiting for her. "That would be lovely," she said again. She turned and walked away, moving through the lobby, up the arced staircase and into the long hallway, past the potted ferns, the ebb and motion. She smiled at the bellhop, who bowed his head a little.

She wondered if William and Edith were home from church yet. She could wait, passing the time with other calls. Lily wasn't in, and the girl who took the message said she didn't know when she'd come back. In the restroom, she fixed her makeup, making sure the rash didn't show, the red nodules. She leaned on the sink and struck a match to melt a bit of wax, but blew the flame out, and drew the spiral on her palm, the one that Dora had shown her. Good luck. She needed that. She would begin again. She filled her teeth. She drank from the sink, cupping her right hand so as not to disturb the spiral on the left. She stood and examined herself.

"Have you got some money? I'd like to go home this spring," she practiced saying it, though she was not sure who she'd ask. Or she'd say something else. She tried to remember what she'd told Adams about the baby and Richard. If she'd added the dog. She got through to William, who said yes, of course they could pick her up. *Of course,* she could stay—but it wouldn't be until later—until Edith came home with the car from church.

Stupid church. She sat in the lobby for a while, smiling. Richard was upstairs. They were on their honeymoon. Richard was just getting the car.

"Edith said she told you the news," William said when she called again. "About the baby."

"Yes, she did. Congratulations." She tried to imagine William and Edith with a baby. She saw them on top of their wedding cake again, the little Bakelite bride and groom, but they were dressed in ordinary clothes and Edith was holding a baby. The sugar from the icing crept up their legs. "You must be thrilled."

"Over the moon," William said. He laughed a little. "Everything is different now."

"Yes."

"Call again in an hour and Edith and I will be around with the car."

After they hung up, she stood in the lobby, beneath the vaulted ceilings, looking up. She was in a palace or on a carousel. A rich woman. A rich woman high in the hills, the sound of her heels clicking across the marble floor. Arriving. Golden as the sun in October. The arched doorway was crowded with sculptures of gods, of women holding shields, of men aiming arrows. There were laurels and wreaths and crowns of ivy. A deer leapt, pursued by hunters. What might a person do in the world? What was impossible, after all, if someone could dream a place like this and then build it? She'd been to dances in the ballroom, but it was always too dark and smoky to see the paintings on the walls. One day, she'd have to go look. The hotel was haunted, that's what everyone said. Maybe it was haunted with dreams. All the dreams of strangers—almost thirty years of nights. And now with her own dreams too.

She phoned William again, but still Edith had not come back with the car. "Sorry, kiddo," he said.

"I'll try Lily," she said, but she didn't try Lily. She took out her address book and opened it, scanning the names there in black ink, scattered in pencil, faded or brand new, like Jack. She put her finger there. So many names, she couldn't remember who half of them were. She wouldn't call Ray.

She called Adams.

She went back to the doors and raised one hand when she saw him. "I've missed you so," he told her when he pushed open the passenger side door without getting out and coming around. Wasn't it strange that he hadn't come around to open it for her? Rude, really, but it was late, or not late but this wasn't a plan they'd had, so she forgave him, and he was smiling. He had on a fresh gray suit. His hair was combed. Jack with his flask and his bold shirts—he couldn't compare. But still there was something—the silliness of the car door?—but later, she'd wonder about it, when she was alone with Adams and he said: "We should never go back. I can't bear to keep sharing you with the world—" He said it as if something were stuck in his throat, he said it as if he'd come to the end of a road and instead of more road there was a high wall that he couldn't find a way around.

Because just before she'd slid across the seat toward him, she thought she might say: "Oh, this is too much trouble. I'll wait for my sister's friends." But it was wrong to inconvenience a fellow like that. It would be terribly rude to get out. He'd driven all the way. But she was queasy—almost frightened—and all that even though he was smiling.

AGNES

The women were chanting. The women were singing.

"Now," Lily said. "It begins." She lifted the grimoire. "Write in the book—" she said. "Write about the death of the Raptor in the book, and when you write it, it will come to pass. Write your name in the book. Write it." She handed Agnes her grimoire. "This is how it ends."

"I can't write about someone's death," Agnes said. She couldn't.

"Just the creature—" Lily explained. "Not a person."

So she did. She wrote of a monstrous night animal. She saw his claws clipped, his wings broken. She passed the book to Dora, who wrote for a long time, and sometimes she laughed as she did. As the other women wrote, Agnes rose and walked toward the sea. The wind was cold, but she'd grown hot by the fire, and the cold wind felt good on her skin. She tried to imagine telling Ben about this night, about the weighted dream of it, the heaviness of intent, the masks in the firelight. What would he say? He would say she was mad. And Danny, what would he say? The world of the morning was another world. It was as far away as the ship that Dora was supposed to be on.

Agnes did not see who threw the book into the flames, but the burning book cracked and whistled. The fire leapt high, and the masks were illuminated around them. The bright light showed each imperfection: the cracks in the paint, the lack of symmetry, the bumps and lines in the papier-mâché. Above them, smoke whipped up into the night, and Agnes, for a moment, standing there, swore that she could see a black shape rise up, the flap of a wing in the swarm of ashes.

"Agnes!" Lily cried. "We've finished now. You'll hear from me again when it's finished. Let's go back to the city."

"Dora—"

"I'm staying here," Dora said. "With the others."

27

MAY

Adams drove with one hand on the wheel, headed north, away from the city. "I'm afraid I spoke too soon," he said. "It's really a good thing you called me. They're awfully upset with you."

"Who?"

"Claude. Ray. Lily. I'm afraid Dora was right about them."

"Claude is the Raptor?"

"I'm afraid so. It's terribly grim. The police are with him right now. It's your tip that got him mixed up in this. I don't think they've got the evidence to lock him up."

"But I didn't tell anyone," she said to Adams. She lifted her hand to her face, afraid. "I only told you. But I didn't tell—"

"The detectives are going to want to interview you. And Dora, if you could get her back here."

"I can't get Dora back here."

"Why not?" he asked, but she didn't want to tell him that it was because she was in Paris.

"How did they find out it was me, Adams?"

"All right, all right." Adams slowed the car down and pulled off the road. He turned the engine off and looked at her. "I told."

"Why?" she yelled. "How could you have done that?"

"I tried not to mention your name. But it came up. You know how persuasive the police can be."

"But you're the police."

"I am."

She kept yelling, so he took her in his arms. "It's all right, shhh—I've got you now. It's all right."

She cried, "I don't see why you had to say it was me."

He lit two cigarettes and handed her one, and she took it, not smoking, holding it awkwardly between her fingers until he'd smoked all his and took it from her and smoked that too. "I swear nothing can happen to you now," he said.

She began to settle down. The night was so big, and the world was bigger. She could leave here. "I don't know where to go," she told Adams.

"You should probably work on getting Dora back here before Claude gets to her."

"All right." She sighed, imagining Dora in an airplane, fast asleep, somewhere over the ocean.

They sat between the mountains and the ocean, the windows down, the air cool, full of the smell of salt and sage. It was getting dark, but she could still see, in the distance, the line the mountains made against each other, the soft bump of hill upon hill. She looked at his profile. He always reminded her of someone—of some boy she knew once a long time ago—or maybe not that, but an actor—not a famous actor, but an actor who was in small roles. He fit the detective type. She wouldn't know his name.

"What?" Adams turned to her. "You're staring at me."

"You remind me of someone."

"I do? Who?"

"I don't know. I can't place it. Look back out at the water." He turned his face away and she studied it for a moment, but she had the feeling that she'd walked into a room and couldn't remember what she was looking for. "Anything?"

"You're so familiar."

"I have one of those faces."

"Do you?"

"People always think they know me. Sometimes I pretend they *do* know me."

"Who do you do that with?"

"Girls, mostly."

"Of course you do." May closed her eyes. "Who did you tell about Claude?"

"No one you know."

"Who did you tell?"

"Another detective. At the top."   ·

"What did he say?"

"It's what he didn't say." He took out another cigarette.

She nodded. "Did we meet in the gardens that day by accident? Were you following me?"

Adams didn't answer. He reached over and put a hand on top of hers. He sighed. "Listen," he finally said. "There are things you don't understand."

"What things?"

"Some of us thought it was Claude all along. Some of us think Claude killed his secretary."

"Do you think it now?"

"It doesn't matter what I think."

"Where will I go?" She glanced at him. He raked his hair back as if it were in his eyes.

"Go back East. Listen. I told anyone who'd listen you'd never say a word."

"Anyone who'd listen? How many people know?" She was embarrassed. It was strange, she thought—to feel so embarrassed—as if she'd been caught stealing. She felt the flush of her cheeks in the dark car. She held her hands tightly together, waiting, wishing she'd gone with Jack to Seattle. Her teeth hurt. "Is Claude going to be arrested? What is this?" She and Jack would be at a bar right now, dancing—or in a hotel room.

"I haven't heard anything like that. Men like Claude don't usually get arrested. They're just questioning him."

"Even if they're guilty?"

"He knows a lot about a lot of important people. Judges, the higher ups. That sort. Any name you've heard, Claude has something on them."

May thought of all the girls, all the girls with secrets. A silvery line of girls circled around him, the dancers from Ray's clubs, and Claude in the center, in the spotlight, placid, protected. *Everyone talks to pretty girls.* She imagined Lily smiling at a girl, holding her hand, saying, "It's going to be just fine." Everyone was forced into silence or complicity. No one was safe.

"Where do you feel safe?" Adams asked. He lit a cigarette. She glanced over at him and saw that his fingers were shaking.

"Safe?" She thought of her room in the Hamilton, the small lock that her key sometimes stuck in, the hook on the bathroom door. She imagined someone kicking the door, filling the bathtub with water. And Lily, whom she could never call, sitting in her perfect replica of an eastern college girl's room in that tall brick house, sitting on a pink bedspread, holding the lines she had to memorize, her glasses on a chain around her neck, a cigarette burning down in the ashtray. Dora whispered to May in the movie theater; William held a light up to illuminate the tunnel—the black wings painted on the wall. The bats silent and sleeping and upside down.

Her underarms were damp. She almost said, "Take me to Lily's," but then she imagined Lily picking up the phone, speaking low, saying, "Yes, she's here." Would Lily do that?

Lily was a liar.

"I don't," May said. "I don't feel safe." She thought of Edith and William, of the long table set for dinner, of two white candles burning, the open window and the smell of limes. She thought of her sister, her mother. "Are they going to kill me?"

"Who? Claude's friends? Oh god no, darling." He shook his head. "No one's going to kill you. Come on. It's a precaution."

"Just keep driving."

"Where do you want me to go?" He began to pull back on to the road. It was night now, and the headlights shone into tangled brush.

She bit her lip. "Up the coast," she said. "We'll go up the coast. I need to lie down." She coughed.

"Would you like to spend the night at a hotel?"

"Yes, I think so."

"You can try Dora from there." They found a motel in the mountains. The motel had low ceilings and small windows, and she thought, as she lay in the tub, how strange it was that she could still hear the ocean this far up. She could hear Adams talking to someone, and she tried to listen, but the words were indistinct, caught in between the hum of the radiator and the drip of the faucet. When she wrapped her hair in a towel and dressed again, she asked him: "Who was that?"

"What was what?" He was sitting on the edge of the bed in his undershirt and trousers. He turned to her. "You can have the bed. Oh, I asked for a cot. That must have been it—what you heard. I was talking to the owner of the hotel." He looked at his hands. They were slack in his lap. "I think we should get you out of here."

"Right now?"

"No. Tomorrow. Get some sleep. Why don't you try Dora now?"

"It's so late there," she said. "I'd like to sleep. I can try her tomorrow."

"I'll stay up."

"Stay up?"

"And watch."

She didn't sleep. What was Adams watching? She could see the shape of him in the big chair by the door. No one had ever brought a cot for him. He said they told him they didn't have cots, but she thought he was lying.

"Adams?" It was past midnight. She could tell he wasn't asleep, but he didn't answer her right away. "Adams?" she said again.

"Yes?"

"I'd like to go to Los Angeles tomorrow. I have family there. They will help me."

"All right. I thought we'd put you on a bus."

"They'll help me."

He didn't say anything else. In the morning, she wondered if he'd ever slept. He had circles under his eyes, and he needed to shave. His face seemed shadowed and changed.

AGNES

When they left the beach, the sun was coming up. Agnes drove. She thought of Claude's grimoire—the blood on the pages, the descriptions of what had been done. The black meandering lines of the tunnels. It was evidence, wasn't it? And she'd watched as they destroyed it. She'd stood by as if she hadn't cared when Lily threw the book into the flames. But wasn't it strange—she thought—that heaviness she'd felt, as if the water were rising around her.

It was gone.

The gray dawn lifted it away, making her lighter. The sea's mist made the world soft, the road ahead, obscure. Lily pulled her hair back into a high ponytail. She took out a compact, and looking at the small silvery mirror, blotted her skin with a white handkerchief. "My pores—" she said mildly, and looked at Agnes. They smelled of smoke and salt air, pungent and pleasant.

"Where shall I take you?" Agnes asked.

Lily lived near the studio lot in a boarding house for actresses. "Listen," Lily said. "I'm desperate to find May. I should have told her what we were up to, but I wanted to leave her out of it, you see. She's not made for this sort of mayhem."

"I rather wish you'd left me out too."

"But I couldn't. You were getting too close."

Agnes was tired. She rolled the window down so that she could feel the cold air on her skin.

"What we did—" Lily went on. "It doesn't entirely change things. It might slow them down, make everyone a little less likely to do what they do, but if they already have it in them to act—there's still such a thing as free will."

"*What* did we just do?"

"We broke the first layer, that's all. The Raptor will be back if we don't watch out."

Agnes drove for a while without saying anything. The sun was higher, and the mist was thin. She didn't understand what Lily meant when she said *the first layer*. All they'd really done on the beach was burn evidence. "Who? Who will be back?"

"You know who."

"The Raptor?" She wished Lily would explain, but she remained stubbornly silent. She sat with her hands in her lap, looking straight ahead. What foolishness—Agnes thought. How preposterous! But then she remembered the black ashes that rose from the fire, the smoke like a being, in the shape of a bird's wing, and a long low call from a place on the beach that she could not see.

"What is the Raptor, Lily?"

"Death. Hate."

Had she imagined it? Ben would say she had. *It was dark,* she imagined him telling her. *You were on a beach with women in circus creature masks! Of course you saw strange things—*

"Claude would never be arrested, you know—" Lily said. She didn't look at Agnes when she said it. She looked straight ahead. "None of them would. If they *were* arrested, if it even got that far—there'd be some show of a trial, some back-room deal. Some lawyer would get them off."

"But you've destroyed the evidence. Now it will never—"

"*We* are the evidence, Agnes. Our bodies. *I* am the evidence. It's they who are destroying the evidence."

When they reached the city, Agnes was glad for the sharp yellow lines of the street, the orderly direction of the stop sign or the green light. "Where do you think May has gone?" Agnes asked.

"I was hoping you'd know. Maybe she's just off with some Henry."

Some fellow, she means, Agnes guessed. She thought of Danny. Perhaps Danny knew—he saw May that last night too. Maybe Danny knew something. At Lily's rooming house, Agnes let the car idle. "When will I hear from you?"

"When it's time." Lily yawned. "*My*, I'm sleepy," she said.

"It's all right. Go on the way you've done. Leave the rest to us."

"What's the rest—what are you going to do?"

"You don't need to know, Agnes. And we don't need you to know, either." She put a finger to her lips. "Shh."

Agnes watched Lily go into the house. She took the front steps lightly, her blond ponytail bouncing as she moved. If her roommates saw her, they would assume she'd been out all night—out having a good time—dancing and laughing.

Agnes didn't want to go home. Not yet—Danny was probably still asleep. It was Sunday, after all. But what did it matter? It might always be too early or too late. If women gathered to burn magical books on beaches, what did it matter if she showed up at Danny's at six o'clock on a Sunday morning?

28

May

Night again, and she'd forgotten what day it was. Adams had stood with his back to the door of the hotel room. He'd kept the curtains closed, and as she fixed her teeth in the bathroom, her hands shook. She traced the spiral into her palm again. Her throat burned from the smoke of his cigarettes, from the car's exhaust. She wanted the small bed at William and Edith's house. May wanted Edith's lemon cake, to see the progress of whatever she'd made with the golden yarn. She would help her if she could. She would give to Edith the same understanding of the world that had been given to her: that to be a person of the world, one had to learn to live in it in the way she wanted— no matter what. No matter who said *no* or banged his fists.

But Adams was making her nervous, and she was glad when they left the hotel and got back in the car. About halfway back, they had car trouble. Something with the oil, and they were stranded for a few hours in a town that had little to recommend, so May took a magazine to the beach and sat on the pink sweater that Jack had given to her, trying to stay warm in the sunshine while Adams saw to the car. No one knows where I am, she thought. She lifted her face to the sun and closed her eyes. Jack would be in Portland now. Claude was looking for May. Claude would do what he would do once he found her, but he would never find her.

And Dora was probably in Paris. She didn't know how much longer she could put off the Dora question. She would call Agnes instead. Agnes was clever. She would understand why May was pretending.

When the car was fixed, they got back on the road. Adams

was quiet. He smoked a lot. One cigarette after the next. May rolled all the windows down, but he did not notice. "Don't you have to be at work?" May said.

"I am at work."

She didn't know what he meant and didn't ask. She thought it would be two hours until she got to Edith's house, but everything seemed to take forever. Adams needed to find a place to buy more cigarettes. He said the map he was using was terrible, the deep creases in the paper made it impossible to read. By the time they finally reached the outskirts of Los Angeles, it was late. May thought Edith was probably already in bed.

"I guess it's too late to call Dora," Adams said. He said it in a mean way, like he was sick of May.

"It is."

When they got to Santa Monica, May was relieved. Soon she'd be with William and Edith.

"Aren't you hungry?" Adams asked.

"Sure, I'm hungry." She was. She hadn't eaten since the car had broken down.

The restaurant was nearly empty. The waitress came over and asked them if they wanted coffee. May ordered two eggs, sunny side up. Adams ordered corned beef hash and toast. They ate in silence. May was tired. She kept thinking about the trundle bed in Edith's spare room, the white spread and the clean sheets.

Adams put his hand on top of hers. He opened her palms and gazed at the spiral she'd drawn on her hand. "What's this?" he asked, but he was smiling, like he knew.

"Oh—it's for good luck."

"Is it?" He lit a cigarette and with the blown-out match, redrew the already lightened circle. "Say," he said when he finished. "I want to tell you something."

"What's that?"

"Don't you remember the first time we met?"

Was he getting sentimental? She tilted her head to the side. "What do you mean?"

"Do you remember the first time we met?"

"We met in the gardens that day."

"No."

"No?" He was being funny, she decided, thinking it must be a joke. "We met in the gardens last July." She tried again.

"August," he corrected. "Yes, and you stood me up."

"I didn't." She winked at him. "You didn't call."

"You *did* stand me up." He didn't smile at her wink. "But that's beside the point. Don't you remember me?"

"I really don't know what you mean."

"We met in Miami."

"You're thinking of someone else."

"No."

"I'm sure you're thinking of someone else."

"You worked as a waitress at that restaurant—the one with the green-and-white awning near the beach. You waited on me all the time. It was that place on the beach with the fake shark over the door and that enormous, terrible needlepoint when you came in." He laughed. "You've never even asked my first name. No one's just called *Adams.*"

"But why didn't you say something?"

He shrugged. "I wanted to see if you remembered."

"I'm sorry," she said, looking into her lap.

"You should be. You hurt a guy's feelings." His face was hard, his jaw set. He squinted at her.

"What's your first name?"

"Marvin."

"Tell me what you ordered when you came in—" she tried. "Maybe then." Her voice shook.

"Hey, it's all right." He laughed and lifted his hand for the waitress. "I'm just fooling you."

"But I did work at a place with an awning." She was confused. Flushed, she reached for water. She held the glass to her cheek and looked at the dark windows.

"It was just a guess."

But it hadn't been. She'd worked all winter at a restaurant

with a needlepoint done in the shape of Florida by the door. It was bordered with oranges, dotted with sandcastles and waves. She rubbed her forehead. "But how did you know about the needlepoint if it was a guess?"

"What needlepoint?"

"The one you just mentioned."

"Why would I talk about a needlepoint?"

"But you did, you said—"

"Sweetheart, you're imagining things." He smiled at the waitress when the check came, and reaching for his wallet, he said: "Why don't we go see if we can take a walk by the docks? In another hour or two it will be light out."

He was serene again—as he had been before, but her thoughts were like a wild animal crashing through a forest—frightened of something unidentifiable. But it was a small thing, wasn't it? And maybe she only imagined the part about the needlepoint after all. Maybe he hadn't actually *said* it. "Oh, I think I'm too tired for a walk."

But she knew the name *Marvin*. She looked at his face, at Marvin Adams's face. How did she know the name Marvin? William has a friend named Marvin, she thought. The tunnels. Marvin Adams. Marvin from the tunnels.

M.A.

The initials in Danny's notepad. *M.A.*

She stood. "Say, I need the little girl's room." She forced herself to smile. She wanted to call Agnes, but first she had to get away.

She went through the kitchen and out the back door. She wanted to run, but Adams was standing in front of her. Marvin Adams. He folded his arms and frowned. "Where are you going?"

Adams took her arm in his and began to walk to the car. "I thought we were going to walk by the water until it got light. I thought you'd like that. You're a romantic girl. You forgot your handbag," he said, but he didn't give it to her.

"Is that true about Florida?" She felt sick to her stomach.

"What does the truth matter to people like you and me?"

"I don't want to be here. I want to leave now."

"You know I love you." He tightened his grip on her arm. "It's all right now," he said. "You're always running from one place to the next. You should slow down."

She pulled away, but he held her fast.

"A man wonders where you are going." His voice was soft. "It's all right," he said again. She almost believed him, but then her dress tore. The fabric gave just beneath the arm.

"Hey now. Take it easy." She tried to pull her arm, but he had her in a grip. "I'm not going anywhere with you."

"I'll fix the dress for you. I'll even get you a new one. Like William did."

"How do you know about William?"

"Oh—" He looked surprised. "I suppose you told me about him."

But she was sure she didn't tell him about William. She didn't tell anyone about William. "I'd like to go." She tried to pull away again, but he held fast, and he guided her to the car. She imagined the two men standing together in the tunnels, both pretending to be someone they weren't. Pretending together. "You know William from the tunnels, don't you?"

"Hey—" He nodded. "You're smarter than you look. Did you just figure that out?"

"Let me go. William will find out."

"William has his own problems. Listen. I'll take you someplace nice, but you'll have to give me your shoes and your handbag."

"What?"

"I'm afraid you'll try to run and hurt yourself. A girl could throw herself from a car. I'd have to come back and get you." He laughed.

"Has that happened?"

"Has what happened?"

"Did you really know me in Florida?" She was shaking. She could get out of it with the right angle. If she could just think—

"Were we friends? I bet we were good friends. Oh, that was a long time ago. Say what were you doing in Florida?" She tried to keep her voice even, but it pitched and careened and cracked. "Were you in the service?"

He imitated her. "Oh, we were the *best* friends. Just like you and Lily."

He opened the car door on his side and pushed her in. She grabbed her handbag, but he pulled it from her. He was strong. She looked for the Adams she had known before, but she didn't see him. He emptied her handbag and put the contents in his pockets.

"Are you really a detective?" she asked.

"Of course. I take care of the big stores. Make sure no one's stealing. Robinson's. That sort. And the smaller ones, but really just the smaller ones, and I suppose not at the moment. No. At the moment, I'm not anything. I'm not a detective, no. Not right now. Well. I watch people. I keep track."

"Were you ever on the police force?"

"Whatever gave you that idea?" He sounded mildly amused. "Give me your shoes."

"No."

"Give me your shoes, May." He was almost patient. He was at the edge of something, and she didn't want him to tip into it, so she reached down and unbuckled her shoes.

"These cost me quite a lot." She thought of the shoe salesman, the way he ran his hand up her leg. "Where are we going?"

"You'll be safe with me. Don't you understand? Claude will never find you." He laughed. "It's for your own good. You've got to find a safe place."

He drove fast, down the long highway that led out of town and into the canyons. Outside of a motel, he parked, and grabbed her arm again, pulling her across the seat on his side. He locked her shoes and purse in the trunk. In a rented room, he sat down across from her and smoked a cigarette. He leaned a little forward in his chair, going through the things he'd taken out of her handbag. She watched him read the page she'd torn from Danny's notepad. He laughed. "That's almost all of us," he said.

The room was square and striped in brown paper. The bed was unmade. There was a dark spot on the pillowcase. The window curtains were shut. There was a painting of two lovers by a stream. Nothing bad could happen in a room where there was a painting like that. A bug crawled out from behind the painting. She thought of screaming, but she couldn't find the place in her throat.

"I'll take care of you." He leaned over and tried to touch the side of her face, but she pulled away. "You'll never want for anything again. I see how you struggle. Do you want a drink?"

"Sure." She thought that if he turned his back to her, she could get out of the room. She could rush to the door, but he pulled a bottle of gin from beneath the chair that he sat in and passed her the bottle. She took it and took a small sip. She wanted her head to be clear. "Is this where you live?"

"Give me your dress," he said.

"No."

His face turned red. He rose from the chair. "Don't make me angry." He leaned over her.

She found the sound in her throat and screamed. She was sure someone would come, but no one did.

"What was that for?"

"Why are you doing this?"

"It's not just me."

"Who is it?"

He smiled. "Tunnel club. They'll be here soon." He looked at his watch.

"Who are they?"

"You'll meet them when they get here. You know some of them already."

"William?"

"Not this time. He can't bear it."

"Are you the Raptor?"

"We're all the Raptor, darling. Me, Claude, Ray. Your William.

He's the Raptor too. We're quite wicked. Ray went and got you that night. It was all planned. Oh, Lily doesn't know that. She was just a lucky coincidence. She's nothing. And William didn't know until me and Claude told him. Each of us plays a part, so none of us are guilty. But really, it's none of your business. It's rude of you to even ask."

"What are you going to do to me?"

"Everyone has different ideas. We'll try some things out. It's nothing personal, doll. After a while—and I tell you this because it might make you feel better. We each play a part, so it looks a little different each time."

"Stop it. My god. Stop it." She covered her ears with her hands. "You don't mean what you're saying. You can't. It's madness. Take me—" But she had nowhere to go. She thought of her mother, far away. She calculated the time. It was late in Boston. It was the middle of the night. Her head hurt.

Adams sat with his palms facing the ceiling, as if he were giving up the argument. "I just don't know why you have to keep running all over the place. Why couldn't you ever just stay in one place and do what you're supposed to do? It's not natural."

"You can't do this. I'm not ready. I don't want it."

"You should have run like Dora did. You came back for a reason. Think. Perhaps this is the reason. Don't you see?" He looked at her. "They'll be here soon. Where is Dora anyway?"

"You'll never find her." She tried to scream again, but he was on her in a moment. He smelled acrid, foul from cigarettes and gin and sweat. He nuzzled his face into her neck like a lover. "We'll pick at your bones long after you're gone," he said.

AGNES

The funny thing was that Danny didn't seem surprised to see her. "Did you feed your cat?" he asked when he opened the door. "I've been calling you. Your line's dead." He was in his pajamas. The room smelled of coffee. He passed her his cup.

"What have you been up to?" He turned back to the narrow counter where he kept a hot plate, a few pieces of cutlery.

"You wouldn't believe me if I told you."

"Did you go out and catch the Raptor on your own?"

She looked at him, her face serious. "I might have. Say—" She sat down in the same spot as she had the night before. "When did you last see May?"

"That night. We went to have dinner, and then I left her at the Nightingale."

"Did she say if she were going somewhere?"

"No. In fact, I didn't even know she was gone. She said her bags were at Union Station."

Agnes drank her coffee. She put her head in her hands. "I'm dead tired," she said.

29

MAY

There were tunnels beneath the city, blasted fissures of stone and upturned roots. There were unfinished basements, hills of raw earth. There were doors that led to alleyways, and alleyways that ended abruptly, that backed up to our walls, to boat landings, to slaughterhouses. There were spaces beneath buildings, corners to fold into; there were pits in the hills, black and yawning, deeper and colder than winter.

She was wrapped inside of her shadow, in and out, above and below. So thirsty, and the stones were cold to touch, damp. Cheek to cool surface. Forehead. It was wonderful how much one could feel. And terrible. The earth was opening up. The grit of dirt, the scalp scabbed, hair tangled. Each cut. She tried to pull her knees into her chest, but she couldn't find herself. She had become a tree. She was forming somewhere deep inside, those roots binding at her ankles, transforming her. She was becoming a tree, and her fingers must find the sun, must branch, must rid themselves of wrapping vines.

The hands are the size of two birds pressed together and sleeping. Feet are only marks left in snow. She was an animal too. Her skin was slashed, like an animal's. She'd been running. And now she could try again. But. She was a tree, and her feet were tied fast by the roots.

The tree was still underground. It must be growing, burrowing. The ground was above her still. It was low or high. The ground was wet. And all around her, things were ending—or beginning, if she were a tree. The light was already there—a white ribbon skirting away into an echo. She watched it go. A door slammed. Or fell. Where had the ocean gone, then? Some trees grow near the ocean. She had seen them along the coast at home, their roots jutting from soil, their white bodies tilting toward forest.

A muffled laugh traveled backward through an echo.

We are not important, Dora said. Dora was standing in the back of Mr. Perry's candy store, near the stacked boxes. There was a child there, a girl, but she didn't want to look at May. *I'm so glad you're all right,* May tried. *Come, be a tree with me.* She moved toward the little girl. She reached her hands out to her, but they were someone else's hands, or they were her hands. Someone was pulling on her branches, tightening the vines.

It happens all the time, Lily said. They were in the trolley and the wind was on May's skin. Her face was warm. *A crime of passion, you know.* Lily was holding a mirror up in front of them, the round one in the bathroom at the Hamilton. There were black cars traveling behind them.

We are all dying, May told Dora, even though she wasn't there. She imagined a blue sky. She looked up into the blue sky above Paris with Dora. Dora turned to her, smiling. She pointed to the Eiffel Tower. *He's up there,* she said, and May knew Dora meant Richard. *You made it.* But it was absurd. This. This way. If Richard looked down and saw her there.

Her father was standing on the edge of a bridge. *This time's for real,* he said.

Mr. Perry plucked her down from the ladder. *My girl.* He called her.

Where was the sun? It was swept into space, pulled into nothing. Richard was crying. He moaned, next to her. *Take the stones out of your mouth so I can hear you. Tell me what this is.* He sat across from her, a black shadow.

Stones and hands and bones and roots.

This is your death.

And then she was alone in a field where Edith's light-filled white tent had stood, but the field was empty and the sky was charcoal and brown and yellow. The field was trash-strewn and rocky and she knew it was another place even though the city

was in the distance. She reasoned it could be an entirely different city. She kept her eyes closed, becoming a tree, but it didn't
matter, because there were two of her, one watching the other,
each waiting for something to happen—standing in the dark
field, the wind blowing, and the two Mays were hovering just
above the ground, the film of herself skipping and reeling until
it finally burned up in a flash of light and disappeared.

AGNES

When Agnes told him about the fire, about the women on the
beach, Danny shook his head in disbelief. He said, "But what
does it mean?"

"I don't know—it's mumbo jumbo, isn't it?" She thought of
Lily saying, *I am the evidence. We are the proof.* Agnes opened one
door only to find another, and so on, a hall of doors. It made
sense, what had happened, in some fantastic way—but it wasn't
going to change anything. Was it?

Here were the facts: Claude's book, before being destroyed,
held descriptions of the Raptor's crimes. The women on the
beach marked it with their blood, wrote of the Raptor's death,
and then burned it. She had not seen what the others had written, but her Raptor died in flames. Her Raptor was broken and
then consumed.

Danny sat by the window. She felt him watching her as she
tried to sleep. He closed the blinds and curtains when the sun
came in, and when she woke late in the day, she found him next
to her. He made her coffee on his hot plate, and she asked him
more questions about May, hoping he'd remember something,
but he only repeated what she'd said about her bags being at
Union Station. "Maybe there will be something there," he said.

At Union Station, she watched the men in their gray suits,
jackets off, shirt sleeves up, pace the station, the smoke from
their cigarettes fractured in the sunlight of the station's high
windows. She sat on a long wooden bench across from a soldier

still in uniform, his hair so short that it was nearly gone, his eyes closed; a woman in her traveling clothes—brown tweed dress and brogans—walked a toddler up and down the space between the benches. Another woman knitted a sweater, her hair plaited and coiled. That one sighed occasionally, as if she were reliving a tragic conversation.

She found an attendant and told him she'd lost the key to her locker. She told him her name, and he brought her to another desk and she repeated the story. She'd been robbed, she said. She lost her claim ticket, her driver's license. "Can't you help?" She smiled at the man, who didn't want to be mean with her, he said, after she'd been robbed. He gave her a key.

At the locker, Agnes put the key in and turned the lock. Inside, she found a battered cardboard suitcase. She took it out and opened it. A blue cotton dress. Night things. White wax candles. She sifted through the contents. Trousers. An old pair of shoes with the tongues loose. A photograph of a man smiling, hands on hips, standing on an airstrip. A plane in the distance. In another photograph, the same man stood with his arm around May. *Richard*, it said on the back. He was broad-shouldered. As handsome as an actor. Letters from a man named Ned O'Neil. Ned O'Neil was in love with May. May had a sister, a mother, but they were in Boston. Far away.

She fastened the suitcase and put it back where she found it.

That night, she dreamed about May. They were lying on the dirt in the lot between the tunnels and the tent church, but everything was gone. The tent was gone, the tunnels—even the city beyond. They lay on their backs, looking up at the bright sky. Agnes could see an airplane there, streaking hot and fast against the blue.

May waved to the plane. "Hello!" she cried. When the plane was gone, May sat up and turned toward Agnes. "Look what they've done to me," she said. "I'm like Humpty Dumpty." But Agnes was afraid to look, and May began to cry. She cried so hard that it woke Agnes up. In the dark room, Agnes thought she could still hear the echo.

30

May

In one of the new bungalows on Norton, Rose was getting too big for the old carriage, so Betty put her into the bright red Taylor Tot stroller instead, the one that sat in the living room on Christmas morning. She and John had taken turns taking pictures of Annie in it, showing her the little tray with the brightly colored beads Rose could play with on their errands.

Betty leaned down to button Rose's coat, counting the number of buttons out loud as she went. "And five!" Rose looked down at her mother's fingers and tried to follow along, repeating vowel sounds like an echo. Betty found the cap that she'd knitted in November. She remembered counting stitches in the new living room, in the new house, a chicken roasting in the brand-new oven and the radio playing an old song with Rose asleep and John at work.

She smiled down at her Rose, who watched her with round eyes. "Momma," she said, reaching up. "Pick me."

"Pick me *up*," Betty corrected.

Rose touched her own cheek, experimented with her jaw, opening, then closing. She reached toward Betty again. "Up."

Betty leaned down and put the cap on, tying the soft cords beneath her daughter's chin. The only sound in the warm house was the tick of the clock in the kitchen. She listened for a few moments before pushing the door open. It was cold and gray out.

And then they were off. The stroller, made of metal, bumped over the stones and cracks in the sidewalk. Rose didn't seem to notice. She pointed at things as they passed. "Yes, darling. Mother sees," Betty said absently. And then Rose growled. The sound was low and strange. No one would expect it to come from such a sweet-faced little girl, but the doctor, when she'd rushed her to him that first morning after she heard it, had said it was perfectly normal.

She pushed Rose's carriage up Norton, answering Rose's vague questions with clucks of approval. She passed the new houses, the bungalows, each with a porch and a garage on the side, the grass neat at the sidewalk's edge. She waved to the other mothers when she saw them. "Hello!" she cried, lifting one hand. "I'm so late today or I'd stop—" She looked down at Rose, at the back of the knitted cap. She is late. She meant to leave a full hour earlier, and now she worried that if she didn't hurry, she'd miss the beginning of Helen Trent. She liked to sit on the big round rug in the living room listening as she folded the laundry, her feet tucked underneath her.

When she reached the strange island where Norton and Degnan merged and then separated, she tried to move more quickly. The houses hadn't been built yet, though the sidewalks were laid. The Taylor Tot jolted along over the uneven patches where weeds grew. At night, couples parked their cars along the unlit street. The families on either side of the empty block pulled their blinds down and waited for the builders to come back. Betty was happy to see boys on bicycles up ahead, shouting to each other as they circled. The island of patchy grass was a spot where children played. There was broken glass and debris left by the workers who'd put the sidewalks in. She hoped the houses were built by the time Rose was old enough to walk to school. She didn't like the idea of her daughter in such an undecided place.

Up ahead, she could make out a shop's mannequin in the dirt. She passed quickly, trying not to look. But she couldn't help but look. There was something awful about it. It wasn't right to leave something like that out. It would scare the children. She looked down at Rose, who pointed at the mannequin as they passed.

She pushed the stroller more quickly. Her brow was damp,

her breath quick. She could see the houses up ahead. When she reached them, she lifted Rose out of her Taylor Tot and ran to the door of the first. She couldn't imagine why she felt so worried about a shop mannequin, but something was moving around in her brain, a shadow trying to find form. She knocked on the door.

When a woman answered, Betty didn't say anything at first, and then: "I saw something strange up the street—a shop mannequin in the lot—where the houses haven't been built yet." The woman peered up the street, but it was too far away to see anything. "I really think it might frighten the children when they come home for lunch. If they see it, they won't—" But she stopped, unsure of the direction of her thought. The shadow pushed forward. "I'd like to call the police."

The woman was confused, her eyes moving over Betty and Rose. "What will the police do with a mannequin?"

"Remove it?"

The woman opened the door all the way and stepped aside to let Betty and Rose in. She smiled at Rose, taking her in her arms as Betty lifted the receiver. Betty turned to the woman. "I don't really know what it was, it's just—" And then she told the police to come. "Hurry," she said. "I'd rather the children didn't see it."

When she hung up, she took Rose. The woman was staring at her. "It was a mannequin? I wonder who would leave a mannequin over here? It seems odd."

She shook her head slowly, wondering what time it was, wondering if she ought to call John.

"Would you like some coffee? I just brewed a pot." Betty tried to say no—after all, she had to get to the store, to make dinner. "You look about as white as a ghost. Sit down."

"I'm fine, really. I don't know why I should be so upset by some silly mannequin." Betty sat in a chair in the living room. The chair was stitched with the deep green shapes of flowers. "I was on my way to the shopping center."

"Yes."

Outside, a car sped by, a boy ran down the street with a camera. Betty and the woman watched. Rose played with her mother's hair, combing it back with her fingers. The tea kettle whistled. A man raced past the window with a camera around his neck. She heard another voice call out, "Is this Norton here, or Degnan?"

Rose growled, but the growl is drowned out by the sound of a police siren. Soon there was another siren, then another. The woman stood in the doorway with the dark kitchen behind her. She was holding a tray with a pot of coffee and a small plate of cookies. Betty shushed Rose and pulled her close to her body. She looked at the woman's eyes, wide with wonder at the sirens, at the yelling. "She must have done something horrible," she said, setting the tray down.

"Who?"

"The—I don't think it's a mannequin."

Betty was confused. How could a girl do something that would leave her like that? Just a girl. Betty's hands were shaking. "No one…"

The woman brought her hands to her mouth. She sat heavily. "Of course not."

They both looked at Rose, who had stopped growling. She looked from her mother's face to the woman's. She clung to her mother's coat as if she would crawl inside, retreat, become small again, and disappear, and then she opened her mouth to cry, but between the intent and the wail, another siren arrived, and the sound was lost.

AGNES

She went to the office on Monday and sat down in front of her photographs. She wasn't long at it when she stood, holding a picture. "Is this some kind of a rotten joke?" she said to the newsroom. It was a photograph of May lying in a field, a blanket over part of her body. "Who did this?"

The men turned in their chairs to look at her. Their eyes

moved from the photograph to Agnes's face, and back again. "It's a shame," Max said. "She was a looker."

"Did you leave this on my desk?" she demanded of Max, whose face betrayed nothing.

Elgin stood in the doorway to his office. "It's for the evening edition," he said. "She was found early this morning. It's another Raptor murder—"

"What—but we—" she began, and then stopped. There was nothing to say. She walked out of the office and started down the stairs. She couldn't. She sat down on a marble step. Dizzy, she held on to the black railing. Her breath was short. May. The Raptor. And Lily—what would Lily do?

It was supposed to end. Wasn't it? They had written in the book. Of course it didn't work! What foolishness!

She remembered May as she'd been that evening, the lie she told about being a hat model, her lovely pale face, the delicacy of her hand as she lifted a drink, or the way she brought the other to her throat as they talked about the murders, as if she were having trouble swallowing.

Agnes didn't know how long she stayed on the steps, but when she got up, she only went back to the newsroom to gather her coat and bag. The men stared after her.

Danny showed up at her door. She let him in, and they sat together without speaking. She held his hand. She didn't go to work the next day, or the next, but when someone shot Ray in his office at the Palace, Elgin called her. "Get in here," he said. "We want you on this." Ray had been found slumped over his desk, wearing the mouse's mask.

Agnes went to the Palace to interview the dancers, who'd decided to do one last show. Ginger winked at her. "It's just terrible how much violence there is in this city," she said.

"How's Lily?" Agnes asked, but Ginger only shrugged. The cigarette girl remarked that Ray was supposed to order the dancers better masks—ones that were easier to wear. Wasn't it strange that someone had left him in that horrible old thing?

Later, Agnes looked at their faces caught in the flat blast of the flashbulb. With her loupe, she examined Ginger's expression. She was looking away, off to the side, a smile on her face.

The following night, Claude Borel was found at the bottom of his basement stairs. He'd died of a morphine overdose. Agnes imagined the women around him in his basement, their garish masks smiling down at him as he realized what was about to happen. This is for Ruth. This is for Beverly. This is for Joan. This is for May.

Elgin put Agnes on the crime desk. She wrote about Ray's murder, but not about Claude's death. She wrote a short piece about Marvin Adams, who'd been walking late at night by the side of the road when a car hit him. No one saw the accident, and Agnes doubted that's what happened. She saw the women again, riding in a convertible, laughing, aiming the car straight at Marvin. That's not what she wrote, though. She wrote about safety controls and the increasing number of cars on the road.

Could it be true? Sometimes the night on the beach felt like a story. It didn't fit into time in the right way. It was the mist—the mist and the half-light. The smoke from the fire. She asked Danny, "Did I tell you about the beach before or after the new year?"

"Come again?" he said.

"The night I went to the beach with Lily—"

"Oh—" he said, absently. "I'm not sure."

The police did not link the men's deaths—had no reason to, and only one was considered a murder. Ray's—but since it was rumored that he had ties to the crime world, it was called a mob hit.

A murder, a drug overdose, a hit and run.

Whenever a man was killed, Agnes wondered if he too had been in Claude's circle. It didn't matter if the death seemed like an accident, or if he wandered off into the sea as Aimsley had—it could be any of them. It could be all of them.

No one else seemed to notice, but she catalogued the deaths.

"Was he in on it?" she asked Danny, when the tent church caught on fire and the preacher with the pink cheeks died. But Danny only looked at her. She had to keep repeating the story about the night on the beach to him. It was maddening. Was he pretending? Did he want to forget it? He wanted to take her away from everything—to drive down to Baja together before it got too hot. "We'll have a dance in every little café we find," he said to her at night. "And we'll sleep under the stars." He bought madras swim trunks and a yellow cotton shirt illustrated with cats with arced backs. "But I don't know who will feed your cat," he joked.

My Raptor died in flames!

She'd written it, hadn't she? She'd described his black flapping wings, imagined him barreling out of the night sky like a downed plane.

She began researching the preacher, and soon she found he was linked to Claude in all sorts of ways: that the land the tent church stood on belonged to Claude, that women from his church had ended up in Claude's circle. The preacher had sent them to do part-time jobs—dictation, cleaning.

Agnes clipped the article and put it in a plain brown manuscript box with the others.

The rest of Los Angeles was still talking about the Raptor and the woman who'd been found in Leimert Park. An intrepid newsman found May's locker in Union Station. The photograph of her and Richard was printed in the newspaper. Agnes tried to call Lily, but her calls went unanswered. When she thought of Lily, she saw her as the woman she'd seen on the beach that night: her hair loose and cutting back in the wind, her chin lifted, the shadow light beyond, the sea moving against the rocks.

What had the others written in Claude's grimoire? In what many ways had they imagined the Raptor would die?

She'd tried again and again to write about the night on the beach, but the details seemed distant, as if she'd heard the story from someone else—who'd also heard it told—and soon she

felt like Hazel asking, "Have you heard about the witches yet?"
She stumbled over her own words. Had the women really worn
masks? Had she seen the ashes leap away from the fire like a
winged creature?

She tried to call Lily again, but Lily never answered. She left
messages at the boarding house. But Lily was filming. Lily was
in a meeting. At lunch. Asleep. Lily was never there.

At the office, she labeled a photograph of May's shoes and
her handbag. They'd been found sitting atop a trashcan in an
alley.

This is the last photograph of her, she thought. Shoes and
a handbag. They were bought for show, but they were private
too. Where you went, how you got there. Who saw when you
arrived.

It was spring. The world was alive, the scent of jasmine thick,
the days hot, but the night was cool. Agnes was thinking about
closing a window, but she didn't feel like getting up. She was
sitting at the kitchen table listening to songs on the radio in the
dark, her typewriter in front of her. She'd tried to write about
the beach again, but each time, it slipped away. Soon she gave
up and got a beer from the refrigerator and turned on the radio.

She'd have to call Lily again. To sit down with her and ask.

But then she couldn't remember what it was exactly she'd
wanted to ask her about. They'd gone somewhere together.
They'd taken a trip—or had it been a dream? Lily had danced
in "The Circus"—that show at the Palace where all the women
had worn masks. They'd gone to the beach together. At night—
to a house where the light was blue and the moon was full. And
then it came back, like a record skipping, and she saw Lily with
her hair blowing back, the creature rising out of the flames.

Finally, Agnes's telephone rang, and when she heard Lily's
voice on the other end, she blurted out. "I can't remember—"

"It's all right," Lily said to her. "It's all right to forget that
night. We did what we did, but no one should have to carry it.
Forget it," she said. "Drink it in. It's a gift."

"But I don't want to. I want to write it down."

"It can't be written," Lily said. "It can't be told."

Then Lily was at Agnes's door. They sat together in front of the window that Agnes hadn't yet closed. Agnes took two brown bottles of beer out of the refrigerator. The red-checked curtains moved in the breeze. Lily began to talk. She told her a story about witches and revenge. She told her a story that sounded like it couldn't be true, but Agnes believed it, and she listened, her chin propped in her hand. Sometimes she said, "Yes. That's how it happened," and other times, she only nodded. She would have to write it down, she thought, when Lily left.

Strangers had always told Agnes stories—the most wonderful stories.

AFTER

On a road through the canyons that leads to the sea, a driver stops to ask a woman walking alone at night if she needs a ride. He thinks of the Raptor, but remembers that there hasn't been a murder in a while. The monster has disappeared. He was pulled back into the fog.

Still.

He slows the car and rolls down the window, calling out, Is everything all right, miss? Can I drive you some place?

The woman doesn't seem to notice. It's obvious she's lost— that something's happened to her. He tries a few more times, calling out to her as he passes, but he only sees her profile. She's looking down, at her shoeless feet. Finally, he gives up, and when he checks in his rearview mirror, the woman has vanished.

When he reaches his friend Gloria's house, he says he wants to call the police. He wants to tell them a woman's had an accident. He tells her the story of seeing the woman—the way the woman turned and looked at him when the lights of his car washed over her, how she touched her hair.

I don't know why I'm telling you this, he says. It was strange. Now that I think of it, I'm not even sure if what I saw was real.

Lily's leaning in the doorway, listening. Which road? she asks, and then, What did the ghost look like?

Ghost? he says, laughing. Why— Well, I wonder. He tells her about the black dress, the pale skin, the dark hair.

Which road? Lily repeats.

The road around the canyon that leads out to the sea. Near the shack on the beach that the studio uses sometimes.

There's a record playing in the next room. Someone laughs. Charlie's seen a ghost—Gloria calls out to the others, and they come, eager to hear the ghost story. As they crowd around

Charlie, Lily backs away. She turns and leaves the house. She drives too fast down Highway 1, toward the long road that leads through the canyons. The shack isn't really a shack at all, but a small house—the one where they burned Claude's grimoire.

May must be trying to find her.

She stops the car and rolls all the windows down. She gets back on the road.

I'm here, she keeps calling. I'm here now.

But May never appears.

The next night, Lily checks in to the Hamilton under an assumed name, wearing a dark wig. She stays in their old room. Strangers say the bath smells of burned wax and matches. Lily sits on the side of the tub and closes her eyes, her wig at her feet. The black hair spirals across the tiled floor. She sniffs. It smells of soap and bleach. She wonders if May will appear in the mirror. She says a few words from the grimoire she took from Agnes's house on the night she visited, willing something—a shape, a shadow—but nothing happens. The only sound is the drip, drip of the faucet.

That morning, the police questioned William, May's sister's friend, and his wife, Edith. Lily saw it in the paper. They're church people. William's shoulders slope forward. Edith looks lost. It's funny May never mentioned them. Lily would watch him. Keep an eye on him.

Maybe even—if she had to, yes.

She'd let the others forget, one by one. The Lethe spell. She would have to take care of him alone.

I was only looking for the gold, William says. Did you know there's gold down there?

He reminds the detective of a child. He's playing a good scout. Of course there's no gold. They both know it. The detective keeps William for a while, sure that he knows something—that he'll slip, and then, when he can't keep him anymore, he has him tailed. But what evidence, in the end, does the detective have? William's prints don't match the ones on May's handbag.

Anyway—Edith says, when she's brought in, He was at home all night, with me. The phone kept ringing, she says. Late into the night. The phone rang, and I remember because William wouldn't answer it. I said it might be an emergency. Maybe it's May—I said—but he wouldn't answer it. He said, It's not May. That's all I remember. How dark it was that night. And how the telephone kept ringing.

How did he know it wasn't May?

She was away, wasn't she? She went to San Francisco for Christmas.

She could have come back. And she never went to San Francisco.

She didn't? That's what she said she was doing.

Why would she lie to you?

Edith doesn't have anything to say. She shakes her head slowly. I don't know why. She made up stories sometimes. About Richard. She tells him about Richard then. And the stories May invented.

The detective looks at his notes. *The phone kept ringing.* He circles back to the phone calls. So who was trying to get in touch with William?

I wish I could tell you more, she says. Edith is pregnant. She's sick all the time. She asks for something cool to drink. She wants his full sympathy. He doesn't like her. He doesn't trust her. There is some duplicity there, some meanness she masks with manners. She's watchful. She attributes pain to her own god's plan.

The detective will never solve it. He'll stay up nights with it.

Why did the Raptor stop killing? Where did he go?

He thinks of the spiral on May's palm. Does it lead anywhere?

There are times, too, that he will drink and make phone calls and smoke too many cigarettes. He has a theory, but it's mad. It's not one man, but many. He dreams of the roots of trees, of the wet earth around them, of a room of men who look through a keyhole at something and laugh. Let me see, they say, jostling. The detective knows that whatever is on the other side of the door is terrible. The room is small and dirty and close with smoke. It is a back room. It is underground. It is a prison cell.

∾

I should have warned you, Lily says to no one, looking at her feet. She's taken her shoes off and sits on the edge of the tub in the small bathroom. For a while, she says, I wasn't sure. I would have told you—I almost told you—after Joan died. But I didn't. I didn't want you to have to be like me.

Lily regards her shoes, which were expensive.

There was a role, and then another role. And then one more. The one she's in is a color movie—*Technicolor,* everyone's sure to say. With a famous director. She doesn't like him, but he does good work. He likes men, and so he leaves her alone.

All your stories—

But Lily knew which were true. Like the time May slept on a beach in Florida. May had gone down with Richard, in the evening, and they watched the sunset, sitting together, wrapped in the woolen government-issued blanket from his quarters. I could get into so much trouble for this, he told her, taking her hand.

I could have stayed there, May told Lily. On that beach with Richard.

Why didn't you? Lily asked.

Why didn't you stay? Lily says, looking in the mirror above the sink at the Hamilton, but she knows the answer.

It got cold. They grew hungry.

May shook the sand out of the blanket. They walked along the edge of the water, holding hands. The blanket was returned.

The day turned to night, night to day. Again.

And Richard left.

There was nowhere to stay, May whispered to Lily through

the faded sheet that hung between their beds, and Lily wondered if the sheet made it easier to say it. Lily lay with her head crooked in her arm, her eyes wide open in the dark room. She imagined May there, standing on the platform, waiting as the other soldiers disembarked. She remained on the platform after everyone else had gone, her smile rigid. She must have got the day wrong, she thought, looking at the hands on her silver wristwatch. Later, there would be a telegram. Black words on white paper.

Lily heard it in May's voice: how she'd dropped down, out of time, how a trap door opened.

But you must be awfully sad, Lily whispered to the pale sheet. About Richard. About how things are.

I've got you, haven't I? The answer came back through time.

I love you only you—Lily sings.

I love you?

The thought reaches her gradually, like a whisper coming across a crowded room. She catches a fragment of it, a hand on her own. Was there a word for that sort of love?

She stands. The room, with its flowered soap and bleached bath towels, tells her nothing. She never liked this room. It was always too hot to close the window, and the garbage collectors woke her up in the morning. She gets up and leaves. It is useless. May isn't here.

May liked to dance—she found the slow-motion places between the quick moves—what the songs said—

I love you.

Lily takes the road along the ocean to the pier. The pier is strewn with lights. Roller coaster cars click up wooden slats. The band is warming up. The air is tinged with burned sugar, sweat, and desire. And then the first song begins. No one can sit still. Everyone dances. They dance on wooden floors, scuffed and worn from other dancers; they dance outside, on the boardwalk, which is trampoline-like beneath soft shoes, the dancers jumping and spinning, the pop and pause of the break toss, the tandem send-out—flight.⁻

May could be among them, Lily thinks. She looks for the still point, but finds none. She stays all night, watching the dancers. Once or twice, she goes out on the floor, and soon she finds someone to dance with. His name is James, and he has a gap between his front teeth. Aren't you that actress? he asks, and she laughs.

Everyone says I look like her.

You do. You look *just* like her.

She likes James. He makes her laugh. In the small hours, they dance on the beach, shoeless, the sand cold between their toes. He lifts her into the air, grasping her waist, staggering below her, his face red. When the sun is coming up, she says they should go into the sea. They stand knee-deep. They are hot from exertion, breathless in the cold water, in the gray scrim of dawn. They go farther, laughing in their wet clothes, the spray of salt on the rocks around them, the birds circling above. And farther—swimming easily in the brine.

It doesn't matter. It doesn't matter that the dress will be ruined, that she has finally lost the coiled bracelet—that she let it slip away in the water like a live thing.

Lily takes James's hand and pulls him under as a wave crests above, and then they are on the beach again, the sun finally and fully risen, golden in the arc of the world.

ACKNOWLEDGMENTS

Thank you, Mary Pacios, Larry Harnisch, and Mark Shostrom for your input, curiosity, and guidance while writing and researching this book. Thank you, Kate Hahn and Andrew Popp, who hosted me on research visits. Thank you to readers Laura Spence-Ash, Meg Bratsch, Lisa Drexler, Mary Downing Hahn, Cindy Lordan, Nora Maynard, Jessica Papin, Allen Rose, Eileen Tomarchio, Tamara Zahaykevich, and Karen Zlotnick. Thank you to the editors at Regal House, who found this novel through their Petrichor Prize. Thank you to the Ragdale Foundation and Wellstone Center at the Redwoods for hosting me while I wrote. Finally, a major thanks to Jacquelyn Mitchard—friend and mentor—who kept the faith that this book would see publication.